Mrs. Henry Wood

Mildred Arkell - A Novel

Vol. I

Mrs. Henry Wood

Mildred Arkell - A Novel
Vol. I

ISBN/EAN: 9783337032265

Printed in Europe, USA, Canada, Australia, Japan

Cover: Foto ©Andreas Hilbeck / pixelio.de

More available books at **www.hansebooks.com**

MILDRED ARKELL.

A Novel.

BY

Mrs. HENRY WOOD,

AUTHOR OF

"EAST LYNNE," "LORD OAKBURN'S DAUGHTERS," "TREVLYN HOLD,"

ETC. ETC.

IN THREE VOLUMES.

VOL. I.

LONDON:

TINSLEY BROTHERS, CATHERINE STREET, STRAND

1865.

CONTENTS.

MILDRED ARKELL.

CHAPTER I.

WHICH IS NOTHING BUT AN INTRODUCTION.

I AM going to tell you a story of real life—one of those histories that in point of fact are common enough; but, hidden within themselves as they generally are, are thought to be so rare, and, if proclaimed to the world in all their strange details, are looked upon as a romance, not reality. Some of the actors in this one are living now, but I have the right to tell it, if I please.

A fair city is Westerbury; perhaps the fairest of the chief towns in all the midland counties. Its beautiful cathedral rises in the midst, the red walls of its surrounding prebendal houses looking down upon the famed river that flows gently past; a cathedral that shrouds itself in its unapproachable exclusiveness, as if it did not belong to the busy town outside. For that town is a manufacturing

one, and the aristocracy of the clergy, with that of
the few well-born families time had gathered round
them, and the democracy of trade, be it ever so
irreproachable, do not, as you know, assimilate.
In the days gone by—and it is to them we must
first turn—this feeling of exclusiveness, this line of
demarcation, if you will, was far more conspicuous
than it is now: it was indeed carried to a pitch that
would now scarcely be believed in. There were
those of the proud old prebendaries, who would
never have acknowledged to knowing a manufacturer
by sight; who would not have spoken to one in
the street, had it been to save their stalls. You don't
believe me? I said you would not. Nevertheless,
I am telling you the simple truth. And yet, some
of those manufacturers, in their intrinsic worth, in
their attainments, ay, and in their ancestors, if
you come to that, were not to be despised.

In those old days no town was more flourishing
than Westerbury. Masters and workmen were
alike enjoying the fruits of their skill and industry:
the masters in amassing a rich competency; the
workmen, or operatives, as it has become the fashion
to call them of late years, in earning an ample
living, and in bringing up their children without a
struggle. But those times changed. The opening
of our ports to foreign goods brought upon
Westerbury, if not destruction, something very

like it; and it was only the more wealthy of the
manufacturers who could weather the storm.
They lost, as others did, a very great deal; but
they had (at least, some few of them) large
resources to fall back upon, and their business was
continued as before, when the shock was over;
and none in the outer world knew how deep it had
been, or how far it had shaken them.

Conspicuous amidst this latter class was Mr.
George Arkell. He had made a great deal of
money—not by the griping hand of extortion;
by badly-paid, or over-tasked workmen; but by
skill, care, industry, and honourable dealing. In
all high honour he worked on his way; he could
not have been guilty of a mean action; to take
an unfair advantage of another, no matter how he
might have benefited himself, would have been
foreign to his nature. And this just dealing in
trade, as in else, let me tell you, generally answers
in the end. A better or more benevolent man than
George Arkell did not exist, a more just or considerate master. His rate of wages was on the
highest scale—and there were high and low scales
in the town—and in the terrible desolation hinted
at above, he had *never* turned from the poor
starving men without a helping hand.

It could not be but that such a man should be
beloved in private life, respected in public; and

some of those grand old cathedral clergy, who,
with their antiquated and obsolete notions, were
fast dropping off to a place not altogether swayed
by exclusiveness, might have made an exception
in favour of Mr. Arkell, and condescended to admit
their knowledge, if questioned, that a man of that
name did live in Westerbury.

George Arkell had one son : an only child. No
expense had been spared upon William Arkell's
education. Brought up in the school attached to
the cathedral, the college school as it was familiarly
called, he had also a private tutor at home, and
private masters. In accordance with the good old
system obtaining in the past days—and not so very
long past either, as far as the custom is concerned
—the college school confined its branches of
instruction to two : Greek and Latin. To teach a
boy to read English and to spell it, would have
been too derogatory. History, geography, any
common branch you please to think of; mathe-
matics, science, modern languages, were not so
much as recognised. Such things probably did
exist, but certainly nothing was known of them in
the college school. Mr. Arkell—perhaps a little
in advance of his contemporaries—believed that
such acquirements might be useful to his son, and
a private tutor had been provided for him.
Masters for every accomplishment of the day were -

also given him; and those accomplishments were less common then than now. It was perhaps excusable: William Arkell was a goodly son: and he grew to manhood not only a thoroughly well-read classical scholar and an accomplished man, but a gentleman. " I should like you to choose a profession, William," Mr. Arkell had said to him, when his schooldays were nearly over. " You shall go to Oxford, and fix upon one while there; there's no hurry." William laughed; " I don't care to go to Oxford," he said; " I think I know quite enough as it is; and I intend to come into the manufactory to you."

And William maintained his resolution. Indulged as he had been, he was somewhat accustomed to like his own way, good though he was by nature, dutiful and affectionate by habit. Perhaps Mr. Arkell was not sorry for the decision, though he laughingly told his son that he was too much of a gentleman for a manufacturer. So William Arkell was entered at the manufactory; and when the proper time came he was taken into partnership with his father, the firm becoming " George Arkell and Son."

Mr. George Arkell had an elder brother, Daniel; rarely called anything but Dan. *He* had not prospered. He had had the opportunity of prospering just as much as his brother had, but he had not done it.

A fatal speculation into which Dan always said he
was "drawn," but which everybody else said he had
plunged into of himself with confiding eagerness,
had gone very far towards ruining him. He did
not fail; he was of the honourable Arkell nature;
and he paid every debt he owed to the uttermost
penny—paid grandly and liberally; but it left him
with no earthly possession except the house he
lived in, and that he couldn't part with. Dan was
a middle-aged man then, and he was fain to accept
a clerkship in the city bank at a hundred a
year salary; and he abjured speculation for the
future, and lived quietly on in the old house with his
wife and two children, Peter and Mildred. But
wealth, as you are aware, is always bowed down to,
and Westerbury somehow fell into the habit of
calling the wealthy manufacturer "Mr. Arkell,"
and the elder "Mr. Dan."

How contrary things run in this world! The one
cherished dream of Peter Arkell's life was to get to
the University, for his heart was set on entering
the Church; and poor Peter could not get to it.
His cousin William, who might have gone had it
cost thousands, declined to go; Peter, who had no
thousands—no, nor pounds, either, at his command,
was obliged to relinquish it. It is possible that
had Mr. Arkell known of this strong wish, he
might have smoothed the way for his nephew, but

Peter never told it. He was of a meek, reticent, somewhat shy nature; and even his own father knew not how ardently the wish had been cherished.

" You must do something for your living, Peter," Mr. Dan Arkell had said, when his son quitted the college school in which he had been educated. "The bank has promised you a clerkship, and thirty pounds a year to begin with; and I think you can't do better than take it."

Poor shy, timid Peter thought within himself he could do a great deal better, had things been favourable; but they were not favourable, and the bank and the thirty pounds carried the day. He sat on a high stool from nine o'clock until five, and consoled himself at home in the evenings with his beloved classics.

Some years thus passed on, and about the time that William Arkell was taken into partnership by his father, Mr. Daniel Arkell died, and Peter was promoted to the better clerkship, and to the hundred a year salary. He saw no escape now; he was a banker's clerk for life.

And now that all this preliminary explanation is over—and I assure you I am as glad to get it over as you can be—let us go on to the story.

In one of the principal streets of Westerbury, towards the eastern end of the town, you might see a rather large space of ground, on which stood a handsome house and other premises, the whole enclosed by iron gates and railings, running level with the foot pavement of the street. Removed from the bustle of the town, which lay higher up, the street was a quiet one, only private houses being in it—no shops. It was, however, one of the principal streets, and the daily mails and other stage-coaches, not yet exploded, ran through it. The house mentioned lay on the right hand, going towards the town, and not far off, behind various intervening houses, rose the towers of the cathedral. This house lay considerably back from the street— on a level with it, at some distance, was a building whose many windows proclaimed it what it was—a manufactory; and at the back of the open-paved yard, lying between the house and the manufactory, was a coach-house and stable—behind all, was a large garden.

Standing at the door of that house, one autumn evening, the red light of the setting sun falling sideways athwart his face, was a gentleman in the prime of life. Some may demur to the expression —for men estimate the stages of age differently— and this gentleman must have seen fifty-five years; but in his fine, unwrinkled, healthy face, his slender, active, upright form, might surely be read the indications that he was yet in his prime. It was the owner of the house and its appendages—the principal of the manufactory, George Arkell.

He was drawing on a pair of black gloves as he stood there, and the narrow crape-band on his hat proclaimed him to be in slight mourning. It was the fashion to remain in mourning longer then than now. Daniel Arkell had been dead twelve months, but the Arkell family had not put away entirely the signs. Suddenly, as Mr. Arkell looked towards the iron gates—both standing wide open—a gentlemanly young man turned in, and came with a quick step across the yard.

There was not much likeness between the father and son, save in the bright dark eyes, and in the expression of the countenance—*that* was the same in both; good, sensitive, benevolent. William was taller than his father, and very handsome, with a look of delicate health on his refined features, and a complexion almost as bright as a girl's. At the same moment that he was crossing the yard, an open carriage, well built and handsome, but drawn by only one horse, was being brought round from the stables. Nearly every afternoon of their lives, Sundays excepted, Mr. and Mrs. Arkell went out for a drive in this carriage, the only one they kept.

"How late you are starting!" exclaimed William to his father.

"Yes; I have been detained. I had to go into

the manufactory after tea, and since then Marmaduke Carr called, and he kept me."

"It is hardly worth while going now."

"Yes, it is. Your mother has a headache, and
the air will do her good; and we want to call in
for a minute on the Palmers."

The carriage had come to a stand-still midway
from the stables. There was a small seat behind
for the groom, and William saw that it was open;
when the groom did not attend them, it remained
closed. Never lived there a man of less pretension
than George Arkell; and the taking a servant with
him for show would never have entered his ima-
gination. They kept but this one man—he was
groom, gardener, anything; his state-dress (in
which he was attired now) being a long blue coat
with brass buttons, drab breeches, and gaiters.

"You are going to take Philip to-night?" observed William.

"Yes; I shall want him to stay with the horse
while we go in to the Palmers'. Heath Hall is a
goodish step from the road, you know."

"I will tell my mother that the carriage is
ready," said William, turning into the house.

But Mr. Arkell put up his finger with a detaining movement.

"Stop a minute, William. Marmaduke Carr's

visit this evening had reference to you. He came to complain."

"To complain!—of me?" echoed William Arkell, his tone betraying his surprise. "What have I done to him?"

"At least, it sounded very like a complaint to my ears," resumed the elder man; "and though he did not say he came purposely to prefer it, but introduced the subject in an incidental sort of manner, I am sure he did come to do it."

"Well, what have I done?" repeated William, an amused expression mingling with the wonder on his face.

"After conversing on other topics, he began speaking of his son, and that Hughes girl. He has come to the determination, he says, of putting a final stop to it, and he requests it as a particular favour that you wont mix yourself up in the matter and will cease from encouraging Robert in it."

"I!" echoed William. "That's good. I don't encourage it."

"Marmaduke Carr says you do encourage it. He tells me you were strolling with the girl and Robert last Sunday afternoon in the fields on the other side the water. I confess I was surprised to hear this, William."

William Arkell raised his honest eyes, so clear and truthful, straight to the face of his father.

"How things may be distorted!" he exclaimed. "Do you remember, sir, my mother asked me, as we left the cathedral after service, to go and inquire whether there was any change for the better in Mrs. Pembroke?"

"I remember it quite well."

"Well, I went. Coming back, I chose the field way, and I had no sooner got into the first field, than I overtook Robert Carr and Martha Ann Hughes. I walked with him through the fields until we came to the bridge, and then I came on alone. Much 'encouragement' there was in that!"

"It was countenancing the thing, at any rate, if not encouraging it," remarked Mr. Arkell.

"There's no harm in it; none at all."

"Do you mean in the affair itself, or in your having so far lent yourself to it?"

"In both," fearlessly answered William. "I wonder who it is that carries these tales to old Carr! We did not meet a soul, that I remember; he must have spies at work."

The remark rather offended Mr. Arkell.

"William," he gravely asked, "do you consider it fitting that Robert Carr should marry that girl?"

William's eyes opened rather wide at the remark.

"He is not likely to do that, sir; he would not make a simpleton of himself."

"Then you consider that he should choose the other alternative, and turn rogue?" rejoined Mr. Arkell, indignation in his suppressed tone. "William, had anyone told me this of you, I would not have believed it."

William Arkell's sensitive cheek flushed red.

"Sir, you are entirely mistaking me: I am sure you are mistaking the affair itself. I believe that the girl is as honest and good a girl as ever lived; and Robert Carr knows she is."

"Then what is it that he proposes to himself in frequenting her society? If he has no end at all in view, why does he do it?"

"I don't think he *has* any end in view. There is really nothing in it—as I believe; we all form acquaintances and drop them. Marmaduke Carr need not put himself in a fever."

"We form acquaintances in our own sphere of life, mind you, young sir; they are the safer ones. I wonder some of the ladies don't give a hint to the two Miss Hughes's to take better care of their sister—she's but a young thing. At any rate, William, do not you mix yourself up in it."

"I have not done it, indeed, sir. As to my walking through the fields with them, when we met, as I tell you, accidentally, I could not help myself, friendly as I am with Robert Carr. There was no harm in it; I should do it again to-morrow under the circumstances; and if old Carr speaks to me, I shall tell him so."

The carriage came up, and no more was said. Philip had halted to do something to the harness. Mrs. Arkell came out.

She was tall, and for her age rather an elegant woman. Her face must once have been delicately beautiful: it was easy to be seen whence William had inherited his refined features; but she was simple in manner as a child.

"What have you been doing, William? Papa was speaking crossly to you, was he not?"

She sometimes used the old fond word to him, "papa." She looked fondly at her son, and spoke in a joking manner. In truth, William gave them little cause to be "cross" with him: he was a good son, in every sense of the term.

"Something a little short of high treason," replied William, laughing, as he helped her in; "Papa can tell you, if he likes."

Mr. Arkell took the reins, Philip got up behind, and they drove out of the yard. William Arkell went indoors, put down a roll of music he had been carrying, and then left the house again.

Turning to his right hand as he quitted the iron gates, he continued his way up the street towards the busier portion of the city. It was not his intention to go so far as that now. He crossed over to a wide, handsome turning on the left, and was speedily close upon the precincts of the cathedral. It was almost within the cathedral precincts that the house of Mrs. Daniel Arkell was situated. Not a large house, as was Mr. Arkell's, but a pretty compact red-brick residence, with a small garden lying before the front windows, which looked out on the Dean's garden and the cathedral elm-trees.

William Arkell opened the door and entered. In a little bit of a room on the left, sat Peter Arkell, deep in some abstruse Greek play. This little room was called Peter's study, for it had been appropriated to the boy and his books ever since he could remember. William looked in, just gave him a nod, and then entered the room on the other side the entrance-passage.

Two ladies sat in this, both of them in mourning: Mrs. Daniel Arkell, a stout, comfortable-looking woman, in widow's weeds; Mildred in a pretty dress of black silk. Peter and William were about the same age: Mildred was two years younger. She was a quiet, sensible, lady-like girl, with a gentle face and the sweetest look possible in her soft brown eyes. She had not been educated fashionably, according to the custom of the present day; she had never been to school, but had received, as we are told of Moses Primrose, a "sort of miscellaneous education at home." She possessed a thorough knowledge of her own language, knew a good deal of Latin, insensibly acquired through being with Peter when he took his earlier lessons in it from his father, read aloud beautifully, wrote an excellent letter, and was a quick arithmetician, made shirts and pastry to perfection, and was well read in our best authors. Not a single accomplishment, save dancing, had she been taught; and yet she was in mind and manners essentially a gentlewoman.

If Mildred was loved by her own mother, so was she by Mrs. George Arkell. Possessing no daughter of her own, Mrs. George seemed to cling to Mildred as one. She cherished within her heart a secret wish that her son might sometime call Mildred his wife. This may be marvelled at—it may seem strange that Mrs. George Arkell should wish to unite her attractive, wealthy, and accomplished son with his portionless and comparatively homely cousin; but *she* knew Mildred's worth and the sunshine of happiness she would bring into any home. Mrs. George Arkell never breathed a hint of this wish: whether wisely or not, perhaps the sequel did not determine.

And what thought Mildred herself? She knew nothing of this secretly-cherished scheme; but if ever there appeared to her a human being gifted with all earthly perfections, it was William Arkell.

Perhaps the very contrast he presented to her brother—a contrast brought palpably before her sight every day of her life—enhanced the feeling. Peter was plain in person, so tall as to be ungainly, thin as a lath, and stooping perpetually, and in manner shy and awkward ; whilst William was all ease and freedom ; very handsome, though with a look of delicate health on his refined features ; danced minuets with Mildred to perfection—relics of the old dancing days, which pleased the two elder ladies ; breathed love-songs to her on his flute, painted her pretty landscapes in water-colours, with which she decorated the walls of her own little parlour, drove her out sometimes in his father's carriage—the one you have just seen start on its expedition ; passed many an evening reading to her, and quoting Shakespeare ; and, in short, made love to her as much as it was possible to make it, not in words. But the misfortune of all this was, that while it told upon *her* heart, and implanted there its never-dying fruit, he only regarded her as a cousin or a sister. Brought up in this familiar intercourse with Mildred, he never gave a thought to any warmer feeling on either side, or suspected that such intimacy might lead to one, still less that it had, even then, led to it on hers. Had he been aware of his mother's hope of uniting them, it is impossible to say whether he would have yielded

to it : he had asked himself the question many a
time in his later life, *and he could never answer.*

The last remains of the setting sun threw a glow
on the room, for the house faced the west. It was
a middling-sized, comfortable apartment, with a
sort of bright look about it. They rarely sat in
any other. There was a drawing-room above, but
it was seldom used.

"Well, aunt! well, Mildred! How are you this
evening ?"

Mildred looked up from her work at the well-
known, cheery voice ; the soft colour had already
mantled in her cheek at the well-known step.
William took a book from his pocket, wrapped in
paper.

"I got it for you this afternoon, Mildred. Mind
and don't spoil your eyes over it : its print is
curiously small."

She looked at him with a smile amidst her glow
of blushing thanks ; she always smiled when he
gave her the same caution. Her sight was remarkably strong—William's, on the contrary, was
not so, and he was already obliged to use glasses
when trying fresh pieces of music.

"William, my dear," began Mrs. Daniel, " I
have a favour to ask your father. Will you carry
it to him for me ?"

"It s granted already," returned William, with

the free confidence of an indulged son. "What is it?"

"I want to get over to see those children, the Carrs. Poor Mrs. John, when she was dying, asked me if I would go over now and then, and I feel as if I were neglecting the promise, for it is full six months since I was there. The coaches start so early in the morning, and I thought, if your father would let me have the carriage for the day, and Philip to drive me; Mildred can sit in the back seat——"

"I'll drive you, aunt," interrupted William. "Fix your own day, and we'll go."

But Mildred had looked up, a vivid blush of annoyance on her cheek.

"I do not care to go, mamma; I'd rather not go to Squire Carr's."

"You be quiet, Mildred," said William. "You are not going to see the squire, you are going to see the squire's grandchildren. Talking about the Carrs, aunt, I have just been undergoing a lecture on their score."

"On the score of the Carrs?"

"It's true. I happened on Sunday to be crossing the opposite fields, on my way from Mrs. Pembroke's, and came upon Robert Carr and Miss Martha Ann Hughes, and walked with them to the bridge. Somebody carried the news to old Marmaduke, and he came down this evening, all flurry and fire, to my father, complaining that I was 'encouraging' the thing. Such nonsense! He need not be afraid that there's any harm in it."

Mrs. Dan Arkell gave her head a shake, as if she were not so sure upon the latter point as her nephew. Prudent age — impulsive youth: how widely different do they judge of things! William was turning to the door.

"You are not going?" said Mrs. Dan, and Mildred looked up from her work, a yearning wistfulness in her eye.

"I must, this evening; I asked young Monk to come in and bring his violin, and he'll be waiting for me, if I don't mind. Good-bye, Aunt Dan ; pleasant dreams to you, Mildred !"

But as William went out, he opened the door of Peter's study, and stood there gossiping at least twenty minutes. He might have stood longer, but for the sight of two gentlemen who were passing along the road arm-in-arm, and he rushed out impulsively, forgetting to say good-evening to Peter.

CHAPTER II.

THE MISS HUGHES'S HOME.

MARMADUKE CARR, of whom mention has been made, was one of the Westerbury manufacturers—a widower, and a wealthy man. He had only one son living—Robert; two other children had died in infancy. Robert Carr, about thirty years of age now, was not renowned for his steadiness of conduct; indeed, he had been a sad spendthrift, and innumerable unpleasant scenes had resulted therefrom between him and his father. It could not be said that his heart was bad; but his head was certainly light. Half the town declared that Robert Carr had no real evil in him; that his faults were but the result of youth and carelessness; that he would make a worthy man yet. The other half prophesied that he would be safe to come to a bad ending, like wicked Harry in the spelling-book. One of his escapades Mr. Carr was particularly sore upon. After a violent quarrel between them—for each possessed a temper of his own—Robert had

started off clandestinely; that is, without saying a
word to anyone.   At the end of a month he returned, and bills to the amount of something like a
hundred pounds came in to his father.   Mr. Robert
had been seeing life in London.

In one sense of the word, the fault was Mr.
Carr's.   There cannot be a greater mistake than to
bring up a son to idleness, and this had been
the case with Robert Carr.   He would settle to
nothing, and his father had virtually winked at it.
Ostensibly, Robert had entered the manufactory;
but he would not attend to the business: he said he
hated it.   One day there, and the other five days
away.   Idling his hours with his friends in the
town; over at his uncle's, Squire Carr's, shooting,
fishing, hunting; going somewhere out by the
morning coach, and in again; anything, in fact, to
avoid work and kill time.   *This* should have been
checked in the onset; it was not, and when Mr.
Carr awoke to the consequences of his indulgent
supineness, the habits had grown to a height that
refused control.   "Let him take his pleasure a bit,"
Mr. Carr had said to his own heart at first, "youth's
never the worse for a little roaming before settling
down. I have made plenty of money, and there's only
Bob to inherit it."   Dangerous doctrine; mistaken
conclusions: and Mr. Carr lived to find them so.

Squire Carr was his elder brother.   He was

several years older than Marmaduke. He possessed a small property, and farmed it himself, and was consequently called "Squire" Carr—as many of those small landed proprietors were called by their neighbours in the days now passing away. Squire Carr, a widower of many years, had one son only— John. This John had made a marriage almost in his boyhood, and had three children born to him— Valentine, Benjamin, and Emma, and then his wife died. Next he married a second wife, and after some years she died, leaving several young children. They all lived with the squire, but the three elder children were now nearly grown up. It was to this house, and to see these younger children, that Mrs. Dan Arkell purposed going, if she could borrow Mr. Arkell's carriage. They lived about eight miles off, near to Eckford, a market town. By the coach road, indeed, it was considerably more.

Squire Carr and his brother were not very intimate. The squire would ride into Westerbury on the market day, or drive in with his son in the dog-cart, but not once in three months did they call at Marmaduke's. There was no similarity between them; there was as little cordiality. The squire was of a grasping, mean, petty nature, and so was his son after him. Marmaduke was open-handed and liberal, despising meanness above every earthly failing.

Robert Carr had plunged into other costly escapades since that first one of the impromptu sojourn
in London, and his father's patience was becoming
exhausted. Latterly he, Robert, had struck up an
acquaintance with a young girl, Martha Ann
Hughes; and there is no doubt that this vexed
Mr. Carr more than any previous aggression had
done. The Carrs, in their way, were proud. They
were really of good family, and in the past generation had been of some account. A horrible fear
had taken hold of Mr. Carr, that Robert, in his
infatuation, might be mad enough to marry this
girl, and he would have deemed it the very worst
calamity that could fall upon his life.

For Robert was seen with this girl in public, and
the girl and her family were, in their station,
respectable people; and the other evening, when
Mr. Carr had spoken out his mind in rather
broad terms, Robert had flown in a passion, and
answered that he'd "shoot himself rather than
hurt a hair of her head." The fear that he might
marry her entered then and there into Mr. Carr's
head; and it grew into a torment.

The two gentlemen, passing Mrs. Dan Arkell's
house as William flew out, were Robert Carr and a
young clergyman with whom he was intimate, the
Reverend John Bell. Mr. Bell had had escapades
of his own, and that probably caused him to

tolerate, or to see no harm in, Robert Carr's. Certain it is they were firm, almost inseparable friends; and rumour went that Mr. Bell was upon visiting terms at Miss Hughes's house, introduced to it by Robert. The Reverend John Bell had had his first year's curacy in Westerbury; he was now in priest's orders, hoping for employment, and, meanwhile, helping occasionally in the services at a church called St. James-the-Less, whose incumbent, one of the minor canons, had fits of gout.

William joined them. He did not say anything to Robert Carr then, in the presence of Mr. Bell; but he did intend, the first opportunity, to recommend him to drop the affair as profitless in every way, and one there seemed to be trouble over. They walked together to the end of the old cathedral outer wall, and there separated. William turned to the left, which would lead him to his home; while Mr. Bell passed through a heavy stone archway on the right, and was then within the precincts of the cathedral, in a large open space, surrounded by the prebendal and other houses; the deanery, the cloisters, and the huge college school-room being on one side. This was the back of the cathedral; it rose towering there behind the cloisters. Mr. Bell made straight for the residence of the incumbent of St. James-the-Less, the Reverend Mr. Elwin—a little old-fashioned house, with no windows to speak of, on the side opposite the deanery.

Robert Carr had turned neither to the right nor the left, but continued his way straight on. Passing an old building called the Palmery—which belonged, as may be said, to the cathedral—he turned into a by-street, and in three or four minutes was at the end of the houses on that side the town. Before him, at some little distance, in the midst of its churchyard, stood the church of St. James-the-Less, surrounded by the open country. The only house near it, a poor little dwelling, was inhabited by the clerk. That is, it had been inhabited by him; but the man was now dead, and a hot dispute was raging in the parish whether a successor should be appointed to him or not. Meanwhile, the widow benefited, for she was allowed to continue in the house until the question should be settled.

Robert Carr, however, had no intention of going as far as the church. He stopped at the last house but one in the street—a small, but very neat dwelling, with two brass plates on the door. You may read them. "Mr. Edward Hughes, Builder," was on one; "The Misses Hughes, Dressmakers," was on the other.

Yes, this was the house inhabited by the young person who was so upsetting the equanimity of Mr. Carr. Edward Hughes was a builder, in business for himself in a small way, and his two elder sisters were the dressmakers—worthy people enough all, and of good report, but certainly not the class from which it might be supposed Robert Carr would take a wife.

Two gaunt, ungainly women were these two elder Miss Hughes's, with wide mouths and standing-out teeth. The eldest, Sophia, was the manager and mistress of the home, and a clever one too, and a shrewd woman; the second, Mary, not in the least clever or shrewd, confined her attention wholly to her business, and went out to work by day at ladies' houses, and sat up half the night working after she got home.

She had been out on this day, but had returned, by some mutual arrangement with her patrons, earlier than usual; for it was a busy time with them at home, and the house was full of work. They were at work at a silk gown now; both sisters bending their heads over it, and stitching away as fast as they could stitch. The parlour faced the street, and some one else was seated at the window, peeping out, between the staves of the Venetian blind.

This was Martha Ann, a young girl of twenty, pretty, modest, and delicate looking; so entirely different was she in person from her sisters, that people might have suspected the relationship,

Perhaps it was from the great contrast she presented to themselves that the Miss Hughes's had
reared her in a superior manner. How they had
loved the pretty little child, so many years younger
than themselves, they alone knew. They had sent
her to school, working hard to keep her there;
and when they brought her home it was, to use
their own phrase, "to be a lady"—not to work.
The plan was not a wise one, and they might yet
live to learn it.

"I wish to goodness you could have put Mrs.
Dewsbury off for to-morrow, Mary!" exclaimed the
elder sister.

"But I couldn't," replied Mary. "The lady's-
maid said I must go to-morrow, whether or
not. In two days Mrs. Dewsbury starts on her
visit."

"Well, all I know is, we shall never get these
dresses home in time."

"I must sit up to-night—that's all," said Mary
Hughes, with equanimity.

"I must sit up, too, for the matter of that,"
rejoined the elder sister. "The worst is, after *no*
bed, one is so languid the next day; one can't get
through half the work."

Martha Ann rose from her seat, and came to the
table.

"I wish you would let me try to help you,

Sophia. I'm sure I could do seams, and such-like straightforward work."

"You'd pucker them, child. No; we are not going to let your eyes be tried over close sewing."

"I'll tell you what you can do, Martha Ann," said the younger of the two. "You can go in the kitchen, and make me a cup of coffee. I feel dead tired, and it will waken me up."

"There now, Mary!" cried the young girl. "I knew you were not in bed last night, and you are talking of sitting up this! I shall tell Edward."

"Yes, I was in bed. I went to bed at three, and slept till six. Go and make the coffee, child."

Martha Ann quitted the room. Mary Hughes watched the door close, and then turned to her sister, and began to speak eagerly, dropping her voice to a half whisper.

"I say, Sophia, I met Mrs. Pycroft to-day, and she began upon me like anything. What do you think she said?"

"How do I know what she said?" returned Miss Sophia, indifferently, and speaking with her mouth full of pins, for she was deep in the intricacies of fitting one pattern to another. "Where did you meet her?"

"Just by the market-house. It was at dinner-time. I had run out for some more wadding, for me and the lady's-maid found we had made a miscalculation, and hadn't got enough to complete the cloak, and I met her as I was running back again. She never said, 'How be you?' or 'How bain't you?' but she begins upon me all sharp— 'What be you doing with Martha Ann?' It took me so aback that for a moment I couldn't answer her, and she didn't give time for it, either. 'Is young Mr. Carr going to marry her?' she goes on. So of course I said he wasn't going to marry her that I knew of; and then——"

"And more idiot you for saying anything of the sort!" indignantly interrupted Sophia Hughes, dropping all the pins in a heap out of her mouth that she might speak freely. "It's no business of Mother Pycroft's, or of anybody else's."

The meeker younger sister—and as a very reed had she always been in the strong hands of the elder—paused for an instant, and then spoke deprecatingly.

"But Mr. Robert Carr is *not* going to marry her that we know of, Sophia. Where was the harm of my saying the truth?"

"A great deal of harm in saying it to that gabbling, interfering Mother Pycroft. She has wanted to put her nose into everything all these years and years since poor mother died. What do you say?"

proceeded Miss Sophia, drowning her sister's feeble attempt to speak. " 'A good heart—been kind to us?' *That* doesn't compensate for the worry she has been. She's a mischief-making old cat."

"She went on like anything to-day," resumed Mary Hughes, when she thought she might venture to speak again; "saying that young Mr. Carr ought not to come to the house unless he came all open and honourable, and had got a marriage-ring at his fingers' ends; and if we didn't mind, we should have Martha Ann a town's talk."

Sophia Hughes flung down her work, her eyes ablaze with anger.

"If you were not my sister, and the poorest, weakest mortal that ever stepped, I'd strike you for daring to repeat such words to me! A town's talk! Martha Ann!"

"Well, Sophia, you need not snap me up so," was the deprecating answer. "She says that folks are talking already of you and me, blaming us for allowing the acquaintance with young Mr. Carr. And I think they are," candidly added the young woman.

"Where's the harm? Martha Ann is as good as Robert Carr any day."

"But if people don't think so? If his folks don't think so? All the Carrs are as proud as Lucifer."

" And a fine lot Robert Carr has got to be proud
of!" retorted Sophia. " Look at the scrapes he
has been in, and the money he has spent! A good,
wholesome, respectable attachment might be the
salvation of him."

" Perhaps so. But then—but then—I wish
you'd not be cross with me, Sophia—there'd be
more chance of it if the young lady were in his own
condition of life. Sophia, we are naturally fond of
Martha Ann, and think there's nobody like her—
and there's not, for the matter of that; but we
can't expect other people to think so. I wouldn't
let Martha Ann be spoken of disparagingly in the
town for the world. I'd lay my life down first."

Sophia Hughes had taken up her work again.
She put in a few pins in silence. Her anger was
subsiding.

" *I'll* take care of Martha Ann. The town knows
me, I hope, and knows that it might trust me. If
I saw so much as the faintest look of disrespect
offered by Robert Carr to Martha Ann, I should tell
him he must drop the acquaintance. Until I do,
he's free to come here. And the next time I come
across old Mother Pycroft she'll hear the length of
my tongue."

Mary Hughes dared say no more. But in the
days to come, when the blight of scandal had tar
nished the fair name of her young sister, she was

wont to whisper, with many tears, that she had warned Sophia what might be the ending, and had not been listened to.

"Here he is!" exclaimed Sophia, as the form of some one outside darkened the window.

And once more putting down her work, but not in anger this time, she went to open the front door, at which Robert Carr was knocking.

CHAPTER III.

THE ADVENT OF CHARLOTTE TRAVICE.

Mrs. GEORGE ARKELL sat near her breakfast-table, deeply intent on a letter recently delivered. The apartment was a rather spacious one, handsomely fitted up. It was the general sitting-room of the family; the fine drawing-room on the other side of the hall being very much kept, as must be confessed, for state occasions. A comfortable room, this; its walls hung with paintings in water-colours, many of them William's doings, and its pleasant window looking across the wide yard, to the iron railings and the street beyond it. The room was as yet in the shade, for it faced due south; but the street yonder lay basking in the bright sun of the September morning; and Mrs. Arkell looked through the open window, and felt almost glad at the excuse the letter afforded her for going abroad in it.

Letters were not then hourly matters, as they are now; no, nor daily ones. Perhaps a quiet country lady did not receive a dozen in a year:

certainly Mrs. Arkell did not, and she lingered on, looking at the one in her hand, long after her husband and son had quitted the breakfast-table for the manufactory.

"It is curious the child should write to me," was her final comment, and the words were spoken aloud. "I must carry it to Mrs. Dan, and talk it over with her."

She rang the bell for the breakfast things to be removed, and presently proceeded to the kitchen to consult with the cook about dinner—for consulting with the cook, in those staid, old-fashioned households, was far more the custom than the present "orders." That over, Mrs. Arkell attired herself, and went out to Mrs. Daniel Arkell's. Mrs. Dan was surprised to see her so early, and laid her spectacles inside the Bible she was reading, to mark the place.

"Betty," began Mrs. Arkell, addressing her sister-in-law by the abbreviation bestowed on her at her baptism, "you remember the Travices, who left here some years ago to make their fortune, as they said, in London?"

"To be sure," replied Mrs. Dan.

"Well, I fear they can't have made much. Here's a letter comes this morning from their eldest girl. It's very odd that she should write to me. A pretty little thing she was, of about

3—2

eight or ten, I remember, when they left Westerbury."

"What does she write about?" interrupted Mrs.
Dan. "I'm sure they have been silent enough
hitherto. Nobody, so far as I know, has ever heard
a word from any of them since they left."

"She writes to me as an old friend of her father's
and mother's, she says, to ask if I can interest myself
for her with any school down here. I infer, from
the wording of the letter, that since their death,
the children have not been well off."

"John Travice and his wife are dead, then?"

"So it would seem. She says—'We have had
a great deal of anxiety since dear mamma died,
the only friend we had left to us.' She must speak
of herself and her sister, for there were but those
two. Will you read the letter, Betty?"

Mrs. Dan took her spectacles from between the
leaves of the Bible, and read the letter, not speaking
immediately.

"She signs herself C. Travice," remarked Mrs.
George; "but I really forget her name. Whether
it was Catherine or Cordelia——"

"It was Charlotte," interposed Mrs. Dan. "We
used to call her Lottie."

"The curious thing in the affair is, why she
should write to *me*," continued Mrs. George Arkell.
"You were so much more intimate with them, that

I can only think she has made a mistake in the address, and really meant the letter for you."

A smile flitted over Mrs. Dan's face. "No mistake at all, as I should believe. You are Mrs. Arkell, you know; I am only Mrs. Dan. She must remember quite well that you have weight in the town, and I have none. She knows which of us is most capable of helping her."

"But, Betty, I and George had little or no acquaintance at all with the Travices," rejoined Mrs. Arkell, unconvinced. "We met them two or three times at your house; but I don't think they were ever inside ours. You brought one of the little girls to tea once with Mildred, I recollect: it must have been this eldest one who now writes. You, on the contrary, were intimate with them. Why, did you not stand godmother to one of the little ones?"

"To the youngest," assented Mrs. Dan, "and quite a fuss there was over it. Mrs. Travice wanted her to be named Betty; short, after me; but the captain wouldn't hear of it. He said Betty was old-fashioned—gone quite out of date. If you'll believe me it was not settled when we started for the church; but I decided it there, for when Mr. Elwin took the baby in his arms, and said, 'Name this child,' I spoke up and said, 'Elizabeth.' She grew to be a pretty little thing, too, meek and mild as a lamb ; Charlotte had a temper."

"Well, I still retain the opinion that she must have been under the impression she was addressing you. 'I write to you as an old friend of papa and mamma's,' you see, she says. Now that can't in any way apply to me. But I don't urge this as a plea for not accepting the letter," Mrs. George hastened to add ; "I'm sure we shall be pleased to do anything we can for her. I have talked the matter over with George, and we think it would be only kind to invite her to come to us for a month or so, while we see what can be done. We shall pay her coach fare down, and any other little matter, so that it will be no expense to her."

"It is exceedingly kind of you," remarked Mrs. Dan Arkell. "And when you write, tell her we will all try and make her visit a pleasant one," she added, in the honest simplicity of her heart. "Mildred will be a companion to her."

"I shall write to-day. The letter is dated Upper Stamford-street : but I'm sure I don't know in what part of London Upper Stamford-street lies," observed Mrs. Arkell, who had never been so far as London in her life, and would as soon have thought of going a journey to Cape Horn. "Where's Mildred ?"

"She's in the kitchen, helping Ann with the

damson jam. I did say I'd not have any made this year, sugar is so expensive, but Mildred pleaded for it. And what she says is true, that poor Peter comes in tired to death, and relishes a bit of jam with his tea, especially damson jam."

"I fear Peter's heart is not in his occupation, Betty."

Mrs. Dan shook her head. "It has never been that. From the time Peter was first taken to the Cathedral, a little fellow in petticoats, his heart has been set upon sometime being one of its clergy; but that is out of the question now: there's no help for it, you know."

Mildred came in, bright and radiant; she always liked the visits of her aunt George. They told her the news about Miss Travice, and showed her the letter.

"Played together when we were children, I and Charlotte Travice," she said, laughing; "I have nearly forgotten it. I hope she is a nice girl; it will be pleasant to have her down here."

"Mildred, I should like to take you back with me for the day. Will you come? Can you spare her, Betty?"

Mildred glanced at her mother, her lips parting with hope; dutiful and affectionate, she deferred to her mother in all things, never putting forth her own wishes. Mrs. Dan could spare her, and

said so. Mildred flew to her chamber, attired herself, and set forth with her aunt through the warm
and sunny streets—warm, sunny, bright as her
own heart.

Very much to the surprise of Mrs. Arkell, as she
turned in at the iron gates, she saw the carriage
standing before the door, and the servant Philip in
readiness to attend it. "Is your master going
out?" she inquired of the man.

"Mr. William is, ma'am."

"Where to, do you know?"

"I think it is only to Mr. Palmer's," returned
Philip. "I know Mr. William said we should not
be away above an hour."

William appeared in the distance, coming from
the manufactory with a fleet step, and a square
flat parcel in his hand.

"I am going to Mr. Palmer's to take this," he
said to his mother, indicating the parcel as he
threw it into the carriage; "it contains some
papers that my father promised to get for him as
soon as possible to-day. He was going to send
Philip alone, but I said I should like the drive.
You have just come in time, Mildred; get up."

The soft pink bloom mantled in her face; but she
rather drew away from the carriage than approached
it. She *never* went out upon William's invitation
alone.

"Why not, my dear?" said Mrs. Arkell, "it
will do you good. You will be back in time for
dinner."

William was looking round all the while, as he
waited to help her up, a half laugh upon his face.
Mildred's roses deepened, and she stepped in.
Philip came round to his young master.

"Am I to go now, sir?"

"Go now? of course; why should you not go?
There's the back seat, isn't there?"

Perhaps Philip's doubts did not altogether refer
to seats. He threw back the seat, and waited.
William took his place by his cousin's side, and
drove away, utterly unconscious of *her* feelings or
the man's thoughts. Had he not been accustomed
to this familiar intercourse with Mildred all his
life?

And Mrs. Arkell went indoors and sat down to
write her letter to Charlotte Travice. Westerbury
had nearly forgotten these Travices; they were not
natives of the place. Captain Travice—but it
should be observed that he had been captain of only
a militia regiment—had settled at Westerbury sometime after the conclusion of the war, and his two
children were born there. His income was but a
slender one, still it was sufficient; but it came
into the ex-captain's head one day, that, for the
sake of his two little daughters, he ought to make

a fortune if he could. Supposing that might be easier of accomplishment in the great metropolis, than in a sober, unspeculative cathedral town, he departed forthwith ; but the fortune, as Mrs. Arkell shrewdly surmised, had never been made ; and after various vicissitudes—ups and downs, as people phrase them—John Travice finally departed this life in their lodgings in Upper Stamford-street, and his wife did not long survive him. Of the two daughters, Charlotte had been the best educated ; what money there was to spare for such purposes, had been spent upon her ; the younger one was made, of necessity, a household drudge.

Charlotte responded at once to Mrs. Arkell's invitation, and within a week of it was travelling down to Westerbury by the day-coach. It arrived in the town at seven o'clock, and rarely varied by a minute. Have you forgotten those old coach days ? I have not. Mr. Arkell and his son stood outside the iron gates, Philip waiting in attendance ; and as the coach with its four fine horses came up the street, the guard blew his horn about ten times, a signal that it was going to stop to set down a passenger—for Mr. Arkell had himself spoken to the guard, and charged him to take good care of the young lady on her journey. The coachman drew up at the gates, and touched his hat to Mr. Arkell, and the guard leaped down and touched his.

"All right, sir. The young lady's here."

He opened the coach door, and she stepped out, dressed in expensive mourning; a tall, showy, handsome girl, affable in manner, ready of speech; altogether fascinating; just the one—just the one to turn the head and win the heart of a young fellow such as William Arkell. They might have foreseen it even in that first hour.

"Oh, how kind it is of you to have me!" she exclaimed, as she quite fell into Mrs. Arkell's arms in the hall, and burst into tears. "But I thought you had no daughter?" she added, recovering herself and looking at the young lady who stood by Mrs. Arkell.

"It is my niece Mildred, my dear; but she is to me as a daughter. I asked her to come and help welcome you this evening."

"I am sure I shall love you very much!" exclaimed Miss Travice, kissing Mildred five or six times. "What a sweet face you have!"

A sudden shyness came over Mildred. The warm greeting and the words were both new to her. She returned a courteous word of welcome, drew a little apart, and glanced at William. He seemed to have enough to do gazing at the visitor.

Philip was coming in with the luggage. Mrs. Arkell took her hand.

"I will show you your room, Miss Travice; and if——"

"Oh, pray don't call me 'Miss Travice,' or anything so formal," was the young lady's interruption. "Begin with 'Charlotte' at once, or I shall fear you are not glad to see me."

Mrs. Arkell smiled; her young visitor was winning upon her greatly. She led her to a very nice room on the first floor.

"This will be your chamber, my dear; it is over our usual sitting-room. My room and Mr. Arkell's is on the opposite side the corridor, over the drawing-room. You face the street, you see; and across there to the right are the cathedral towers."

"What a charming house you have, Mrs. Arkell! So large and nice."

"It is larger than we require. Let me look at you, my dear, and see what resemblance I can trace. I remember your father and mother."

She held the young lady before her. A very pretty face, certainly—especially now, for Charlotte laughed and blushed.

"Oh, Mrs. Arkell, I am not fit to be seen; I feel as dusty as can be. You cannot think how dusty the roads were; I shall look better to-morrow."

"You have the bright dark eyes and the clear complexion of your father; but I don't see that you are like him in features—yours are prettier.

But now, my dear, tell me—in writing to me, did you not think you were writing to Mrs. Daniel Arkell?"

"Mrs. Daniel Arkell! No, I did not. Who is she? I don't remember anything about her."

"But Mrs. Daniel was your mother's friend—far more intimate with her than I was. I am delighted at the mistake, if it was one; for Mrs. Dan might otherwise have gained the pleasure of your visit, instead of me."

"I don't *think* I made a mistake," said Charlotte, more dubiously than she had just spoken; "I used to hear poor mamma speak of the Arkells of Westerbury; and one day lately, in looking over some of her old letters and papers, I found your address. The thought came into my mind at once to write to you, and ask if you could help me to a situation. I believe papa was respected in Westerbury; and it struck me that somebody here might want a teacher, or governess, and engage me for his sake. You know we are of gentle blood, Mrs. Arkell, though we have been so poor of late years."

"I will do anything to help you that I can," was the kind answer. "Have you lost both father and mother?"

"Why yes," returned Charlotte, with a surprised air, as if she had thought all the world knew that.

"Papa has been dead several months—twelve, I think, nearly; mamma has been dead five or six."

"And—I suppose—your poor papa did not leave much money?"

"Not a penny," freely answered Charlotte. "He had a few shares in some mining company at the time of his death; they were worth nothing then, but they afterwards went up to what is called a premium, and the brokers sold them for us. They did not realize much, but it was sufficient to keep mamma as long as she lived."

"And what have you done since?"

"Not much," sighed Charlotte; "I had a situation as daily governess; but, oh! it was so uncomfortable. There were five girls, and no discipline, no regularity; it was at a clergyman's, too. They live near to us, in Upper Stamford-street. I am so glad I wrote to you! Betsey did not want me to write; she thought it looked intrusive."

"Betsey!" echoed Mrs. Arkell.

"My sister Elizabeth—we call her Betsey. She is younger than I am."

"Oh yes, to be sure. I wondered you did not speak of her in your letter; Mrs. Daniel Arkell is her godmother. Where is she?"

"At Mrs. Dundyke's."

"Who is Mrs. Dundyke?"

"She keeps the house where we live, in Stamford-street. She is not a lady, you know; a worthy sort of person, and all that, but quite an inferior woman. Not but that she was always kind to us; she was very kind and attentive to mamma in her last illness. I can't bear her," candidly continued the young lady, " and she can't bear me ; but she likes Betsey, and has asked her to stop there, free of cost, for a little while. Her daughter died and left two little children, and Betsey is to make herself useful with them."

" But why did you not mention Betsey? why did you not bring her?" cried Mrs. Arkell, feeling vexed at the omission. " She would have been as welcome to us as you are, my dear."

Miss Charlotte Travice shook back her flowing hair, and there was a little curl of contempt on her pretty nose. "You are very kind, Mrs. Arkell, but Betsey is better where she is. I could not think of taking her out with me."

" Why so ?" asked Mrs. Arkell, rather surprised.

" Oh, you'd not say, why so, if you saw her. She is quite a plain, homely sort of young person : she has not been educated for anything else. Nobody would believe we were sisters; and Betsey knows that, and is humble accordingly. Of course some one had to wait upon mamma and me, for lodging-house servants are the most unpleasant things upon earth, and there was only Betsey."

Mrs. Arkell went downstairs, leaving her young guest to follow when she was ready. Mrs. Arkell did not understand the logic of the last admissions, and certainly did not admire the spirit in which they appeared to be spoken.

The hours for meals were early at Mr. Arkell's; dinner at one, tea at five; but the tea had this evening been put off, in politeness to Miss Travice. She came down, a fashionable-looking young lady, in a thin black dress of some sort of gauze, with innumerable rucheings and quillings of crape upon it. Certainly her attire—as they found when the days went on—betrayed little symptom of a straitened purse.

She took her place at the tea-table, all smiles and sweetness; she glanced shyly at William; she captivated Mr. Arkell's heart; she caused Mrs. Arkell completely to forget the few words concerning Betsey which had so jarred upon her ear; and before that tea-drinking was over, they were all ready to fall in love with her. All, save one.

Then she went round the room, a candle in her hand, and looked at the pictures; she freely said which of them she liked best; she sat down to the piano, unasked, and played a short, striking piece from memory. They asked her if she could sing; she answered by breaking into the charming old song "Robin Adair;" it was one of William

Arkell's favourites, and he stood by enraptured, half bewildered with this pleasant inroad on their quiet routine of existence.

"You play, I am sure," she suddenly said to him.

He had no wish to deny it, and took his flute from its case. He was a finished player. It is an instrument very nearly forgotten now, but it never would have been forgotten had its players managed it as did William Arkell. They began trying duets together, and the evening passed insensibly. William loved music passionately, and could hardly tear himself away from it to run with Mildred home.

"Well, Mildred, and how do you like her?" was Mrs. Dan's first question.

"I—I can hardly tell," was the hesitating answer.

"Not tell!" repeated Mrs. Dan: "you have surely found out whether she is pleasant or disagreeable?"

"She is very pretty, and her manners are perfectly charming. But—still——"

"Still, what?" said Mrs. Dan, wondering.

"Well, mother—but you know I never like to speak ill of anyone—there is something in her that strikes me as not being *true*."

CHAPTER IV.

ROBERT CARR'S REQUEST.

THE time went on. The month for which Charlotte Travice had been invited had lengthened itself into nearly three, and December had come in.

Mrs. Dan Arkell (wholly despising Mildred's acknowledged impression of the new visitor, and treating her to a sharp lecture for entertaining it) had made a call on Miss Travice the following morning, and offered Mildred's services as a companion to her. But in a very short time Mildred found she was not wanted. William was preferred. *He* was the young lady's companion, and nothing loth so to be; and his visits to Mildred's house, formerly so frequent, became rare almost as those of angels. It was Charlotte Travice now. She went out with him in the carriage; she was his partner in the dance; and the breathings on the flute grew into strains of love. Worse than all to Mildred—more hard to bear—William would laugh at the satire the London lady was pleased to tilt at her. It is true Mildred had no great pretension to beauty; not half as much as Charlotte; but William had found it enough before. In figure and manners Mildred was essentially a lady; and her face, with its soft brown eyes and its sweet expression, was not an unattractive one. It cannot be denied that a sore feeling arose in Mildred's heart, though not yet did she guess at the full calamity looming for that heart in the distance. She saw at present only the temporary annoyance; that this gaudy, handsome, off-hand stranger had come to ridicule, rival, and for the time supplant her. But she thought, then, it was but for the time; and she somewhat ungraciously longed for the day when the young lady should wing her flight back to London.

That expression we sometimes treat a young child to, when a second comes to supplant it, that "its nose is put out of joint," might decidedly have been now applied to Mildred. Charlotte Travice took her place in all ways. In the winter evening visiting—staid, old-fashioned, respectable visiting, which met at six o'clock and separated at midnight —Mildred was accustomed to accompany her uncle and aunt. Mrs. Dan Arkell's visiting days were over; Peter, buried in his books, had never had any; and it had become quite a regular thing for Mildred to go with Mr. and Mrs. Arkell and

4—2

William. They always drove round and called for her, leaving her at home on their return; and Mildred was generally indebted to her aunt for her pretty evening dresses—that lady putting forth as an excuse the plea that she should dislike to take out anyone ill-dressed. It was all altered now. Flies—as everybody knows—will hold but four, and there was no longer room for Mildred : Miss Travice occupied her place. Once or twice, when the winter parties were commencing, the fly came round as usual, and William walked ; but Mildred, exceedingly tenacious of anything like intrusion, wholly declined this for the future, and refused the invitations, or went on foot, well cloaked, and escorted by Peter. William remonstrated, telling Mildred she was growing obstinate. Mildred answered that she would go out with them again when their visitor had returned to London.

But the visitor seemed in no hurry to return. She made a faint sort of pleading speech one day, that really she ought to go back for Christmas ; she was sure Mr. and Mrs. Arkell must be tired of her : just one of those little ·pseudo moves to go, which, in politeness, cannot be accepted. Neither was it by Mr. and Mrs. Arkell : had the young lady remained with them a twelvemonth, in their proud and stately courtesy they would have pressed her to stay on longer. Mrs. Arkell had once or twice

spoken of the primary object of her coming—the
looking out for some desirable situation for her :
but Miss Travice appeared to have changed her
mind. She thought now she should not like to be
in a country school, she said ; but would get something in London on her return.

Mildred, naturally clear-sighted, felt convinced
that Miss Travice was playing a part ; that she was
incessantly *labouring* to ingratiate herself into the
good opinion of Mr. and Mrs. Arkell, and especially into that of William. " Oh, that they could
see her as she really is !" thought Mildred ; " false
and false !" And Miss Travice took out her re-
creation tilting lance-shafts at Mildred.

" How is it you never learned music, Miss
Arkell ?" she was pleased to inquire one day, as
she finished a brilliant piece, and gave herself a
whirl round on the music-stool to speak.

" I can't tell," replied Mildred ; " I did not
learn it."

" Neither did you learn drawing ?"

" No."

" Well, that's odd, isn't it ? Mr. and Mrs. Dan
Arkell must have been rather neglectful of you."

"I suppose they thought I should do as well
without accomplishments as with them," was the
composed answer. " To tell you the truth, Miss
Travice, I dare say I shall."

"But everybody is accomplished now—at least, ladies are. I was surprised, I must confess, to find William Arkell a proficient in such things, for men rarely learn them. I wonder they did not have you taught music, if only to play with him. He has to put up with a stranger, you see—poor me."

Mildred's cheek burnt. "I have *listened* to him," she said; "hitherto he has found that sort of help enough, and liked it."

"He is very attractive," resumed Charlotte, throwing her bright eyes full at Mildred, a saucy expression in their depths; "don't you find him so?"

"I think you do," was Mildred's quiet answer.

"Of course I do. Haven't I just said it? And so, I dare say, do a great many others. Yesterday evening—by the way, you ought to have been here yesterday evening."

"Why ought I?"

"Mrs. Arkell meant to send for you, and told William to go; I heard her. He forgot it; and then it grew too late."

Mildred did not raise her eyes from her work. She was hemming a shirt-frill of curiously fine cambric—Mr. Arkell, behind the taste of his day, wore shirt-frills still. Mrs. Arkell rarely did any plain sewing herself; what her maid-servants did not do, was consigned to Mildred.

"Do you *like* work?" inquired Miss Charlotte, watching her nimble fingers, and quitting abruptly the former subject.

"Very much indeed."

Charlotte shrugged her shoulders with a spice of contempt. "I hate it; I once tried to make a tray-cloth, but it came out a bag; and mamma never gave me anything more."

"Who did the sewing at your house?"

"Betsey, of course. Mamma also used to do some, and groan over it like anything. I think ladies never ought——"

What Charlotte Travice was about to say ladies ought not to do was interrupted by the entrance of William. He had not been indoors since the early dinner, and looked pleased to see Mildred, who had come by invitation to spend a long afternoon.

"Which of you will go out with me?" he asked, somewhat abruptly; and his mother came into the room as he was speaking.

"Out where?" she asked.

"My father has a little matter of business at Purford to-day, and is sending me to transact it. It is only a message, and wont take me two minutes to deliver; but it is a private one, and must be spoken either by himself or me. I said I'd go if Charlotte would accompany me," he

added, in his half-laughing, half-independent manner. "I did not know Mildred was here."

"And you come in and ask which of them will
go," said Mrs. Arkell. "I think it must be Mildred. Charlotte, my dear, you will not feel
offended if 1 say it is her turn ? I like to be just
and fair. It is you who have had all the drives
lately ; Mildred has had none."

Charlotte did not answer. Mildred felt that it
was her turn, and involuntarily glanced at William ;
but he said not a word to second his mother's
wish. The sensitive blood flew to her face, and
she spoke, she hardly knew what—something to
the effect that she would not deprive Miss Travice
of the drive. William spoke then.

"But if you would like to go, Mildred ? It *is*
a long time since you went out, now I come to
think of it."

Now I come to think of it! Oh, how the admission of indifference chilled her heart !

"Not this afternoon, thank you," she said, with
decision. "I will go with you another opportunity."

"Then, Charlotte, you must make haste, or we
shall not be home by dark," he said. "Philip is
bringing the carriage round."

Mildred stood at the window and watched the
departure, hating herself all the while for standing

there; but there was fascination in the sight, in the midst of its pain. Would she win the prize, this new stranger? Mildred shivered outwardly and inwardly as the question crossed her mind.

She saw them drive away—Charlotte in her new violet bonnet, with its inward trimming of pretty pink ribbons, her prettier face raised to his—William bending down and speaking animatedly—sober old Philip, who had been in the family ten years, behind them. Purford was a little place, about five miles off, on the road to Eckford; and they might be back by dusk, if they chose. It was not much past three now, and the winter afternoon was fine.

Would she win him? Mildred returned to her seat, and worked on at the cambric frill, the question running riot in her brain. A conviction within her—a prevision, if you will—whispered that it would be a marriage particularly distasteful to Mr. and Mrs. Arkell. *They* did not yet dream of it, and would have been thankful to have their eyes opened to the danger. Mildred knew this; she saw it as clearly as though she had read it in a book; but she was too honourable to breathe it to them.

When the frill was finished, she folded it up, and told her aunt she would take her departure; Peter had talked of going out after banking hours with a friend, and her mother, who was not well, would be alone. Mrs. Arkell made but a faint resistance to this: Mildred came and went pretty much as she liked.

Peter, however, was at home when she got there, sitting over the fire in the dusk, in a thoughtful mood. On two afternoons in the week, Tuesdays and Thursdays, the bank closed at four; this was Thursday, and Peter had come straight home. Mildred took her seat at the table, against five o'clock should strike, the signal for their young maid-servant to bring the tea-tray in. It was quite dark outside, and the room was only lighted by the fire.

"What are you thinking of, Peter?" Mrs. Dan presently broke the silence by asking.

Peter took his chin from his hand where it had been resting, and his eyes from the fire, and turned his head to his mother. "I was thinking of a proposal Colonel Dewsbury made to me to-day," he answered; "deliberating upon it, in fact, and I think I have decided."

This was something like Greek to Mrs. Dan; even Mildred was sufficiently aroused from her thoughts to turn to him in surprise.

"The colonel wants me to go to his house in an evening, mother, and read the classics with his eldest son."

" Peter !"

" For about three hours, he says, from six till nine.   He will give me a guinea a week."

" But only think how you slave and fag all day at that bank," said Mrs. Dan, who in her ailing old age thought work (as did Charlotte Travice) the greatest evil of life.

" And only think what a many additional comforts a guinea a week could purchase for you, mother," cried Peter in his affection ; " our house would be set up in riches then."

" Peter, my dear," she gravely said, " I do not suppose I shall be here very long ; and for comforts, I have as many as I require."

" Well, put it down to my own score, if you like," said Peter, with as much of a smile as he ever attempted ; " I shall find the guinea useful."

" But if you thus dispose of your evenings, what time should you have for your books ?" resumed Mrs. Arkell.

" I'll make that ; I get up early, you know ; and in one sense of the word, I shall be at my books all these three hours."

" How came Colonel Dewsbury to propose it to you ?"

" I don't know. I met him as I was returning to the bank after dinner, and he began saying he was trying to find some one who would come in and read with Arthur. Presently he said, ' I wish you would come yourself, Mr. Arkell.' And after a little more talk I told him I would consider of it."

" I thought Arthur Dewsbury was to go into the army," remarked Mrs. Dan, not yet reconciled to the thing. " Soldiers don't want to be so very proficient in the classics."

" Not Arthur; he is intended for the church: the second son will be brought up for the army. Mildred, what do you say—should you take it if you were me?"

" I should," replied Mildred : " it appears to me to be a wonderfully easy way of earning money. But it is for your own decision entirely, Peter : do not let my opinion sway you."

" I think I had decided before I hung up my top-coat and hat on the peg at the bank," answered Peter. " Yes, I shall take it; I can but resign it later, you know, mother, if I find it doesn't work well."

The cathedral clock, so close to them, was chiming the quarters, and the first stroke of five boomed out; Peter rose and stretched himself with a relieved air. "It's always a weight off my mind when I get any knotty point decided," quoth he, rather simply ; and in truth Peter was not good for much, apart from his Latin and Greek.

At the same moment, when that melodious col

lege clock was striking, William Arkell was driving in at his own gates. He might have made more haste had he so chosen ; and Mr. Arkell had charged him to be home "before dark ;" but William had not hurried himself.

He was driving in quickly now, and stopped before the house-door. Philip left his seat and went to the horse's head, and William assisted out Miss Travice.

"Have you enjoyed your drive, Charlotte?" he whispered, retaining her hand in his, longer than he need have done ; and there was a tenderness in his tone that might have told a tale, had anyone been there to read it.

"Oh ! very, very much," she answered, in the soft, sweet, earnest voice she had grown to use when alone with William. "Stolen pleasures are always sweetest."

"Stolen pleasures?"

"*This* was a stolen one. You know I usurped the place of your cousin Mildred. She ought to have come."

"No such thing, Charlotte. She can go anytime."

"I felt quite sorry for her. I am apt to think those poor seamstresses require so much air. They——"

"Those what?" cried out William—and Miss Charlotte Travice immediately knew by the tone, that she had ventured on untenable ground. "Are you speaking of my cousin Mildred?"

"She is so kind and good; hemming cambric frills, and stitching wristbands! I wish I could do it. I was always the most wretched little dunce at plain sewing, and could never be taught it. My sister on the contrary——"

"I want to speak a word to you, Arkell."

William turned hastily, wondering who was at his elbow. At that moment the hall-door was thrown open, and the rays of the lamp shone forth, revealing the features of Robert Carr. Charlotte ran indoors, vouchsafing no greeting. She had taken a dislike to Robert Carr. He was free of speech, and the last time he and the young lady met, he had said something in her ear for which she would be certain to hate him for his life—"How was the angling going on? Had Bill Arkell bit yet?"

"Hallo!" exclaimed William as he recognised him. "I thought you were in London! I heard you went up on Tuesday night!"

"And came down last night. I want you to do me a favour, Arkell."

He put his arm within William's as he spoke, and began pacing the yard. William thought his manner unusual. There seemed a nervous restlessness about it—if he could have fancied such a thing of Robert Carr. William waited for him to speak.

"I have had an awful row with the governor to-day," he began at length. "I don't intend to stand it much longer."

"What about?"

"Oh! the old story—my extravagance. He was angry at my running up to town for a day, and called it waste of money and waste of time. So unreasonable of him, you know. Had I stayed a month, he'd not have made half the row."

"It does seem like waste, to go so far for only a day," said William, "unless you have business. That is a different thing."

"Well, I had business. I wanted to see a fellow there. You never heard any one make such a row about nothing. I have the greatest mind in the world to shake off the yoke altogether, and start for myself in life."

William could not help laughing. "You start?"

"You think I couldn't? If I do, rely upon it I succeed. I'm nearly sick of knocking about. I declare I'd rather sweep a crossing, and get ten shillings a week and keep myself upon it, than I'd continue to have my life bothered out by him. I shall tell him so one of these first fine days if he doesn't let me alone. Why doesn't he!"

"I suppose the fact is you continue to provoke him," remarked William.

"What about?" was the fierce rejoinder.

"Oh! you know, Carr. What I spoke to you of, before—though it is not any business of mine. Why don't you drop it?"

"Because I don't choose," returned Robert Carr, understanding the allusion. "I declare, before Heaven, that there's no wrong in it, and I don't choose to submit myself, abjectly, to the will of others. The thing might have been dropped at first but for the opposition that was raised. So long as fools continue that, I shall go there."

"For the girl's own sake, you should drop it. I presume you can't intend to marry her——"

"Marry her!" scoffingly interrupted Robert Carr.

"Just so. But she is a respectable girl, and——"

"I'd knock any man down that dared to say she wasn't," said Robert, quietly.

"But don't you know that the very fact of your continuing to go there must tend to damage her in public opinion? Edward Hughes must be foolish to allow it."

"Where's the wrong, or harm, of my going there?" demanded Robert, condescending to argue the question. "I like the girl excessively; I like talking to her. She has been as well reared as I have."

"Nonsense," returned William. "You can't separate her from her family; from what she is. I say you ought to drop it."

"What on earth has made you so squeamish all on a sudden? The society of that fine London lady, Miss Charlotte Travice?"

They were passing in a ray of light at the moment, thrown across the yard from one of the carriage lamps. Philip had left the carriage and the lamps outside, and was in the stable with the horse. Robert Carr saw his companion's face light up at the allusion, but William replied, without any symptom of anger—

"I will tell you what, people are beginning to talk of it from one end of the town to the other. I don't think you have any right to bring the scandal upon her. You bring it *needlessly*, as you yourself admit. A girl's good name, once lost, is not easy to regain, although it may be lost unjustly."

"I told you months ago, that there was nothing in it."

"I believe you; I believe you still. But now that the town has taken the matter up, and is passing its opinion upon it, I say that for the young girl's sake you should put a stop to it, and let the acquaintance cease."

"The town may be smothered for all I care— and serve it right!" was Robert Carr's reply. " But look here, Arkell, I didn't come to raise up this discussion, I have no time for it; and you may just take one fact into your note-book—that all you can say, though you talked till doomsday, would not alter my line of conduct by a hair's breadth. I came to ask you a favour."

"What is it?"

"Will you lend me the carriage for an hour or so to-morrow morning? It's to go to Purford."

"To Purford! Why that's where I have just been. I dare say you may have it. I will ask my father."

"But that is just what I don't want you to ask. I have to go there on a little private business of my own, and I don't wish it known that I have gone."

William hesitated. Only son, and indulged son though he was, he had never gone the length of lending out his father's carriage without permission; and he very much disliked the idea of doing so now. Robert Carr did not give him much time for consideration.

"You will be rendering me a service which I shan't forget, Arkell. If Philip will drive me over——"

"Philip! Do you want Philip with you?"

"Philip must go to bring back the carriage; I shan't return until the afternoon. Why, he will be there and home again almost before Mr. Arkell's up. I must go pretty early."

This, the going of Philip, appeared to simplify

the matter greatly. To allow Robert Carr or anyone else to take the carriage off for a day without
permission was one thing; for Philip to drive him
to Purford early in the morning, and be back again
directly, was another. "I think you may have it,
Carr," he said; "but if my father misses the
carriage and Philip—as he is sure to do—and asks
where they are——"

"Oh, you may tell him then," interrupted
Robert Carr.

"Very well. Shall Philip bring the carriage to
your house?"

"No need of that; I'll come here and get up.
I'd better speak to Philip myself. Don't stay out
any longer in the cold, Arkell. Good night, and
thank you."

William went indoors; and Robert Carr sought
Philip in the stable to give him his instructions for
the morning.

5—2

CHAPTER V.

THE FLIGHT.

In a quiet and remote street of the city was situated the house of Mr. Carr. Robert Carr walked towards it, with a moody look upon his face, after quitting William Arkell—a plain, dull-looking house, as seen from the street, presenting little in aspect beyond a dead wall, for most of the windows looked the other way, or on to the side garden—but a perfect bijou of a house inside, all on a small scale, with stained glass illuminating the hall, and statues and pictures ornamenting the rooms. The fretwork in the hall, and the devices on the windows—bright in colours when the sun shone through them, but otherwise dark and sombre—imparted the idea of a miniature chapel, when seen by a stranger for the first time. Old Mr. Carr had spent much time and money on his house, and was proud of it.

Robert swung himself in at the outer door in the wall, and then in at the hall door, which he shut

with a bang; things, in fact, had arrived at a
pitch of discomfort between him and his father
hardly bearable by the temper of either. Neither
would give way—neither would conciliate the other
in the smallest degree. The disputes—arising, in
the first place, from Robert's extravagance and un-
steady habits—had continued for some years now;
but during the past two or three months they had
increased both in frequency and violence. Robert
was idle—Robert spent—Robert did hardly anything that he ought to do, as member of a respectable community; these complaints made the basis
of the foundation in all the disputes. But graver
sins, in old Mr. Carr's eyes, of some special nature
or other, cropped up to the surface from time to
time. Latterly, the grievance had been this acquaintance of Robert's with Martha Ann Hughes;
and it may really be questioned whether Robert, in
his obstinate spirit, did not continue it on purpose
to vex his father.

On the Tuesday (this was Thursday, remember)
Robert had been, to use his father's expression,
" swinging about all day"—meaning that Mr.
Robert had passed it out of doors, nobody knew
where, only going in to his meals. Their hours
were early—as indeed was the general custom at
Westerbury, and elsewhere, also, in those days—
dinner at one o'clock, tea at five. About half-

past four, on the Tuesday, Robert had gone in, ordered himself some tea made at once, and something to eat with it, and then went out again, taking a warm travelling rug, and telling the servant to say he was gone to London. And he proceeded to the coach-office, took his seat in the mail, then on the point of starting, and departed.

Mr. Carr came in from the manufactory at five to *his* tea, and received the message—" Mr. Robert had gone to London by the mail." He was very wroth. It was an independent, off-hand mode of action, calculated to displease most fathers; but it was not the first time, by several, that Robert had been guilty of it. "He's gone off to spend that money," cried Mr. Carr, savagely; " and he wont come back until there's not a farthing of it left." Mr. Carr alluded to a hundred pounds which Robert had received not many days previously. A twelvemonth before, an uncle of Mr. Carr's and of Squire Carr's had died, leaving Robert Carr a legacy of a hundred pounds, and the same sum *between* the two sons of Mr. John Carr. This, of course, was productive of a great deal of heart-burning and jealousy in the Squire's family, that Robert should have the most; but it has nothing to do with our history just now. At the expiration of a year from the time of the death, the legacies were paid, and Robert had been in possession of his since the previous Saturday.

"He's gone to spend the money," Mr. Carr repeated. No very far-fetched conclusion; and Mr. Carr got over his wrath, or bottled it up, in the best way he could. He certainly did not expect Robert back again for a month at least; very considerably astonished, therefore, was he, to find Mr. Robert arrive back by the mail that took him, and walk coolly in to breakfast on the Thursday morning, having only stayed a few hours in London. A little light skirmishing took place then—not much. Robert said he had been to London to see a friend, and, having seen him, came back again; and that was all Mr. Carr could obtain. For a wonder, Robert spent the morning in the manufactory, but not in the presence of his father, who was shut in his private room. At dinner they met again, and before the meal was over the quarrel was renewed. It grew to a serious height. The old housekeeper, who had been in her place ever since the death of Mrs. Carr, years before, grew frightened, and stole to the door with trembling limbs and white lips. The clock struck three before it was over; and, in one sense, it was not over then. Robert burst out of the room in its very midst, an oath upon his lips, and strode into the street. Where he passed the time that after-

noon until five o'clock could never be traced. Mr.
Carr endeavoured afterwards to ascertain, and could
not. Mr. Carr's opinion, to his dying day, was that
he passed it at Edward Hughes's house; but Miss
Hughes positively denied it, and she was by nature
truthful. She stated freely that Robert Carr had
called in that afternoon, and was for a few minutes
alone with Martha Ann, she herself being upstairs
at the time; but he left again directly. At five
o'clock, as we have seen, he was with William
Arkell, and then he went straight home.

Mr. Carr had nearly finished tea when he got
in. The meal was taken in a small, snug room,
at the end of the hall—a *round* room, whose
windows opened upon the garden in summer, but
were closed in now behind their crimson-velvet
curtains.

Robert sat down in silence. He looked in the
tea-pot, saw that it was nearly empty, and rang the
bell to order fresh tea to be made for him. Whether the little assumption of authority (though it
was no unusual circumstance) was distasteful to
Mr. Carr, and put him further out of temper, cannot be told; one thing is certain, that he—he, the
father—took up again the quarrel.

It was not a seemly one. Less loud than it had
been at dinner-time, the tones on either side were
graver, the anger more real and compressed. It

seemed too deep for noise. An hour or so of this unhappy state of things, during which many, many bitter words were said by both, and then Robert rose.

"Remember," he said to his father, in a low, firm tone, "if I am driven from my home and my native place by this conduct of yours, I swear that I will never come back to it."

"And do you hear me swear," retorted Mr. Carr, in the same quiet, concentrated voice of passion, "if you marry that girl, Martha Ann Hughes, not one penny of my money or property shall you ever inherit; and you know that I will keep my word."

"I never said I had any thought of marrying her."

"As you please. Marry her; and I swear that I will leave all I possess away from you and yours. Before Heaven, I will keep my oath!"

And now we must go to the following morning, to the house of Mr. Arkell. These little details may appear trivial to the reader, but they bear their significance, as you will find hereafter; and they are remembered and talked of in Westerbury to this day.

The breakfast hour at Mr. Arkell's was nine o'clock. Some little time previous to it, William was descending from his room, when in passing his father's door he heard himself called to. Mr. Arkell appeared at his door in the process of dressing.

"William, I heard the carriage go out a short while ago. Have you sent it anywhere?"

Just the question that William had anticipated would be put. Being released now from his promise, he told the truth.

"Over to Purford! Why could he not have gone by the coach?"

"I don't know I'm sure," said William; and the same thought had occurred to himself. "I did not like to promise him without speaking to you, but he made such a favour of it, and—I thought you would excuse it. I fancy he is on worse terms than ever with his father, and feared you might tell him."

"He need not have feared that: what should I tell him for?" was the rejoinder of Mr. Arkell as he retreated within his room.

Now it should have been mentioned that Mary Hughes was engaged to work that day at Mr. Arkell's. It was regarded in the town as a singular coincidence; and, perhaps, what made it more singular was the fact that Mrs. Arkell's maid, Tring (who had lived in the house ever since William was a baby, and was the only female servant kept besides the cook), had arranged with Mary Hughes

that she should go *before* the usual hour, eight
o'clock, so as to give a long day. The fact was,
Mary Hughes's work this day was for the maids.
It was Mrs. Arkell's custom to give them a gown
apiece for Christmas, and the two gowns were this
day to be cut out and as much done to them as the
dressmaker, and Tring at odd moments, could accomplish. Mary Hughes, naturally obliging, and
anxious to stand well with the servants in one of
her best places, as Mrs. Arkell's was, arrived at
half-past seven, and was immediately set to work
in what Tring called her pantry—a comfortable
little boarded room, a sort of offshoot of the
kitchen.

Mr. Arkell spoke again at breakfast of this expedition of Robert Carr's. It wore to him a
curious sound—first, that Robert could not have
gone by the coach, which left Westerbury about the
same hour, and had to pass through Purford on its
way to London; and, secondly, why the matter of
borrowing the carriage need have been kept from
him. William could not enlighten him on either
point, and the subject dropped.

Breakfast was over, and Mr. Arkell had gone
into the manufactory, when the carriage came
back. Philip drove at once to the stables, and
William went out.

"Well," said he, "so you are back!"

" Yes, sir."

Philip began to unharness the horse as he spoke, and did not look up. William, who knew the man and his ways well, thought there was something behind to tell.

" You have driven the horse fast, Philip."

" Mr. Carr did, sir ; it was he who drove. I never sat in front at all after we got to the three-cornered field. He drove fast, to get on pretty far before the coach came up."

" What coach ?" asked William.

" The London coach, sir. He's gone to London in it."

" What ! did he take it at Purford ?"

" We didn't go to Purford at all, Mr. William. He ain't gone alone, neither."

" Philip, what do you mean ?"

" Miss Hughes—the young one—is gone with him."

" No !" exclaimed William.

" It was this way, sir," began the man, disposing himself to relate the narrative consecutively. " I had got the carriage ready and waiting by a few minutes after eight, as he ordered me ; but it was close upon half-past before he came, and we started. ' I'll drive, Philip,' says he ; so I got in beside him. Just after we had cleared the houses, he pulls up before the three-cornered field, saying he was waiting for a friend, and I saw the little Miss Hughes come scuttering across it—it's a short cut from their house, you know, Mr. William—with a bit of a brown-paper parcel in her hand. 'You'll sit behind, Philip,' he says; and before I'd got over my astonishment, we was bowling along—she in front with him, and me behind. Just on this side Purford he pulled up again, and waited—it was in that hollow of the road near the duck-pond—and in two minutes up came the London coach. It came gently up to us, stopping by degrees; it was expecting him—as I could hear by the guard's talk, a saying he hoped he'd not waited long—and they got into it, and I suppose he's gone to London. Mr. William, I don't think the master will like this?"

William did not like it, either; it was an advantage that Robert Carr had no right to take. Had the girl forgotten herself at last, and gone off with him? Too surely he felt that such must be the case. He saw how it was. They had not chosen to get into the coach at Westerbury, fearing the scandal—fearing, perhaps, prevention; and Robert Carr had made use of this *ruse* to get her away. That there would be enough scandal in Westerbury, as it was, he knew—that Mr. Arkell would be indignant, he also knew; and he himself would come in for a large portion of the blame.

" Philip," he said, awaking from his reverie, " did the girl appear to go willingly?"

" Willingly enough, sir, for the matter of that, for she came up of her own accord—but she was crying sadly."

" Crying, was she?"

" Crying dreadfully all the way across the field as she came up, and along in this carriage, and when she got into the coach. He tried to persuade and soothe her; but it wasn't of any good. She hid her face with her veil as well as she could, that the outside passengers mightn't see her state as she got in; and there was none o' the inside."

William Arkell bit his lip. " Carr had no business to play me such a turn," he said aloud, in his vexation.

" Mr. William, if I had known what he was up to last night, I should just have told the master, in spite of the half-sovereign he gave me."

" Oh, he gave you one, did he?"

" He gave me one last evening, and he gave me another this morning; but, for all that, I should have told, if I'd thought she was to be along of him. I know what the master is, and I know what he'll feel about the business. And the two other Miss Hughes's are industrious, respectable young women, and it's a shabby thing for Mr. Carr to go and do. A fine way they'll be in when they find the young one gone !"

" They can't have known of it, I suppose," observed William, slowly, for a doubt had crossed his mind whether Robert could be taking the young girl away to marry her.

" No, that they don't, sir," impulsively cried the man. " I heard him ask her whether she had got away without being seen ; and she said she had, as well as she could speak for her tears."

William Arkell, feeling more annoyed than he had ever felt in his life, not only on his own score, but on that of the girl herself, turned towards the manufactory with a slow step. The most obvious course now—indeed, the only honourable one—was to tell his father what he had just heard. He winced at having it to do, and a feeling of relief came over him, when he found that Mr. Arkell was engaged in his private room with some gentlemen, and he could not go in. There was to be also a further respite : for when they left Mr. Arkell went out with them.

" William did not see him again until they met at dinner, for Mr. Arkell only returned just in time for it. Charlotte Travice was rallying William for being " absent," " silent," asking him where his thoughts had gone ; but he did not enlighten her.

Barely had they sat down to dinner when Marmaduke Carr arrived—pale, fierce, and deeply agitated. Ignoring ceremony, he pushed past Tring into the dining-room, and stood before them, his lips apart, his words coming from them in jerks. Mr. Arkell rose from his seat in consternation.

"George Arkell, you and I have been friends since we were boys together. I had thought if there was one man in the whole town whom I could have depended on, it was you. Is this well done?"

"Why, what has happened?" exclaimed Mr. Arkell, rather in doubt whether Marmaduke Carr had suddenly gone deranged. "Is what well done?"

"So! it is you who have helped off my son."

"Helped him where? What is the matter, Carr?"

"Helped him *where?*" roared Mr. Carr, "why, on his road to London. He is gone off there with that—that——" Mr. Carr caught timely sight of the alarmed faces of Mrs. Arkell and Miss Travice, and moderated his tone—"that Hughes girl. You pretend to ask me where he's gone, when it was you sent him!—conveyed him half-way on his road."

"I protest I do not know what you mean," cried Mr. Arkell.

"Not know! Did your chaise and your servant take him and that girl to Purford, or did they not?"

For reply, Mr. Arkell cast a look on his son—a look of stern inquiry. William could only speak the truth now, and Mr. Arkell's brow darkened as he listened.

"And you knew of this—this elopement?"

"No, on my word of honour. If I had known of it, I should not have lent him the carriage. Robert"—he raised his eyes to Mr. Carr's—"was not justified in playing me this trick."

"I don't believe a word of your denial," roughly spoke Mr. Carr, in his anger; "you and he planned this escape together; you were in league with him."

It is useless to contend with an angry man, and William calmly turned to his father: "All I know of the matter, sir, I told you this morning. I never suspected anything amiss until Philip came back with the carriage and related what had occurred."

George Arkell knew that his son's veracity might be depended on, nevertheless he felt terribly annoyed at being drawn into the affair. Mrs. Arkell did not mend the matter when she inquired whither Robert had gone.

Mr. Carr answered intemperately, speaking out the truth more broadly than he need have done:

his scamp of a son and the shameless Hughes girl
had taken flight together.

Tring, who had stood aghast during the short colloquy, not at first understanding what was amiss,
stole away to her pantry, where the dressmaking was
going on. Tring sunk down in a chair at once,
and regarded the poor seamstress with open mouth
and eyes, in which pity and horror struggled together. Tring was of the respectable school, and
really thought death would be a light calamity in
comparison with such a flight.

"I have been obliged to cut your sleeves a little
shorter than Hannah's, for the stuff ran short;
but I'll put a deeper cuff, so you wont mind," said
Miss Mary Hughes.

Surprised at receiving no answer, she looked up,
and saw the expression on Tring's face. "Oh,
Mary Hughes!"

There was so genuine an amount of pity in the
tone, of some unnamed dread in the look, that Mary
Hughes dropped her needle in alarm. "Is anybody took ill?" she asked.

"Not that, not that," answered Tring, subduing her
voice to a whisper, and leaning forward to speak;
"your sister, Martha Ann—I can't tell it you."

"What of her?" gasped Mary Hughes, a dreadful prevision of the truth rushing over her heart,
and turning it to sickness.

"She has gone away with Mr. Robert Carr."

Mary Hughes, not of a strong nature, became faint. Tring got some water for her, and related to her as much as she had heard.

"But how is it known that she's gone? How did Mr. Carr learn it?" asked the poor young woman.

Tring could not tell how he learnt it. She gathered from the conversation that it was known in the town; and Mr. William seemed to know it.

"You'll spare me while I run home for a minute, Tring," pleaded Mary Hughes; "I can't live till I know the rights and the wrongs of it. I can't believe that she'd do such a thing. I'll be back as soon as I can."

"Go, and welcome," cried Tring, in her sympathy; "don't hurry back. What's our gowns by the side of this dreadful shock? Poor Martha Ann!"

"I can't believe she's gone; I can't believe it," reiterated the dressmaker, as she hastily flung on her cloak and bonnet; "there was never a modester girl lived than Martha Ann. It's some dreadful untruth that has got about."

The way in which Mr. Carr had learnt it so soon was this—one of the outside passengers of the coach, a young man of the name of Hurt, had been only going as far as Purford, where the coach dropped him. He hurried over his errand there, and hurried back to Westerbury, big with the importance of what he had seen, and burning to make it known. Taking his course direct to Mr. Carr's, and only stopping to tell everybody he met on the way, he found that gentleman at home, and electrified him with the recital. From thence he ran to the house of Edward Hughes, and found Miss Hughes in a sea of tears, and her brother pacing the rooms in what Mr. Hart called a storm of passion. The young lady, it seems, had been already missed, and one of the gossips to whom Mr. Hart had first imparted his tale, had flown direct with it to the brother and sister.

"Why don't you go after her?" asked Hart; "I'd follow her to the end of the world if she was my sister. I'd take it out of him, too."

Ah, it was easy to say, why don't you go after her? But there were no telegraphs in those days, and there was not yet a rail from London to Westerbury. Robert Carr and the girl were halfway to London by that time; and the earliest conveyance that could be taken was the night mail.

"It's of no use," said Edward Hughes, moodily; "they have got too great a start. Let her go, ungrateful chit! As she has made her bed, so must she lie on it."

Mary Hughes got back to Mrs. Arkell's: she

had found it all too true. Martha Ann had taken her opportunity to steal out of the house, and was gone. Mary Hughes, in relating this, could not speak for sobs.

"My sister says she could be upon her Bible oath, if necessary, that at twenty-five minutes past eight Martha Ann was still at home. She called out something to her up the stairs, and Martha Ann answered her. She must have crept down directly upon that, and got off, and run all the way along the bank, and across the three-cornered field. She—she——" the girl could not go on for sobs.

Tring's eyes were full. "Is your sister much cut up?" she asked.

"Oh, Tring!"—and indeed the question seemed a bitter mockery to Mary Hughes—"I'm sure Sophia has had her death-blow. What a thing it is that I was engaged out to work to-day! If I had been at home, she might not have got away unseen."

Tring sighed. There was no consolation that she could offer.

"I was always against the acquaintance," Mary Hughes resumed, between her tears and sobs: "Sophia knows I was. I said more than once that even if Mr. Robert Carr married her, they'd never be equals. I'd have stopped it if I could, but I've no voice beside Sophia's, and I couldn't stop it. And now, of course, it's all over, and Martha Ann is lost; and she'd a deal better have never been born."

Nothing more satisfactory was heard or seen of the fugitives. They stayed a short time in London, and then went abroad, it was understood, to Holland. Those who wished well to the girl were in hopes that Robert Carr married her in London, but there appeared no ground whatever for the hope. Indeed, from certain circumstances that afterwards transpired, it was quite evident he did not. Westerbury gradually recovered its equanimity; but there are people living in it to this day who never have believed, and never will believe, but that William Arkell was privy to the flight.

CHAPTER VI.

A MISERABLE MISTAKE.

THE time again went on—went on to March—and still Charlotte Travice lingered. It was some little while now that both Mr. and Mrs. Arkell had come to the conclusion within their own minds that the young lady's visit had lasted long enough, but they were of that courteous nature that shrunk not only from hinting such a thing to her, but to each other. She was made just as welcome as ever, and she appeared in no hurry to hasten her departure.

One afternoon Mildred, who had been out on an errand, was accosted by her mother before she had well entered.

" Whatever has made you so long, child ?"

" Have I been so long ?" returned Mildred. " I had to go to two or three shops before I could match the ribbon. I met Mary Pembroke, and she went with me ; but I walked fast."

" It is past five."

"Yes, it has struck. But I did not go out until four, mother."

"Well, I suppose it is my impatience that has made me think you long," acknowledged Mrs. Dan. "Sit down, Mildred; I wish to speak to you. Mrs. George has been here."

"Has she?" returned Mildred, somewhat apathetically; but she took a chair, as she was told to do.

"She came to talk to me about future prospects. And I am glad you were out with that ribbon, Mildred, for our conversation was confidential."

"About her prospects, mamma?" inquired Mildred, raising her mild dark eyes.

"Hers!" repeated Mrs. Dan. "Her prospects, like mine, will soon be drawing to a close. Not that she's as old as I am by a good ten years. She came to speak of yours, Mildred."

Mildred made no rejoinder this time, but a faint colour arose to her face.

"Your Aunt George is very fond of you, Mildred."

"Oh, yes," said Mildred, rather nervously; and Mrs. Dan paused before she resumed.

"I think you must have seen, child, for some time past, that we all wanted you and William to make a match of it."

The announcement was, perhaps, unnecessarily

abrupt. The blush on Mildred's face deepened to a glowing crimson.

"Mrs. George never spoke out freely to me on the subject until this afternoon, but her manner was enough to tell me that it was in their minds. I saw it coming as plainly as I could see anything."

Mildred made no remark. She had untied her bonnet, and began to play nervously with the strings as they hung down on either side her neck.

"But though I felt sure that it was in their minds," continued Mrs. Dan, "though I saw the bent of William's inclinations—always bringing him here to you—I never encouraged the feeling; I never forwarded it by so much as the lifting of a finger. You must have seen, Mildred, that I did not. In one sense of the word, you are not William's equal——"

Mrs. Dan momentarily arrested her words, the startled look of inquiry on her daughter's face was so painful.

"Do not misunderstand me, my dear. In point of station you and he are the same, for the families are one. But William will be wealthy, and William is accomplished; you are neither. In that point of view you may be said not to be on an equality with him; and there's no doubt that William Arkell might go a-wooing into families of higher pretension than his own, and be successful. It

may be, that these considerations have withheld me
and kept me neuter; but I have not—I repeat it,
as I did twice over to Mrs. George just now—I
have not forwarded the matter by so much as the
lifting of a finger."

Mildred knew that.

"The gossiping town will, no doubt, cast ill-
natured remarks upon me, and say that I have
angled for my attractive nephew, and caught him;
but my conscience stands clear upon the point
before my Maker; and Mrs. George knows that
it does. They have come forward of themselves,
unsought by me; unsought, as I heartily believe,
Mildred, by you."

" Oh, yes," was the eager, fervent answer.

" No child of mine would be capable, as I trust,
of secret, mean, underhand dealing, whatever the
prize in view. When I said this to Mrs. George just
now, she laughed at what she called my earnestness, and said I had no need to defend Mildred,
she knew Mildred just as well as I did."

Mildred's heart beat a trifle quicker as she
listened. They were only giving her her due.

" But," resumed Mrs. Dan, " quiet and undemonstrative as you have been, Mildred, your
aunt has drawn the conclusion—lived in it, I may
say—that the proposal she made to-day would not
be unacceptable to you. I agreed with her, say-

ing that such was my conviction. And let me tell you, Mildred, that a more attractive and a better young man than William Arkell does not live in Westerbury."

Mildred silently assented to all in her heart. But she wondered what the proposal was.

"You are strangely silent, child. Should you have any objection to become William Arkell's wife?"

"There is one objection," returned Mildred, almost bitterly, as the thought of his intimacy with Charlotte Travice flashed painfully across her— " he has never asked me."

" But—it is the same thing—he has asked his mother for you."

A wild coursing on of all her pulses—a sudden rush of rapture in every sense of her being—and Mildred's lips could hardly frame the words—

" For *me* ?"

" He asked for you after dinner to-day—I thought I said so—that is, he broached the subject to his mother. After Mr. Arkell went back to the manufactory, he stayed behind with her in the dining-room, and spoke to her of his plans and wishes. He began by saying he was getting quite old enough to marry, and the sooner it took place now, the better."

" Is this true?" gasped Mildred.

"True!" echoed the affronted old lady. "Do you suppose Mrs. George Arkell would come here upon such an errand only to make game of us? True! William says he loves you dearly."

Mildred quitted the room abruptly. She could not bear that even her mother should witness the emotion that bid fair, in these first moments, to overwhelm her. Never until now did she fully realize how deeply, how passionately, she loved William Arkell—how utter a blank life would have been to her had the termination been different. She shut herself in her bed-chamber, burying her face in her hands, and asking how she could ever be sufficiently thankful to God for thus bringing to fruition the half-unconscious hopes which had entwined themselves with every fibre of her existence. The opening of the door by her mother aroused her.

"What in the world made you fly away so, Mildred? I was about to tell you that Mrs. George expects us to tea. Peter will join us there by and by."

"I would rather not go out this evening, mamma," observed Mildred, who was really extremely agitated.

"I promised Mrs. George, and they are waiting tea for us," was the decisive reply. "What is the matter with you, Mildred? You need not be so struck at what I have said. Did it never occur to yourself that William Arkell was likely to choose you for his wife?"

" I have thought of late that he was more likely to choose Miss Travice," answered Mildred, giving utterance in her emotion to the truth that lay uppermost in her mind.

" Marry that fine fly-away thing!" repeated Mrs. Dan, her astonishment taking her breath away. " Charlotte Travice may be all very well for a visitor—here to-day and gone to-morrow; but she is not suitable for the wife of a steady, gentlemanly young man, like William Arkell, the only son of the first manufacturer in Westerbury. What a pretty notion of marriage you must have!"

Mildred began to think so. too.

" I shall not be two minutes putting on my shawl; I shan't change my gown," continued Mrs. Dan. " You can change yours if you please, but don't be long over it. It is past their tea-time."

Implicit obedience had been one of the virtues ever practised by Mildred, so she said no more. The thought kept floating in her mind as she made herself ready, that it had been more appropriate for William to visit her that evening than for her to visit him; and she could not help wishing that he had spoken to her himself, though it had been but a single loving hint, before the proposal could reach

her through another. But these were but minor
trifles, little worth noting in the midst of her intense
happiness. As she walked down the street by her
mother's side, the golden light of the setting sun,
shining full upon her, was not more radiantly
lovely than the light shining in Mildred Arkell's
heart.

"I can't think what you can have been dreaming
of, Mildred, to imagine that that Charlotte Travice
was a fit wife for William Arkell," observed Mrs.
Dan, who could not get the preposterous notion
out of her head. "You might have given William
credit for better sense than that. I don't like her.
I liked her very much at first, but, somehow, she
is one who does not gain upon you on prolonged
acquaintance; and it strikes me Mr. and Mrs.
George are of the same opinion. Mrs. George just
mentioned her this afternoon—something about
her being your bridesmaid."

"She my bridesmaid!" exclaimed Mildred, the
very idea of it unpalatable.

"Mrs. George said she supposed she must ask
Charlotte Travice to stay and be bridesmaid; that
it would be but a mark of politeness, as she had
been so intimate with you and William. It would
not be a very great extension of the visit," she
added, "for William seemed impatient for the wedding to take place shortly, now that he had made

up his mind about it. It does not matter what bridesmaid you have, Mildred."

Ah! no; it did not matter! Mildred's happiness seemed too great to be affected by that, or any other earthly thing. Mrs. George Arkell kissed her fondly three or four times as she entered, and pressed her hand, as Mildred thought, significantly. Another moment, and she found her hand taken by William.

He was shaking it just as usual, and his greeting was a careless one—

"How d'ye do, Mildred? You are late."

Neither by word, or tone, or look, did he impart a consciousness of what had passed. In the first moment Mildred felt thankful for the outward indifference, but the next she caught herself thinking that he seemed to take her consent as a matter of course—as if it were not worth the asking.

When tea was over, and the lights were brought, Mr. and Mrs. Arkell and Mrs. Dan sat down to cribbage, the only game any of the three ever played at.

"Who will come and be fourth?" asked Mr. Arkell, looking over his spectacles at the rest. " You, Mildred?"

It had fallen to Mildred's lot lately to be the fourth at these meetings, for Miss Travice always held aloof, and William never played if he could

help it ; but on this evening Mildred hesitated, and
before she could assent—as she would finally have
done—Miss Travice sprang forward.

"I will, dear Mr. Arkell—I will play with you
to-night."

"She knows of it, and is leaving us alone,"
thought Mildred. "How kind of her it is! I
fear I have misjudged her."

"I say, Mildred," began William, as they sat
apart, his tone dropped to confidence, his voice to
a whisper, "did my mother call at your house this
afternoon?"

Mildred looked down, and began to play with
her pretty gold neckchain. It was one William
had given her on her last birthday, nearly a year
ago.

"My aunt called, I believe. I was out."

William's face fell.

"Then I suppose you have not heard anything—
anything particular? I'm sure I thought she had
been to tell you. She was out ever so long."

"Mamma said that Aunt George had been—had
been—speaking to her," returned Mildred, not very
well knowing how to make the admission.

William saw the confusion, and read it aright.

"Ah, Mildred! you sly girl, you know all, and
wont tell!" he cried, taking her hand half-fondly,
half-playfully, and retaining it in his.

She could not answer; but the blush on her cheek was so bright, the downcast look so tender, that William Arkell gazed at her lovingly, and thought he had never seen his cousin's face so near akin to perfect beauty. Mildred glanced up to see his gaze of fond admiration.

"Your cheek tells tales, cousin mine," he whispered; "I see you have heard all. Don't you think it is time I married?"

A home question. Mildred's lips broke into a smile by way of answer.

"What do you think of my choice?"

"People will say you might have made a better."

"I don't care if they do," returned Mr. William, firing up. "I have a right to please myself, and I will please myself. I am not taking a wife for other people, meddling mischief-makers!"

The outburst seemed unnecessary. It struck Mildred that he must have seriously feared opposition from some quarter, the tone of his voice was so sore a one. She looked up with questioning eyes.

"I have plenty of money, you know, Mildred," he added, more quietly. "I don't want to look out for a fortune with my wife."

"Very true," murmured Mildred.

"I wonder whether she has brought it out to my father?" resumed William, nodding towards his

mother at the card-table. " I don't think she has ;
he seems only just as usual. She'll make it the
subject of a curtain-lecture to-night, for a guinea!"

Mildred stole a glance at her uncle. He was
intent on his cards, good old man, his spectacles
pushed to the top of his ample brow.

"Do you know, Mildred, I was half afraid to
come to the point with them," he presently said.
" I dreaded opposition. I——"

" But why ?" timidly interrupted Mildred.

" Well, I can't tell why. All I know is, that
the feeling was there—picked up somehow. I
dreaded opposition, especially from my mother ;
but, as I say, I cannot tell why. I never was more
surprised than when she said I had made her happy
by my choice—that it was a union she had set her
heart upon. I am not sure yet, you know, that
my father will approve it."

"He may urge against it the want of money,"
murmured Mildred ; "it is only reasonable he
should. And——"

"It is not reasonable," interposed William
Arkell, in a tone of resentment. " There's nothing
at all in reason that can be urged against it ; and I
am sure you don't really think there is, Mildred."

"And yet you acknowledge that you dreaded
opening the matter to them ?"

"Yes, because fathers and mothers are always

so exacting over these things. Every crow thinks
its own young bird the whitest, and many a mother
with an only son deems him fit to mate with a prin-
cess of the blood-royal. I declare to you, Mildred,
I felt a regular coward about telling my mother—
foolish as the confession must sound to you; and
once I thought of speaking to you first, and getting
you to break it to her. I thought she might listen
to it from you better than from me."

Mildred thought it would have been a novel
mode of procedure, but she did not say so. Her
cousin went on :—

"We must have the wedding in a month, or so ;
I wont wait a day longer, and so I told my mother.
I have seen a charming little house just suitable
for us, and——"

"You might have consulted me first, William,
before you fixed the time."

"What for ? Nonsense ! will not one time do
for you as well as another ?"

Miss Arkell looked up at her cousin ; he seemed
to be talking strangely.

"But where is the necessity for hurrying on the
wedding like this ?" she asked. "Not to speak of
other considerations, the preparations would take
up more time."

"Not they," dissented Mr. William, who had
been accustomed to have things very much his own

way, and liked it. "I'm sure you need not raise a barrier on the score of preparation, Mildred. You wont want much beside a dress and bonnet, and my mother can see to yours as well as to Charlotte's. Is it orthodox for the bride and bridesmaid to be dressed alike?"

"Who was it fixed upon the bridesmaid?" asked Mildred. "Did you?"

"Charlotte herself. But no plans are decided on, for I said as little as I could to my mother. We can go into details another day."

"With regard to a bridesmaid, Mary Pembroke has always been promised——"

"Now, Mildred, I wont have any of those Pembroke girls playing a conspicuous part at my wedding," he interrupted. "What you and my mother can see in them, I can't think. Provided you have no objection, let it be as Charlotte says."

"I think Charlotte takes more upon herself than she has any cause to do," returned Mildred, the old sore feeling against Miss Travice rising again into prominence in her heart.

"I'll tell her if you don't mind, Mildred," laughed William. "But now I think of it, it was not Charlotte who mentioned it, it was my mother. She——"

"Mr. Peter Arkell."

The announcement was Tring's. It cut off Wil-

liam's sentence in the midst, and also any further
elucidation that might have taken place. Peter
came forward in his usual awkward manner, and
was immediately pressed into the service of cribbage,
in the place of Miss Travice, who never " put out "
to the best advantage, and could not count. As
Peter took her seat, he explained that his early
appearance was owing to his having remained but
an hour with Mr. Arthur Dewsbury, who was going
out that evening.

Charlotte Travice sat down to the piano, and
William got his flute. Sweet music ! but, nevertheless, it grated on Mildred's ear. His whole attention became absorbed with Charlotte, to the
utter neglect of Mildred. Now and then he seemed
to remember that Mildred sat behind, and turned
round to address a word to her; but his whispers
were given to Charlotte. " It is not right," she
murmured to herself in her bitter pain ; " this
night, of all others, it is not surely right. If she
were but going back to London before the
wedding !"

Supper came in, for they dined early, you remember; and afterwards Mrs. Dan and Mildred
had their bonnets brought down.

" What a lovely night it is !" exclaimed Peter,
as he waited at the hall door.

" It is that !" assented William, looking out ; " I

think I'll have a run with you. Those stars are enough to tempt one forth. Shall I go, Mildred?"

"Yes," she softly whispered, believing she was the attraction, not the stars.

But Mrs. Dan lingered. The fact was, Mrs. Arkell had drawn her to the back of the hall.

"Did you speak to her, Betty?"

"I spoke to her as soon as she came home. It was that that made us late."

"Well? She does not object to William?"

"Not she. I'll tell you a secret," continued Mrs. Dan; "I could see by Mildred's agitation when I told her to-day, that she already loved William. I suspected it long ago."

Mrs. Arkell nodded her head complacently. "I noticed her face when he was talking to her as they sat apart to-night; and I read love in it, if it ever was read. Yes, yes, it is all right. I thought I could not be mistaken in Mildred."

"I say, Aunt Dan, are you coming to-night or to-morrow?" called out William.

"I am coming now, my dear," replied Mrs. Dan; and she walked forward and took her son's arm. William followed with Mildred.

"Now, Mildred, don't you go and tell all the world to-morrow about this wedding of ours," he began; "don't you go chattering to those Pembroke girls."

" How can you suppose it likely that I would ?" was the pained answer.

" Why, I know all young ladies are fond of gossiping, especially when they get hold of such a topic as this."

" I don't think I have ever deserved the name of gossip," observed Mildred, quietly.

" Well, Mildred, I do not know that you have. But it is not all girls who possess your calm good sense. I thought it might be as well to give even you a caution."

" William, you are scarcely like yourself to-night," she said, anxiously. " To suppose a caution in this case necessary for me !"

He had begun to whistle, and did not answer. It was a verse of " Robin Adair," the song Charlotte was so fond of. When the verse was whistled through, he spoke—

" How very bright the stars are to-night ! I think it must be a frost."

Inexperienced as Mildred was practically, she yet felt that this was not the usual conversation of a lover on the day of declaration, unless he was a remarkably cool one. While she was wondering, he resumed his whistling—a verse of another song this time.

Mildred looked up at him. His face was lifted towards the heavens, but she could see it perfectly

in the light of the night. He was evidently thinking more of the stars than of her, for his eyes were
roving from one constellation to another. She
looked down again, and remained silent.

"So you like my choice, Mildred!" he presently
resumed.

"Choice of what?" she asked.

"Choice of what! As if you did not know!
Choice of a wife."

"How is it you play so with my feelings this
evening?" she asked, the tears rushing to her eyes.

"I have not played with them that I know of.
What do you mean, Mildred? You are growing
fanciful."

She could not trust her voice to reply. William
again broke into one of his favourite airs.

"I proposed that we should be married in
London, amidst her friends," he said, when the few
bars were brought to a satisfactory conclusion.
"I thought she might prefer it. But she says
she'd rather not."

"Amidst whose friends?" inquired Mildred, in
amazement.

"Charlotte's. But in that case I suppose you
could not have been bridesmaid. And there'd have
been all the trouble of a journey beforehand."

"*I* bridesmaid!" exclaimed Mildred; and all the
blood in her body seemed to rush to her brain as a

faint suspicion of the terrible truth stole into it. "Bridesmaid to whom?"

William Arkell, unable to comprehend a word, stopped still and looked at her.

"You are dreaming, Mildred!" he exclaimed.

"What do you mean? Who is it you are going to marry?" she reiterated.

"Why, what have we been talking of all the evening? What did my mother say to you to-day? What has come to you, Mildred? You certainly are dreaming."

"We have been playing at cross purposes, I fear," gasped Mildred, in her agony. "Tell me who it is you are going to marry."

"Charlotte Travice. Whom else should it be?"

They were then turning round by what was called the boundary wall; the old elms in the dean's garden towered above them, and Mildred's home was close in sight. But before they reached it, William Arkell felt her hang heavily and more heavily on his arm.

Ah! how she was struggling! Not with the pain—that could not be struggled with for a long, long while to come—but with the endeavour to suppress its outward emotion. All, all in vain. William Arkell bent to catch a glimpse of her features under the bonnet—worn large in those days—and found that she was white as death, and appeared to be losing consciousness.

"Mildred, my dear, what ails you?" he asked, kindly. "Do you feel ill?"

She felt dying; but to speak was beyond her, then. William passed his arm round her just in time to prevent her falling, and shouted out, excessively alarmed—

"Peter! Aunt! just come back, will you? Here's something the matter with Mildred."

They were at the door then, but they heard him, and hastened back. Mildred had fainted.

"What can have caused it?" exclaimed Peter, in his consternation. "I never knew her faint in all her life before."

"It must have been that rich cream tart at supper," lamented Mrs. Dan, half in sympathy, half in reproof. "I have told Mildred twenty times that pastry, eaten at night, is next door to poison."

And so this was to be the ending of all her cherished dreams! Mildred lay awake in her solitary chamber the whole of that live-long night. There was no sleep, no rest, no hope for her. Desolation the most complete had overtaken her —utter, bitter, miserable desolation.

CHAPTER VII.

A HEART SEARED.

MILDRED ARKELL, in the midst of her agony, had the good sense to see that some extraordinary misapprehension had occurred, either on her mother's part or on Mrs. Arkell's; that William had not announced his wish of marrying her, but Charlotte Travice. From that time forward, Mildred would have a difficult part to play in the way of *concealment*. Her dearest feelings, her bitter mortification, her sighs of pain must be hidden from the world; and she prayed God to give her strength to go through her task, making no sign. The most embarrassing part would be to undeceive her mother; but she must do it, and contrive to do it without suspicion that *she* was anything but indifferent to the turn affairs had taken. Commonplace and insignificant as that little episode was—the partaking of a rich cream tart at Mrs. Arkell's supper-table—Mildred was thankful for it. Her mother, remarkably single-minded by nature, unsuspicious as the day, would never think of attributing the fainting fit to any other cause.

It may at once be mentioned that the singular misapprehension was on the part of Mrs. Arkell. She was so thoroughly imbued with the hope—it may be said with the notion—that her son would espouse Mildred, that when William broached the subject in a hasty and indistinct manner, she somehow fell into the mistake. The fault was probably William's. He did not say much, and his own fear of his mother's displeasure caused him to be anything but clear and distinct. Mrs. George Arkell caught at the communication with delight, believing it to refer to Mildred. She mentioned a word herself, in her hasty looking forward, about a bridesmaid. The names of Mildred and Charlotte, not either of them mentioned above once, got confused together, and altogether the mistake took place, William himself being unconscious of it.

William ran home that night, startling them with the news of the indisposition of Mildred. She had fainted in the street as they were going home. Mr. and Mrs. Arkell, loving Mildred as a daughter, were inexpressibly concerned; Charlotte Travice sat listening to the tale with wondering ears and eyes. "My aunt said it must be the effect of the cream tart at supper," he observed, "but I think that must be all rubbish. As if cream tart would make people faint! And Mildred has eaten it before."

"It was the agitation, my dear. It was nothing else," whispered Mrs. Arkell to her guest, confidentially, as she bid her good night in the hall. "A communication like that must cause agitation to the mind, you know."

"What communication?" asked Charlotte, in surprise. For Mrs. Arkell spoke as if her words must necessarily be understood.

"Don't you know? I thought William had most likely told you. It's about her marriage. But there, we'll talk of it to-morrow, I wont keep you now, Miss Charlotte, and I have to speak to Mr. Arkell."

Charlotte continued her way upstairs, wondering excessively; not able, as she herself expressed it, to make head or tail of what Mrs. Arkell meant. Mrs. Arkell returned to the dining-room, asked her husband to sit down again for a few minutes, for he was standing with his bed-candle in his hand, and she made the communication.

Elucidation was, however, near at hand, as it of necessity must be. On the following morning nothing was said at the breakfast-table: but on their going into the manufactory, Mr. Arkell took his son into his private room. Mr. Arkell sat down before his desk, and opened a letter that waited on

it before he spoke.   William stood by the fire,
rather nervous.

"So, young sir! you are wanting, I hear, to
encumber yourself with a wife!   Don't you think
you had better have taken one in your leading-
strings?"

"I am twenty-five, sir," returned William, drawing himself up in all the dignity of the age. "And
you have often said you hoped to see me settled
before——"

"Before I died.   Very true, you graceless boy.
But you don't want me to die yet, I suppose?"

"Heaven forbid it!" fervently answered William.

"Well," continued the good man—and William
had known from the first, by the tone of the voice,
the twinkle in the eye, that he was pleased instead
of vexed—"I cannot but say you have chosen
worthily.   I suppose I must look over her being
portionless."

"Our business is an excellent one, and you have
saved money besides, sir," observed William.
"To look out for money with my wife would be
superfluous."

"Not exactly that," returned Mr. Arkell, in his
keen, emphatic tone.   "But I suppose you can't
have everything.   Few of us can.   She has been a
good and affectionate daughter, William, and she
will make you a good wife.   I should have been

better pleased though, had there been no relationship between you."

"Relationship!" repeated William.

"For I share in the popular prejudice that exists against cousins marrying. But I am not going to make it an objection now, as you may believe, when I tell you that I foresaw long ago what your intimacy would probably end in. Your mother says it has been her cherished plan for years."

William listened in bewilderment. "She is no cousin of mine," he said.

"No what?" asked Mr. Arkell, pushing his glasses to the top of his forehead, the better to stare at his son—for those glasses served only for near objects, print and writing—"is the thought of this marriage turning your head, my boy?"

"I don't understand what you are speaking of," returned William, perfectly mystified; "I only said she was not my cousin."

"Why, bless my heart, what do you mean?" exclaimed Mr. Arkell. "She has been your cousin ever since she was born; she is the daughter of my poor brother Dan; do you want to disown the relationship now?"

"Are you talking of Mildred Arkell?" exclaimed the astonished young man. "I don't want to marry *her*. Mildred is a very nice girl as

a cousin, but I never thought of her as a wife.   I
want Charlotte Travice!"

"Charlotte Travice!"

The change in the tone, the deep pain it betrayed,
struck a chill on William's heart.   Mr. Arkell
gazed at him before he again broke the silence.

"How came you to tell your mother yesterday
that you wanted to marry Mildred?"

"I never did tell her so, sir; I told her I wished
to marry Charlotte."

Mr. Arkell took another contemplative stare at
his son.   He then turned short away, quitted the
manufactory by his own private entrance, walked
across the yard, past the coach-house and
stable, and went straight into the presence of his
wife.

"A pretty ambassador you would make at a
foreign court!" he began; "to mistake your
credentials in this manner!"

Mrs. Arkell was seated alone, puzzling herself
with a lap-full of patchwork, and wishing Mildred
was there to get it into order.   Every now and
then she would be taken with a sewing fit, and do
about two stitches in a morning.   She looked up
at the strange address, the mortified tone.

"You told me William wanted to marry Mildred!"

"So he does."

"So he does *not*," was Mr. Arkell's answer.

"He wants to marry your fine lady visitor, Miss Charlotte Travice."

Mrs. Arkell rose up in consternation, disregardful of the work, which fell to the ground. "You must be mistaken," she exclaimed.

"No; it is you who have been mistaken. William says he did not speak to you of Mildred: never thought of her as a wife at all; he spoke to you of Charlotte Travice."

"Dear, dear!" exclaimed Mrs. Arkell, a feeling very like unto faintness coming over her spirit: "I hope it is not so! I hope still there may be some better elucidation."

"There can be no other elucidation, so far, than this," returned Mr. Arkell, his tone one of sharp negation. "The extraordinary part of the affair is, how you could have misinterpreted his meaning, and construed Charlotte Travice into Mildred Arkell! I said we kept the girl here too long."

He turned away again with the last sentence on his tongue. He was not sufficiently himself to stay and talk then. Mrs. Arkell, in those first few minutes, was as one who has just received a blow. Presently she despatched a message for her son; she was terribly vexed with him; and, like we all do, felt it might be a relief to throw off some of her annoyance upon him.

"How came you to tell me yesterday you wanted

to marry Mildred?" she began when he appeared, her tone quite as sharp as ever was Mr. Arkell's.

"I did not tell you so. My father has been saying something of the same sort, but it is a mistake."

"You must have told me so," persisted Mrs. Arkell; "how else could I have imagined it? Charlotte's name was never mentioned at all. Except—yes—I believe I said that she could be the bridesmaid."

"I understood you to say that Mildred could be the bridesmaid," returned William. "Mother, indeed the mistake was yours."

"We have made a fine mess of it between us," retorted Mrs. Arkell, in her vexation, as she arrived at length at the conclusion that the mistake was hers; "you should have been more explicit. What a simpleton they will think me! Worse than that! Do you know what I did yesterday?"

"No."

"I went straight to Mrs. Dan Arkell's as soon as you had spoken to me, and asked for Mildred to marry you."

"Mother!"

"I did. It is the most unpleasant piece of business I was ever mixed up in."

"Mildred will only treat it as a joke, of course?"

"Mildred treated it in earnest. Why should she

not ? When she came here last evening, she came expecting that she would shortly be your wife."

They stood looking at each other, the mother and son, their thoughts travelling back to the past night, and its events. What had appeared so strange in William's eyes was becoming clear; the cross-purposes, as Mildred had expressed it, in their conversation with each other, and Mildred's fainting-fit, when the elucidation came. He very much feared, now that he knew the cause of that fainting-fit—he feared that Mildred's love was his.

Mrs. Arkell's thoughts were taking the same course, and she spoke them:—"William, that fainting-fit must in some way have been connected with this. Mildred is not in the habit of fainting."

He made no reply at first. Loving Mildred excessively as a cousin, he would not have hurt her feelings willingly for the whole world. A half-wish stole over him that it was the fashion for gentlemen to cut themselves in half when two ladies were in the case, and so gallantly bestow themselves on both. Mrs. Arkell noted the mortification in his expressive face.

"What is to be done, William? Mrs. Dan told me she felt sure Mildred had been secretly attached to you for years."

Mrs. Arkell might not have spoken thus openly

to her son, but for a hope, now beginning to dawn within her—that his choice might yet fall upon Mildred. William made no reply. He smoothed his hand over his troubled brow ; he recalled more and more of the previous evening's scene ; he felt deeply perplexed and concerned, for the happiness of Mildred was dear to him as a sister's. But the more he reflected on the case, the less chance he saw of mending it.

"You must marry Mildred," Mrs. Arkell said to him in a low tone.

"Impossible !" he hastily rejoined ; "I cannot do that."

"But I made the offer for her to her mother ! Made it on your part."

"And I made one for myself to Charlotte."

An embarrassed, mortified silence. Mrs. Arkell, an exceedingly honourable woman, did not see a way out of the double dilemma any more than William did.

"Do you know that I do not like her?" resumed Mrs. Arkell, in a voice hoarse with emotion. "That I have grown to *dislike* her? And what will become of Mildred ?"

"Mildred will get over it in no-time," he answered, already beginning to reason himself into a satisfactory state of composure and indifference, as people like to do. "She is a girl of excellent common sense, and will see the thing in its proper light."

Strange perhaps to say, Mrs. Arkell fell into the same train of reasoning when the first moments of mortification had cooled down. She saw Mrs. Dan, and intimated that she had been under an unfortunate mistake, which she could only apologise for. Mrs. Dan, a sober-minded, courteous old lady, who never made a fuss about anything, and had never quarrelled in her life, said she hoped she had been mistaken as to Mildred's feelings. And when Mrs. Arkell next saw Mildred, the latter's manner was so quiet, so unchanged, so almost indifferent, that Mrs. Arkell repeated with complacency William's words to herself: "Mildred will get over it in no-time."

What mattered the scaring of one heart? How many are there daily blighted, and the world knows it not! The world went on its way in Westerbury without reference to the feelings of Mildred Arkell; and poor Mildred went on hers, and made no sign.

The marriage went on—that is, the preparations for it. When a beloved and indulged son announces that he has fixed his heart upon a lady, and intends to make her his wife, consent and approval generally follow, provided there exists no very grave objection against her. There existed none

against Miss Travice ; and she made herself so
pleasant and delightful to Mr. and Mrs. Arkell,
when once it was decided she was to marry
William, that they nearly fell in love with her
themselves, and became entirely reconciled to the loss
of Mildred as a daughter-in-law.   The " charming
little house" spoken of by William, was taken and
furnished ; and the wedding was to take place
the end of April, Charlotte being married from Mr.
Arkell's.

One item in the original programme was not
carried out: Mildred refused to act as bridesmaid.
Mrs. Arkell was surprised.   The intimacy of the
two families had been continued as before ; for
Mildred, in all senses of the word, had condemned
herself to suffer in silence ; and she was so quiet,
so undemonstrative, that Mrs. Arkell believed the
blow was quite recovered—if blow it had been.
Mildred placed her refusal on the plea of her
mother's health, which was beginning seriously to
decline.   Mrs. Arkell did not press it, for a half-
suspicion of the true cause arose in her mind.

" Your sister must come down now, whether or
not," she said to Charlotte.

Charlotte looked up hastily, a flush of annoyance on her bright cheek.   Miss Charlotte had per-
sistently refused Mrs. Arkell's proposal to invite
her sister to the wedding ; had turned a deaf ear

to Mrs. Arkell's remonstrance that it was not fit or seemly this only sister should be excluded. Charlotte had carried her point hitherto; but Mrs. Arkell intended to carry hers now.

"Betsey can't bear visiting," she said, with pouting lips; "she would be sure to refuse if you did ask her."

"She would surely not refuse to come to her sister's marriage! You must be mistaken, Charlotte."

"She has never visited anywhere in all her life; has not been out, so far as I can call to mind, for a single day—has never drank tea away from home," urged Charlotte, who seemed strangely annoyed. "I have said so before."

"All the more reason that she should do so now," returned Mrs. Arkell. "Charlotte, my dear, don't be foolish; I shall certainly send for her."

"Then I shall write and forbid her to come," returned Charlotte; and she bit her lip for saying it as soon as the words were out.

"My dear!"

"I did not mean that, dear Mrs. Arkell," she pleaded, with a winning expression of repentance and a merry laugh; "but indeed it will not do to invite poor Betsey here."

"Very well, my dear."

But in spite of the apparently acquiescent "very

well," Mrs. Arkell remained firm. Whether it was that she detected something false in the laugh, or that she chose to let her future daughter-in-law see which was mistress, or that she deemed it would not be right to ignore Miss Betsey Travice on this coming occasion, certain it was that Mrs. Arkell wrote a pressing mandate to the younger lady, and enclosed a five-pound note in the letter. And she said nothing to Charlotte of what she had done.

It was about this time that some definite news arrived in Westerbury of Robert Carr. He, the idle, roving, spendthrift spirit, had become a clerk in Holland. He had obtained a situation, he best knew how, in a merchant's house in Rotterdam, and appeared, so far, to have really settled down to steadiness. It would seem that the remark to William Arkell, "If I do make a start in life, rely upon it, I succeed," was likely to be borne out. He had taken this clerkship, and was working as hard as any clerk ever worked yet. Whether the industry would last was another thing.

Mr. John Carr, the squire's son, was the one to bring the news to Westerbury. Mr. John Carr appeared to be especially interested in his cousin's movements and doings : near as he was known to be in money matters, he had actually gone a journey to Rotterdam, to find out all about Robert. Mr. John Carr did not fail to remember, and hardly cared to conceal from the world that he remembered, that, failing Robert, who had been threatened times and again with disinheritance, *he* might surely look to be his uncle's heir. However it may have been, Mr. John Carr went to Rotterdam, saw Robert, stayed a few days in the place, and then came home again.

"Has he married the girl?" was Squire Carr's first question to his son.

"No," replied John, gloomily; for, of course it would have been to his interest if Robert had married her. Squire Carr and his son knew of Marmaduke's oath to disinherit Robert if he did marry Martha Ann Hughes; and they knew that he would keep his word.

"Is the girl with him still?"

"She's with him fast enough; I saw her twice."

"John, he may have married her in London."

"He did not, though. I said to Robert I supposed they had been married in London. He flew into one of his tempers at the supposition, and said he had never been inside a church in London in his life, or within fifty miles of it; and I am sure he was speaking the truth. He told me afterwards, when we were having a little confidential talk together, that he never should marry her, at any rate as long as his father lived; and she did not expect him to do it. He had no mind, he added, to be disinherited."

This news oozed out to Westerbury, and Mr. John was vexed, for he did not intend that it should ooze out. Amidst other ears, it reached that of Mr. Carr. "A cunning man in his own conceit," quoth he to a friend, alluding to his brother's son, "but not quite cunning enough to win over me. If Robert marries that girl, I'll keep my word, and not bequeath him a shilling of my money; but I'll not leave it to John Carr, or any of his brood."

Had this news touching Robert's life in Holland needed confirmation, such might have been supplied to it by a letter received from Martha Ann Hughes by her sister Mary. The shock to Mary Hughes had been, no doubt, very great, and she had written several letters since, begging and praying Martha Ann to urge Mr. Robert Carr to marry her, even now. For the first time Martha Ann sent an answer, just about the period that Mr. John Carr was in Holland. It was a long and very nicely-written letter; but to Mary Hughes's ear there was a vein of repentant sadness running throughout it. It was not likely Mr. Robert would marry her now, she said, and to urge it upon him would be worse than useless. She had chosen her own path and must abide by it; and she did not see that what she had done ought to cause people to reflect upon her sisters. Mary's saying that it did, must be all nonsense—or ought to be. Her sisters had done their part by her well; and if she had repaid them ill, that ought to be only the more reason for the world showing them additional kindness and respect: Mary would no doubt live to prove this. For herself she was not unhappy. Robert was quite steady, and had a good clerkship in a merchant's house. He was as kind to her as if they had been married twice over ; and her position was not so unpleasant as Mary seemed to imagine, for nobody knew but what she was his wife—though, for the matter of that, they had made no acquaintances in the strange town.

Mary Hughes blinded her eyes with tears over this letter, and in her unhappiness lent it to anyone who cared to see it. And her strong-minded but more reticent sister, when she found out what she was doing, angrily called her a fool for her pains, and tore the letter to pieces before her face. But not before it had been heard of by Mr. Carr. For one, who happened to get hold of it, reported the contents to him.

CHAPTER VIII.

BETSEY TRAVICE.

THEY were grouped together in Mrs. Arkell's sitting-room, their faces half-indistinct in the growing twilight. Mrs. Arkell herself, doing nothing as usual; Mildred by her side, sewing still, although Mrs. Arkell had told her she was trying her eyes; Charlotte Travice, with a flush upon her face and a nervous movement of the restless foot—signs of anger suppressed, to those who knew her well; and a stranger, a young lady, whom you have not seen before.

Had anyone told you this young lady and Charlotte were sisters, you had disputed the assertion, so entirely dissimilar were they in all ways. A quiet little lady, this, of twenty years, with a smooth, fair face, somewhat insipid, for all its good sense; light blue eyes, truthful as Charlotte's were false; small features, and light hair, worn plainly. Perhaps what might have struck a beholder as the most prominent feature in Betsey Travice was her excessive natural meekness; nay, humility would be the better word. She was meek in mind, in temper, in look, in manner, in speech; humble always. She sat there at the fire, her black bonnet laid beside her, for the girl had felt cold after her journey, and the fire was more welcome to her than the going upstairs to array herself for attraction would have been to Charlotte. The weather was very cold for the close of April, and the coach— it was a noted circumstance in its usual punctuality —had been half an hour behind its time. She sat there, sipping the hot cup of tea that Tring had brought her, declining to eat, and feeling miserably uncomfortable, as she saw that, to one at least, she was not welcome.

That one was her sister. Mrs. Arkell had kept the secret well; and not until the evening of the arrival—but an hour, in fact, before the coach was expected in—was Charlotte told of it.

"Tring, or somebody, has been putting two pillows upon my bed," remarked Charlotte, who had run up to her bedroom to get a book. "I wonder what that's for."

"You are going to have a bedfellow to-night, my dear," said Mrs. Arkell.

"A bedfellow!" echoed Charlotte, in wonder. "Who is it?"

"Your sister."

"Who?" cried out Charlotte; and the sharp, passionate, uncontrolled tone struck on their ears unpleasantly.

"I told you I should have your sister down to the wedding," quietly returned Mrs. Arkell. "In my opinion it would have been unseemly and unkind not to do so. She is on her road now. Mildred has come in to help me welcome her. Betsey is Mrs. Dan's godchild, you know."

"And Mildred knew she was coming?" retorted Charlotte, as if that were a further grievance; and she spoke as fiercely as she dared, compatible with her present amiability as bride-elect.

"Mildred knew it from the first."

Of course there was no help for it now. Betsey was on her road down, as Mrs. Arkell expressed it, and it was too late to stop her, or to send her back again. Charlotte made the best of it that she could make, but never had her temper been nearer an explosion; and when Betsey arrived she took care to let *her* see that she had better not have come.

"And now, my dear, that you are warmed and refreshed a little, tell me if you were not glad to come," said Mrs. Arkell, kindly, as Betsey Travice put the empty cup on the table, and stretched out one small, thin hand to the blazing warmth.

"I was very glad, ma'am," was the reply, delivered in the humble, gentle, deprecatory tone which cha-

racterized Betsey Travice, no matter to whom she
spoke. " I was glad to have the opportunity of
seeing Charlotte, she had been gone away so long :
and I shall like to see a wedding, for I have never
seen one ; and I was very glad to come also for
another thing."

" What is that ?" asked Mrs. Arkell, yearning to
the pleasant, single-minded tone—to the truthful,
earnest eyes.

" Well, ma'am, I'm afraid I was getting over-
worked. Though it would have seemed ungrateful
to kind Mrs. Dundyke to say so, and I never did
say it. The children were heavy to carry about the
kitchen, and up and down stairs ; and the waiting
on the lodgers was worse than usual. I used to
have such a pain in my side and back towards
night, that I did not know how to keep on."

Charlotte Travice was in an agony. It was pre-
cisely these revelations that she had dreaded in a
visit from Betsey. That Betsey had to work like a
horse at Mrs. Dundyke's, Charlotte thought extremely probable : but she had no mind that this
state of things should become known at Mrs.
Arkell's. In her embarrassment, she was unwise
enough to attempt to deny the fact.

" Where's the use of your talking like this,
Betsey ?" she indignantly asked. " If you did attend a little to the children—as nursery governess—

you need not have carried them about, making a slave of yourself."

" But you know how young they are, Charlotte! You know that they need to be carried. I would not have cared had it been only the children. There was all the house work and the waiting."

" But what had you to do with this, my dear ?" asked Mrs. Arkell, a little puzzled, while Charlotte sat with an inflamed face.

Betsey Travice entered on the explanation in detail. Mrs. Dundyke cooked for her lodgers herself—and she generally had two sets of lodgers in the house—and kept a servant to wait upon them. Six weeks ago the servant had left—she said the place was too hard for her—and Mrs. Dundyke had not found one to her mind since. She got a charwoman in two or three times a week, and Betsey Travice had put herself forward to help with the work and the waiting. She had made beds and swept rooms, and laid cloths for dinner, and carried up dishes, and handed bread and beer at table, and answered the door ; in short, had been, to all intents and purposes, a maid of all work.

To see her sitting there, and quietly telling this, was not the least curious portion of the tale. She looked a lady, she spoke as a lady—nay, there was something especially winning and refined in her voice ; and she herself seemed altogether so incom-

patible with the work she confessed to have passed
her later days in, that even Mildred Arkell gazed at
her in fixed surprise.

"You are a fool!" burst forth Charlotte, between
rage and crying. "If that horrible woman, that
Mrs. Dundyke, thrust such degrading work upon
you, you ought not to have done it."

"Oh! Charlotte, don't call her that! She is a
kind woman; you know she is. If you please,
ma'am, she's as kind as she can be," added Betsey,
turning to Mrs. Arkell, in her anxiety for justice to
be done to Mrs. Dundyke. "And for the work, I
did not mind it. It's not as if I had never done
any. I had to do all sorts of work in poor mamma's
time, and I am naturally handy at it. I am sorry
you should be angry with me, Charlotte."

"I don't think it was exactly the sort of work
your friend Mrs. Dundyke should have put upon
you," remarked Mrs. Arkell.

"But there was no help for it, ma'am," represented Betsey. "The work was there, and had to
be done by somebody. That servant left us at a
pinch. She had a quarrel with her mistress about
some dripping that was missing, and she went off
that same hour. I began to do what I could of
myself, without being asked. Mrs. Dundyke did
not like my doing it, any more than Charlotte does,
but there was nobody else, and I could not bear to

seem ungrateful.   When Charlotte came here I had
but sixpence left in my purse, and Mrs. Dundyke
has bought me shoes and things that I have wanted
since, from her own pocket."

A dead silence.   Charlotte Travice felt as if she
were going to have brain fever.   Could the earth
have opened then, and swallowed up Betsey, it had
been the greatest blessing, in Charlotte's estimation, ever accorded her.

"What are your prospects for the future,
Betsey?" quietly asked Mrs. Arkell.

"Prospects, ma'am? I have not any.   At least"
—and a sudden blush overspread the fair face—
"not at present."

"But you cannot go on waiting on Mrs. Dundyke's lodgers. It is not a desirable position for
yourself, nor a suitable one for your father's
daughter."

"I shall not have to do that again.   Mrs. Dundyke has engaged a good servant now; indeed, I
could not else have come away; when I return, I
shall only attend to the two children, and do the
sewing."

"I think we must try and find you something
better, Betsey."

"Oh, ma'am, you are very kind to interest yourself for me," was the reply; "but I have promised
myself to Mrs. Dundyke for twelve months to

come. I am very happy there; and when the work's over at night, we sit in her little parlour; she goes to sleep, and David does his accounts, and I darn the socks and stockings. You cannot think how comfortable and quiet it is."

"Who is David?" inquired Mrs. Arkell.

"Mrs. Dundyke's son. He is clerk in a house in Fenchurch-street, in the day; and he keeps books and that, for anybody who will employ him at night. Sometimes he has to bring them home to do. He is very industrious."

"What did you mean by saying you had promised yourself to Mrs. Dundyke for a twelve-month?"

"It was when I was coming away. She cried at parting, and said she supposed she should never see me again, now I was coming to be with Charlotte and her grand acquaintances. I told her I should be sure to come back to her very soon, and I would stop a whole year with her, if she liked. She said, was it a promise; and I told her it was. Oh! ma'am, I would not be ungrateful to Mrs. Dundyke for the world! I should have had no home to go to when Charlotte came here, but for her. All our money was gone, and Mrs. Dundyke had been letting us stop on then, ever so long, without any pay. Besides, I shall like to be with her."

9—2

If Charlotte could have cut her sister's tongue out, she would most decidedly have done it. To own such a sister at all, was bad enough ; but to be compelled to sit by while these revelations were made to her future mother-in-law, to her rival Mildred, was dreadful. If Charlotte had disliked Mildred before, she hated her now. The implied superiority of position which it had been her plea- sure from the first to assume over Mildred, would now be taken for what it was worth. She flung her arms up with a gesture of passionate pain, and approached Mrs. Arkell. Had Betsey confessed to having passed her recent months in housebreaking, it had sounded less despicable to Charlotte's pre- tentious mind than this ; and a dread had rushed over her, whether Mrs. Arkell might not, even at that eleventh hour, break off the union with her son.

"Mrs. Arkell, I pray you, do not notice this !" she said, her voice a wail of passion and despair. " It has, I am sure, not been as bad as Betsey makes it out ; she could not have degraded herself to so great an extent. But you see how it is. She is but half-witted at best, and anyone might impose upon her."

Half-witted ! Mrs. Arkell smiled at the look of surprise rising to Betsey's eyes at the charge. Charlotte's colour was going and coming.

"On the contrary, Charlotte, I should give your sister credit for a full portion of good plain sense. Why should you be angry with her? The sort of work was not suitable for her; but it seems she could not help herself."

"I'd rather hear that she had gone out and swept the crossings in the streets! I knew how it would be if you had her down! I knew she would disgrace me!"

Mrs. Arkell took Betsey's hand in hers. The young face was distressed; the blue eyes shone with tears. "I do not think you have disgraced anyone, Betsey; I think you have been a good girl. Charlotte," Mrs. Arkell added, very pointedly, "I would rather see your sister what she is, than a fine lady, stuck up and pretentious."

Did Charlotte understand the rebuke? She made no sign. Tring came in with lights: it caused some little interruption, and while they were calming down again from the past excitement, Betsey Travice took the opportunity to approach Mrs. Arkell with a whisper.

"I don't know how to thank you for your kindness to me, ma'am, not only in inviting me here, but in sending me the money in the letter. If ever I have it in my power to repay it, you will not find me ungrateful. I do not mean the money; I mean the kindness.

"Hush, child!" said Mrs. Arkell, and patted her smooth fair hair.

"There was always something deficient in Betsey's mind," Charlotte was condescending to say to Mildred Arkell. "It is a great misfortune. Papa used to say times and again that Betsey was not a lady; never would be one. Will you believe me, that once, when she was about ten I think, she fell into a habit of curtseying to gentlepeople when she met them in the street, and we could hardly break her of it! Papa would have been quite justified, in my opinion, had he then put her into an asylum or a reformatory, or something of the kind."

"She does not strike me—as my aunt has just remarked—as being deficient in sense."

"In plain, rough, every-day sense perhaps she is not. But there's something wanting in her, for all that. Her *notions* are not those of a lady, if you can understand. You hear her speak of the work that horrid landlady has made her do—well, she feels no shame in it."

Before Mildred could answer, Mr. Arkell and William entered, big with some local news. They kindly welcomed the meek-looking young stranger, and then spoke it out.

Edward Hughes, the brother of the sisters so frequently mentioned, had bid adieu to Westerbury

for ever. Whether he had at length become sick of
the condemnatory comments the town had not yet
forgotten to pass on Martha Ann, certain it was,
that he had suddenly sold off his stock in trade,
and gone away, en route for Australia. For some
little time past he had said it was his intention to
go; the two sisters also had spoken of it with a
kind of dread; but it was looked upon by most
people as idle talk. However, an opportunity
arose for the disposing advantageously of his
business and stock; he embraced it without an
hour's delay, and was already on his road to
Liverpool to take ship. The town could hardly
believe it, and concluded he was gone to escape
the reflections on Martha Ann—although he had
shown sufficient equanimity over them in general.
People needn't bother him about it, he had been
wont to say. They should talk to the one who
had been the cause of the mischief, Mr. Carr's
fine gentleman of a son.

"What a blow for the two sisters!" exclaimed
Mildred. "What will they do?"

"Nay, my dear, they have their business," said
Mr. Arkell. "I don't suppose their brother con-
tributed at all to their support. On the contrary,
people say he had been saving all he could to
emigrate with."

"I don't know that I altogether alluded to

money, Uncle George. It seems very sad for them to be left alone."

"It is sad for them," said Mrs. Arkell, agreeing with Mildred. "First Martha Ann, and now Edward!—it is a cruel bereavement. Tring says—and I have noticed it myself—that Mary Hughes has not been the same since that day's misfortune, three or four months ago."

"Ah," said Mr. Arkell, drawing a long breath, "I wish 1 had had the handling of Mr. Robert Carr that day!" The subject was a sore one with him, and ever would be. William believed, in his heart, that he had never been forgiven for having given the permission for the carriage that unlucky morning.

They continued to speak of the Hughes's and their affairs, and the interest of Betsey Travice appeared to be awakened. She had risen to go up-stairs, but halted near the door, listening still.

"And now tell me," began Charlotte, when they were alone together in the chamber, "how you dared so to disgrace me!"

"Oh, Charlotte, how have I disgraced you? Do not be unkind to me. I wish I had not come."

"I wish it too with all my heart! Why *did* you come? How on earth could you *think* of coming? What possessed you to do it?"

"Mrs. Arkell wrote for me. She wrote to Mrs.

Dundyke, asking her to see me off. I should never else have thought of coming."

"Did I write for you, pray? Could you not have known that if you were wanted I *should* have written, and, failing that, you were not to come? You wicked girl!"

Betsey burst into tears. She had been domineered over in this manner, by Charlotte, all her life; and she took it with appropriate humility and repentance.

"Charlotte, you know I'd lay down my life to do you any good; why are you so angry with me?"

"And you *do* do me good, don't you!" retorted Charlotte. "Look at the awful disgrace you have this very evening brought upon me!"

"What disgrace?" asked Betsey, her blue eyes bespeaking compassion from the midst of her tears.

"Good heavens! what an idiot!" uttered the exasperated Charlotte. "She asks what disgrace! Did you not proclaim yourself before them a servant of all work—a scourer of rooms, a blacker of grates, a——"

"Stop, Charlotte; I have not done either of those things—Mrs. Dundyke would not let me. I made beds and waited on the drawing-room, and such-like light duties. I did this, but I did not black grates."

"And if you did do it, was there any necessity for your proclaiming it? Had you not the sense to know that for my sister to avow these things was to me the very bitterest humiliation? Not for your doing them," tauntingly added Charlotte, in her passion, "for you are worth nothing better; but because you are a sister of mine."

Betsey's sobs were choking her.

"Where did you get the money to come down?" resumed Charlotte.

"Mrs. Arkell sent it me, Charlotte. There was a five-pound note in her letter."

It seemed to be getting worse and worse. Charlotte sat down and poked the fire fiercely, Tring having lighted one in compassion to the young visitor's evident chilly state. Betsey checked her sobs, and bent down to kiss her sister's neck.

"Somehow I always offend you, Charlotte; but I never do it intentionally, as you know, and I hope you will forgive me. I so try to do what I can for everybody. I always hope that God will help me to do right. There was the work to be done at Mrs. Dundyke's, and it seemed to fall to me to do it."

Charlotte was not all bad, and the tone of the words could but conciliate her. Her anger was subsiding into fretfulness.

"The annoying thing is this, Betsey—that *you* feel no disgrace in doing these things."

"I should not do them by choice, Charlotte. But the work was there, as I say; the servant was gone, and there was nobody but me to do it."

"Well, well, it can never be mended now," returned Charlotte, impatiently. "Why don't you let it drop?"

Betsey sighed meekly. She would have been too glad to let it drop at first. Charlotte pointed imperiously to a chair near her.

"Sit down there. You have tried me dreadfully this evening. Don't you know that in a few days I shall be Mrs. William Arkell? His father is one of the largest manufacturers in Westerbury, and they are rolling in money. It was not pleasant, I can tell you, for my sister to show herself out in such a light. What do you think of him?"

"Oh, Charlotte! I think you must be so happy! I am so thankful, dear! Working, and all that, does not matter for me; but it would not have done for you. I never saw anyone so nice-looking."

"As I?"

"As Mr. William Arkell. How pleasant his manner is! And, Charlotte, who is that young lady down there? I did not quite understand. What a sweet face she has!"

"You never do understand. It is the cousin:

Mildred. *She* thought to be Mrs. William Arkell,"
continued Charlotte, triumphantly. " The very
first night I came here I saw it as plain as glass,
and I took my resolution—to disappoint her. She
has been loving William all her life, and fully
meant him to marry her. I said I'd supplant her,
and I've done it; and I know our marriage is just
breaking her heart."

Betsey Travice—than whom one more generous-
hearted, more unselfishly forgetful of self-interest,
more earnestly single-minded, did not exist—felt
frightened at the avowal. Had it been possible
for her to recoil from her imperious sister, she had
recoiled then.

" Oh, Charlotte !" was all she uttered.

" Why, you don't think I should allow so good
a match to escape me, if I could help it ! And,
besides, I love him," added Charlotte, in a deeper
voice.

" But if——oh, Charlotte ! pardon me for speaking—I cannot help it—if that sweet young lady
loved him before you came ? had loved him for
years ?"

" Well ?" said Charlotte, equably.

" It *cannot* be right of you to take him from her."

" Right or not right, I have done it," said Charlotte, with a passing laugh. " But it *is* right, for
he loves me, and not her."

"What will she do?" cried Betsey, after a pause of concern; and it seemed that she asked the question of her own heart, not of Charlotte.

"Dwindle down into an old maid," was the careless answer: spoken, it is to be hoped, more in carelessness than heartlessness. "There, that's enough. Have you seen anything of Mrs. Nicholson?" resumed Charlotte.

"We have seen her a great many times, Charlotte; she has been very troublesome to Mrs. Dundyke. She wanted your address here: but for me, Mrs. Dundyke would have given it to her. She said—but, perhaps, I had better not tell it you."

: "What who said? Mrs. Dundyke? Oh, you may tell anything *she* said. I know her delight was to abuse me."

"No, no, Charlotte; it never was. She only said it was not right of you to order so many new things when you were coming here, unless you could pay for them. I went to Mrs. Nicholson and paid her a sovereign off the account."

"How did you get the sovereign?"

"Mrs. Dundyke made me a present of it—as a little recompense for my work, she said. I did not so very much want anything for myself, for I had just had new shoes, and I had not worn my best clothes; so I took it to Mrs. Nicholson."

Did the young girl's generosity strike no chord of gratitude in Charlotte's heart? This money, owing to Mrs. Nicholson, a fashionable dressmaker, had been Charlotte's worry during her visit. She would soon have it in her power to pay now.

"I wonder what you'll do in future?" resumed Charlotte, looking at her sister. "You can't expect to find a home with me, you know. It would be entirely unreasonable. And you can't expect to marry, for I don't think you'd be likely to get anyone to have you. If——"

The exceedingly vivid blush that overspread the younger sister's cheek, the wondrous look of intelligence in the raised eyes, brought Charlotte's polite speech to a summary conclusion. "What's the matter?" she asked.

"Charlotte, if you would let me tell you," was the whispered answer. "Papa is dead, and mamma is dead, and there is no one left but you; and I suppose I *ought* to tell you. I have promised to marry David."

"Promised——what?" repeated Charlotte, in an access of consternation.

"To marry David Dundyke. Not yet, of course; not for a long while, I dare say. When he shall be earning enough to keep a wife."

For once speech failed Charlotte Travice, and she sat gazing at her sister. Her equanimity had received several shocks that evening; but none had been like this. She had seen but little of this David Dundyke; but, a vision of remembrance rose before her of an inferior, common young man, carrying coal-scuttles upstairs in his shirt-sleeves, who could not speak a word grammatically.

"Are you really mad, Betsey?"

"I feared you would not like it, Charlotte; and I know I can't expect to be as you are. But we shall be more than a hundred miles apart, so that it need not annoy you."

Betsey had unconsciously put the matter in the right light. It was not because Mr. Dundyke was unfit to be Betsey's husband, but because he was unfit to be her brother-in-law, that the matter so grated on the ear of Charlotte.

"I cannot expect much better, Charlotte; I have not been educated as you have. Perhaps if I had been——"

"But the man is utterly beneath you!" burst forth Charlotte. "He is a common man. He used—if I am not mistaken—to black the boots and shoes for the house at night, and carry up the coal before he went out in the morning!"

"But not as a servant, Charlotte; only to save work for his mother. Just as I helped with the rooms and waited, you know. He does it all still. They were very respectable once; but Mr. Dundyke died, and she had to struggle on, and she took this house in Upper Stamford-street. You have heard her tell mamma of it many a time."

"You *can't* think of marrying him, Betsey? You are something of a lady, at any rate; and he—— cannot so much as speak like a Christian."

"He is very steady and industrious; he will be sure to get on," murmured Betsey. "Some of the clerks in the house he is in get a great deal of money."

"What house is it?" snapped Charlotte, beginning to feel cross again. "A public-house?—an eating-house?"

"It is a tea-house," said Betsey, mildly. "They are large wholesale tea-dealers; whole shiploads of tea come consigned to them from China. He went into it first of all as errand-boy, and——"

"You need not have told *that*, I think."

"And has got on by attention and perseverance to be a clerk. He is twenty-two now."

"If he gets on to be a partner—if he gets on to be sole proprietor—you cannot separate him from himself!" shrieked Charlotte. "Look here, Betsey; sooner than you should marry that low man, I'll have you to live with me. You can make yourself useful."

"Thank you kindly, Charlotte, all the same; but I could not come to you. You see, you and I do not get on together. It is my fault, I know, being so inferior; but I can't help it. Besides, I have promised David Dundyke."

Charlotte looked at her. "You do not mean to tell me that you have any *love* for this David Dundyke?"

Another bright blush, and Betsey cast down her pretty blue eyes. "We have seen so much of each other, Charlotte," she said, in a tone of apology; "he brings the books home nearly every evening now, instead of doing them out."

"Well, I shan't stop with you," concluded Charlotte, moving to the door. "I'm afraid to stop, for I truly believe you are going on for Bedlam. And *you'd* better make haste, if you want to do anything to yourself. Supper will be ready directly."

"One moment, Charlotte," said Betsey, detaining her—"I want to say only a word. They were speaking downstairs this evening of a family of the name of Hughes—a Mr. Edward Hughes, and some sisters."

"Well?" cried Charlotte.

"I think they are related to Mrs. Dundyke. She has relatives in Westerbury of that name; she has mentioned it several times since you came down. One or two of the sisters are dressmakers."

"Pleasant!" ejaculated Charlotte. "Are they intimate?"

"Not at all. I don't think they have met for

years, and I am sure they never correspond. But
when you were all speaking of the Hughes's to-
night, I thought it must be the same. I did not
like to say so."

"And it's well you did not," was Charlotte's
comment. "Those Hughes people have not been
in good odour in Westerbury since last December."

She went downstairs in a thoughtful mood,
her brain at work upon the question of whether
Betsey *could* be in her right mind. The revelation
regarding Mr. David Dundyke caused her really to
doubt it. She, Charlotte Travice, had a sufficiently
correct taste—to give her her due—and it would
have been simply impossible to her to have associ-
ated herself for life with anyone not possessing,
outwardly at any rate, the attributes of a gentleman

CHAPTER IX.

DISPLEASING EYES.

THE wedding day of Mr. William Arkell and Miss Travice dawned. All had gone well, and was going on well towards completion. You who have learnt to like Mildred Arkell, may probably have been in hopes that some impediment might arise to frustrate the wedding—that the bride, after all, might be Mildred, not Charlotte. But it is in the chronicles of romance chiefly that this sort of poetical justice takes place. Weddings are not frustrated in real life; and when I told you at the beginning that this was a story of real life, I told you the truth. The day dawned—one of the finest the close of April has ever seen—and the wedding party went to church to the marriage, and came home again when it was over.

It was quite a noted wedding for those quiet days, and guests were bidden to it from far and near. That the bride looked charmingly lovely

10—2

was indisputable, and they called William Arkell a lucky fellow.

A guest at the breakfast-table, but not in the church, was Mildred Arkell. She had wholly declined to be the bridesmaid; but it was next to impossible for her to decline to be at the breakfast. Put the case to yourselves, as Mildred had put it to herself in that past March night, that now seemed to be so long ago. Her resolve to pass over the affliction in silence; to bear, and make no sign, involved its consequences—and *they* were, that social life must go on just as usual, and she must visit at her uncle's as before. Worse than any other thought to Mildred, was the one, that the terrible blow to her might become known. She shrank with all the reticence of a pure-minded girl from the baring of her heart to others—shrank from it with a shivering dread—and Mildred felt that she would far rather die, than see her love suspected for one, who, as it now turned out, had never loved her. So she buried her misery within her, and went to Mr. Arkell's as before, not quite so frequently perhaps, but sufficiently so to excite no observation. She had joined in the plans and preparations for the wedding; had helped to fix upon the bride's attire, simply because she could not help herself. How she had borne it, and suppressed within her heart its own agony, she never knew. Charlotte's keen bright eyes would at times be fixed on hers, as if they could read her soul's secret; perhaps they did. William's rather seemed to shun her. But she had gone through it all, and borne it bravely; and none suspected how cruel was the ordeal.

And here was Mildred at the wedding-breakfast! There had been no escape for it. Peter went to church, but Mrs. Dan and Mildred arrived for breakfast only. Mildred, regarded and loved almost as a daughter of the house, had the place of honour assigned her next to William Arkell, his bride being on his other hand. None forgot how chaste and pretty Mildred looked that day; paler it may have been than usual, but that's expected at a wedding. She wore a delicate pearl-grey silk, and her gentle face, with its sweet, sad eyes, had never been pleasanter to look upon. " A little longer! a little longer!" she kept murmuring to her own re-bellious heart. " May God help me to bear!"

Perhaps the one who felt the most out of place at that breakfast-table, was our young friend, Miss Betsey Travice. Miss Betsey had never assisted at a scene of gaiety in her life—or, as she called it, grandeur; and perhaps she wished it over nearly as fervently as another was doing. She wore a new shining silk of maize colour, the gift of Mrs. Arkell—for maize was then in full fashion for bridesmaids—and Betsey felt particularly stiff and ashamed in it. What if the young gentleman on her left, who seemed to partake rather freely of the different wines, and to be a rollicking sort of youth, should upset something on her beautiful dress! Betsey dared not think of the catastrophe, and she astonished him by suddenly asking him if he'd please to move his glasses to the other side.

For answer, he turned his eyes full upon her, and she started. Very peculiar eyes they were, round and black, showing a great deal of the white, and that had a yellow tinge. His face was sallow, but otherwise his features were rather fine. It was not the colour of the eyes, however, that startled Betsey Travice, but their expression. A very peculiar expression, which made her recoil from him, and it took its seat firmly thenceforth in her memory. A talkative, agreeable sort of youth he seemed in manner, not as old by a year or two, Betsey thought, as herself; but, somehow, she formed a dislike to him—or rather to his eyes.

"I beg your pardon—I did not catch what you asked me."

"Oh, if you please, sir," meekly stammered Betsey, "I asked if you would mind moving the wine glasses to the other side; all three of them are full."

"And you are afraid of your dress," he said,

good-naturedly, doing what she requested. "Such accidents do happen to me sometimes, for I have a trick of throwing my arms about."

"But, in spite of the good nature so evident on the surface, there was a hidden vein of satire apparent to Betsey's ear. She blushed violently, fearing she had done something dreadfully incongruous. "I wonder who he is?" she thought; amidst the many names of guests she had not caught his.

Later, when all had left, save the Arkell family, and the bride and bridegroom were some miles on their honeymoon tour, Betsey ventured to put the question to Mildred—Who was the gentleman who had sat next to her at breakfast?

Poor Mildred could not recollect. The breakfast was to her one scene of confused remembrance, and she knew nothing save that she and William Arkell sat side by side.

"I don't remember where you sat," she was obliged to confess to Betsey.

" Nearly opposite to you, Miss Arkell. He had great black eyes, and he talked loud."

"Oh, that was Ben Carr," interrupted Peter; "he did sit next to you. He is Squire Carr's grandson. Did you see an old gentleman with a good deal of white hair, at the end of the table, near my mother?"

"Yes, I did," said Betsey; "I thought what beautiful hair it was."

"That was Squire Carr. I wonder, by the way, what brought Ben at the breakfast. Aunt," added Peter, turning to Mrs. Arkell; "did you invite Benjamin Carr?"

"No, Peter, Benjamin was not invited," was the reply. "Squire Carr and his son were invited, but John declined. I don't much think he likes going out."

"Afraid of being put to the expense of a coat," interrupted Peter.

There was a general laugh, John Carr's propensity to closeness in expenditure was well known. Mrs. Arkell resumed—

" So when John Carr declined, your uncle asked for his eldest son, young Valentine, to come with the squire; it seems, however, the squire brought Benjamin instead."

"Report runs that the squire favours his younger grandson more than he does his elder," remarked Peter. "For that matter, I don't know who does like young Valentine: I don't, he is too mean-spirited. Why did you wish to know who it was, Miss Betsey?"

"Not for anything in particular, sir. What curious eyes he has got!"

It was late when Mrs. Dan and her children went

home. The evening had been a quiet one ; in no way different from the usual evenings at Mr. Arkell's. Mildred had borne up bravely, and been cheerful as the rest.

But, oh ! the tension it had been to every nerve of her frame, every fibre of her heart ! Not until she was shut up in the quiet of her own room, did she know the strain it had been. She took her pretty dress off, threw a shawl on her shoulders, and sat down ; her brain battling with its misery, her hands pressed upon her throbbing temples.

How long she thus sat she could not tell. I believe—I honestly and truly believe—that no sorrow the world knows, can be of a nature more cruel than was Mildred's that night ; certainly none could be more intensely felt. " How can I bear it ?" she moaned, " how can I bear it ? To see them come back here in their wedded happiness, and have to witness it, and live. Perhaps— after a time, if God will help me, I shall be——"

" What on earth are you doing, Mildred ?"

She started from her chair with a scream. So entirely had she believed herself secure from interruption, that in the first confused moments it seemed as if her thoughts and anguish had been laid bare. Mrs. Dan stood there in her night-dress, a candle in her hand.

" You were moaning, Mildred. Are you ill ?"

"I—I am quite well, mamma," stammered Mildred, her words confused, and her face a fiery red. "Do you want anything?"

"But how is it you are not undressed? I had been in bed ever so long."

"I suppose I had fallen into a train of thought, and let the time slip away," answered Mildred, beginning to undo her hair in a heap, as if to make up for the lost time. "Why have you come out of your bed, mamma?"

"Child, I don't feel myself, and I thought I'd come and call you. It is well, as it happens, that you are not undressed, for I think I should like a cup of tea made. If I drink it very hot, it may take away the pain."

"Where is the pain?" asked Mildred, beginning to put up her hair again, as hurriedly as she had undone it.

"I scarcely know where it is; I feel ill all over. The fact is, I never ought to go to these festivities," added Mrs Dan, hastening back to her own room. "They are sure to upset me."

Alas! it was not the festivity that had "upset" Mrs. Dan; but that her time was come. Another hour, and she was so much worse, that Peter had to be aroused from his bed, and go for their doctor. Mrs. Daniel Arkell was in danger.

It may be deemed unfeeling, in some measure,

to say it, but it was the best thing that could have happened for Mildred. It took her out of her own thoughts—away from herself. There was so much to do, even in that first night, which was only the commencement; and it all fell on Mildred. Peter, with his timid heart, and unpractised hands, was utterly useless in a sick room, as book-worms in general are; and their one servant, Ann, a young, inexperienced, awkward girl, was nearly as much so. Mustard poultices had to be got, steaming hot flannels, and many other things. Before Mildred had made ready one thing, another called for her, It was well it was so!

At seven o'clock, Peter started for his uncle's, and told the news there. Mr. Arkell went up directly; Mrs. Arkell a little later. Mrs. Dan's danger had become imminent then, and Mr. Arkell went himself, and brought back a physician.

Later in the morning, Mildred was called down stairs to the sitting-room. Betsey Travice was standing there. The girl came forward, a pleading light in her earnest eye.

"Oh, Miss Arkell! if you will only please to let me! I have come to ask to help you."

"To help me!" mechanically repeated Mildred.

"I am so good a nurse; I am indeed! Poor papa died suddenly, but I nursed mamma all through her last long illness; there was only me to do everything, and she used to say that I was as handy as if I had learnt it in the hospitals. Let me try and help you!"

"You are very, very kind," said Mildred, feeling inclined to accept the offer as freely as it was made, for she knew that she should require assistance if the present state of things continued. "How came you to think of it?"

"When Mrs. Arkell came home to breakfast this morning, she said how everything lay upon you, and that you would never be able to do it. I believe she was thinking of sending Tring; but I took courage to tell her what a good nurse I was, and to beg her to let me come. I said—if you will not think it presuming of me, Miss Arkell— that Mrs. Daniel was my Godmother, and I thought it gave me a sort of right to wait upon her."

Mildred, undemonstrative Mildred, stooped down in a sudden impulse, and kissed the gentle face. "I shall be very glad of you, Betsey. Will you stay now?"

There was no need of further words. Betsey's bonnet and shawl were off in a moment, and she stood ready in her soft, black, noiseless dress.

"Please to put me to do anything there is to do, Miss Arkell. *Anything*, you know. I am handy in the kitchen. I do any sort of rough work as

handily as I can nurse. And perhaps your servant
will lend me an apron."

Three days only; three days of sharp, quick
illness, and Mrs. Daniel Arkell's last hour arrived.
Betsey Travice had not boasted unwarrantably, for
a better, more patient, ay, or more skilful nurse
never entered a sick chamber. She really was of
the utmost use and comfort, and Mildred righteously
believed that Heaven had been working out its
own ends in sending her just at that time to
Westerbury.

It was somewhat singular that Betsey Travice
should again be brought into the presence of the
young gentleman to whose eyes she had taken so
unaccountable a dislike. On that last day, when
the final scene was near at hand, the maid came
to the dying chamber, saying that Miss Arkell was
wanted below; a messenger had come over from
Mr. John Carr, and was asking to see her in person.

"I cannot go down now," was Mildred's answer;
"you might have known that, Ann."

"I did know it, miss, and I said it; that is, I
said I didn't think you could. But he wouldn't
take no denial: he said Mr. Carr had told him
not."

Giving herself no trouble as to who the "he"
might be, Mildred whispered to Betsey Travice to
go down for her, and mention the state of things.

Excessively to Betsey's discomfiture, she found herself confronted by the gentleman of the curious eyes, who held out his hand familiarly.

His errand was nothing particular, after all; but his father had expressly ordered him to see Miss Arkell, and convey to her personally his sympathy and inquiries as to her mother's state. For the news of Mrs. Dan's danger had travelled to Squire Carr's, and urgent business at home had alone prevented John Carr's coming over in person. As it was, he sent his son Ben.

Betsey, more meek than ever, thanked him, and told him how ill Mrs. Daniel was; that, in point of fact, another hour or two would bring the end. It was quite impossible Miss Arkell could, under the circumstances, leave the chamber.

"Of course she can't," he answered; "and I'm very sorry to hear it. My father will go on at me, I dare say, saying it was my fault, as he generally does when anything goes contrary to his orders. But he'd not have seen her any the more had he come himself. You will tell me who you are?" he suddenly continued to Betsey, without any break; "I sat by you at the breakfast, but I forget your name."

"If you please, sir, it is Betsey Travice," was the reply, and the girl quite cowered as she stood under the blaze of those black and piercing eyes.

" Betsey Travice! and a very pretty name. too.
You'll please to say everything proper for us up
there," jerking his head in the direction of the
upper floors. "Oh! and I say, I forgot to add
that my grandfather, the squire, intends to ride in
to-morrow, and call."

He shook hands with her in the passage, and
vaulted out at the front door, a tall, strong, fine
young fellow. And those eyes, which had so un-
accountably excited the disfavour of Miss Betsey,
were generally considered the handsomest of the
handsome.

Betsey stole upstairs again, and whispered the
message into Mildred's ear. "It was that tall,
dark young man, with the black eyes, that sat by
me at Charlotte's wedding breakfast."

They waited on, in the hushed chamber: Peter,
Mildred, Mr. and Mrs. Arkell, and Betsey Travice. And at two o'clock in the afternoon the
shutters were put up to the windows, through
which Mrs. Daniel Arkell would never look again.

CHAPTER X.

GOING OUT AS LADY'S MAID.

A WEEK or two given to grief, and Mildred Arkell sat down to deliberate upon her plans for the future. It was impossible to conceal from herself, dutiful, loving, grieving daughter though she was, how wonderfully her mother's death had removed the one sole impediment to the wish that had for some little time lain uppermost in her heart. She wanted to leave Westerbury; it was misery to her to remain in it; but while her mother had lived, her place was there. All seemed easy now: and in the midst of her bitter grief for that mother, Mildred's heart almost leaped at the thought that there was no longer any imperative tie to bind her to her home.

She would go away from Westerbury. But how? what to do? For a governess Mildred had not been educated; and accomplishments were then getting so very general, even the daughters of the petty tradespeople learning them, that Mildred felt

in that capacity she should stand but little chance
of obtaining a situation. But she might be a
companion to an invalid lady, might nurse her,
wait upon her, and be of use to her; and that sort
of situation she determined to seek.

Quietly, and after much thought, she arranged
her plans in her own mind; quietly she hoped and
prayed for assistance to be enabled to carry them
out. Nobody suspected this. Mildred seemed to
others just as she had ever seemed, quiet, unobtru-
sive Mildred Arkell, absorbed in the domestic
cares of her own home, in thought for the comfort
of her not at all strong brother. Mildred went
now but very little to her aunt's. Betsey Travice
had returned to London, to the enjoyments of
Mrs. Dundyke's household, which she had refused
to abandon; and William Arkell and his bride
were not yet come home.

"Peter," she said, one late evening that they were
sitting together—and it was the first intimation of
the project that had passed her lips—"I have been
thinking of the future."

"Yes?" replied Peter, absently, for he was as
usual disputing some knotty point in his mind,
having a Greek root for its basis. "What about it?"

"I am thinking of leaving home; leaving it for
good."

The words awoke even Peter. He listened to

her while she told her tale, listened without in-
terrupting, he was so amazed.

"But I cannot understand why you want to go,"
he said at last.

"To be independent." Of course she was ready
to assign any motive but the real one.

Peter could not understand this. She was independent at home. "I don't know what it is
you are thinking of, Mildred! Our house will go
on just the same; my mother's death makes no
difference to it. I kept it before, and I shall keep
it still."

"Oh yes, Peter, I know that. That is not it.
I—in point of fact, I wish for a change of scene.
I think I am tired of Westerbury."

"But what can you do if you go away from it?"

"I intend to ask Colonel and Mrs. Dewsbury:
I suppose you have no objection. They have many
influential friends in London and elsewhere, and
perhaps they might help me to a situation."

"Why do you want to go to London?" rejoined
Peter, catching at the word. "It's full of traps
and pitfalls, as people say. I don't know; I never
was there."

"I don't want to go to London, in particular; I
don't care where I go." Anywhere—anywhere that
would take her out of Westbury, she had nearly
added; but she controlled the words, and resumed

calmly. " I would as soon go to London as to any other place, Peter, and to any other place as to London. I don't mind where it is, so that I find a —a—sphere of usefulness."

" I don't like it at all," said Peter, after a pause of deliberation. " There are only two of us left now, Mildred, and I think we ought to continue together."

" I will come and see you sometimes."

" But, Mildred——"

" Listen, Peter," she imperatively interrupted, "it may save trouble. I have made up my mind to do this, and you must forgive me for saying that I am my own mistress, free to go, free to come. I wished to go out in this way some time before my mother died; but it was not right for me to leave her, and I said nothing. I shall certainly go now. I heard somebody once speak of the ' fever of change," she added, with a poor attempt at jesting; " I suppose I have caught it."

" Well, I am sorry, Mildred: it's all I can say. I did not think you would have been so eager to leave me."

The ready tears filled her eyes. " I am not eager to leave *you*, Peter; it will be my greatest grief. And you know if the thing does not work well, and I get too much buffeted by the world, I can but come back to you."

It never occurred to Peter Arkell to interpose any sort of veto, to say you shall not go. He had not had a will of his own in all his life; his mother and Mildred had arranged everything for him, and had Mildred announced her intention of becoming an opera dancer, he would never have presumed to gainsay it.

The following morning Mildred called at Mrs. Dewsbury's. They lived in a fine house at the opposite side of the river; but only about ten minutes' walk distance, if you took the near way, and crossed the ferry.

One of the loveliest girls Mildred had ever in her life seen was in the drawing-room to which she was shown, to wait for Mrs. Dewsbury. It was Miss Cheveley, an orphan relative of Mrs. Dewsbury's, who had recently come to reside with her. She rose from her chair in courteous welcome to Mildred; and Mildred could not for a few moments take her eyes from her face—from the delicate, transparent features, the rich, loving brown eyes, and the damask cheeks. The announcement, "Miss Arkell," and the deep mourning, had no doubt led the young lady to conclude that it was the tutor's sister. Mrs. Dewsbury came in immediately.

"Lucy, will you go into the school-room," she said, as she shook hands with Mildred, whom she knew, though very slightly. "The governess is giving Maria her music lesson, and the others are alone."

As Miss Cheveley crossed the room in acqui escence, Mildred's eyes followed her—followed her to the last moment; and she observed that Mrs. Dewsbury noticed that they did.

"I never saw anyone so beautiful in my life," she said to Mrs. Dewsbury by way of apology.

"Do you think so? A lovely face, certainly; but you know face is not everything. It cannot compensate for figure. Poor Miss Cheveley!"

"Is Miss Cheveley's not a good figure?"

"Miss Cheveley's! Did you not notice? She is deformed."

Mildred had not noticed it. She had been too absorbed in the lovely face. She turned to Mrs. Dewsbury, apologized for calling upon her, told her errand, that she wished to go out in the world, and craved the assistance of herself and Colonel Dewsbury in endeavouring to place her.

"I know, madam, that you have influential friends in many parts of England," she said, "and it is this——"

"But in what capacity do you wish to go out?" interrupted Mrs. Dewsbury. "As governess?"

"I would go as *English* governess," answered Mildred, with a stress upon the word. "But I do not understand French, and I know nothing of music or drawing : therefore I fear there is little chance for me in that capacity. I thought perhaps I might find a situation as companion ; as humble companion, that is to say, to make myself useful."

Mrs. Dewsbury shook her head. " Such situations are rare, Miss Arkell."

" I suppose they are ; too rare, perhaps, for me to find. Rather than not find anything, I would go out as lady's maid."

" As lady's maid !" repeated Mrs. Dewsbury.

Mildred's cheek burnt, and she suddenly thought of what the town would say. " Yes, as lady's maid, rather than not go," she repeated, firm in her resolution. " I think I have not much pride; what I have, I must subdue."

" But, Miss Arkell, allow me to ask—and I have a motive in it—whether you would be capable of a lady's-maid's duties ?"

" I think so," replied Mildred. " I would endeavour to render myself so. I have made my own dresses and bonnets, and I used to make my mother's caps until she became a widow; and I am fond of dressing hair."

Mrs. Dewsbury mused. " I think I have heard that you are well read, Miss Arkell ?"

" Yes, I am," replied Mildred. " I am a thoroughly good English scholar ; and my father, whose taste in literature was excellent, formed mine. I could teach Latin to boys until they were ten or eleven," she added, with a half smile.

"Do you read aloud *well* ?"

"I believe I do. I have been in the habit of reading a great deal to my mother."

"Well now I will tell you the purport of my putting these questions, which I hope you have not thought impertinent," said Mrs. Dewsbury. "The last time Lady Dewsbury wrote to us—you may have heard of her, perhaps, Miss Arkell, the widow of Sir John ?"

Mildred did not remember to have done so.

"Sir John Dewsbury was my husband's brother. But that is of no consequence. Lady Dewsbury, the widow, is an invalid ; and the last time she wrote to us she mentioned in her letter that she was wishing to find some one who would act both as companion and maid. It was merely spoken of incidentally, and I do not know whether she is suited. Shall I write and inquire ?"

"Oh, thank you, thank you !" cried Mildred, her heart eagerly grasping at this faint prospect. "I shall not care what I do, if Lady Dewsbury will but take me."

Mrs. Dewsbury smiled at the eagerness. She concluded that Mrs. Dan's death had made a difference in their income, hence the wish to go out. Mildred returned home, said nothing to anybody of what she had done, and waited, full of hope.

A short while of suspense, and then Mrs. Dewsbury sent for her. Lady Dewsbury's answer was favourable. She was willing to make the engagement, provided Miss Arkell could undertake what was required.

"First of all," said Mrs. Dewsbury to her, "Lady Dewsbury asks whether you can bear confinement?"

"I can indeed," replied Mildred. "And the better, perhaps, that I have no wish for aught else."

"Are you a good nurse in sickness?"

"I nursed my mother in her last illness," said Mildred, with tears in her eyes. "It was a very short one, it is true; but she had been ailing for years, and I attended on her. She used to say I must have been born a nurse."

"Lady Dewsbury is a great invalid," continued the colonel's wife, "and what she requires is a patient attendant; a maid, if you like to call it such; but who will at the same time be to her a companion and friend. 'A thoroughly-well-brought-up person,' she writes, 'lady-like in her manners and habits; but not a *fine lady* who would object to make herself useful.' I really think you would suit, Miss Arkell."

Mildred thought so too. "I will serve her to the very best of my power, Mrs. Dewsbury, if she will but try me;" and Mrs. Dewsbury noted the same eagerness that had been in her tone before, and smiled at it.

"She is willing to try you. Lady Dewsbury has, in fact, left the decision to the judgment of myself and the colonel. She has described exactly what she requires, and has empowered us to engage you, if we think you will be suitable."

"And will you engage me, Mrs. Dewsbury?"

"I will engage you now. The next question is about salary. Lady Dewsbury proposes to give at the rate of thirty pounds per annum for the first six months; after that at the rate of forty pounds; and should you remain with her beyond two years, it would be raised to fifty."

"Fifty!" echoed Mildred, in her astonishment. "Fifty pounds a year! For me!"

"Is it less than you expected?"

"It is a great deal more," was the candid answer. "I had not thought much about salary. I fancied I might be offered perhaps ten or twenty pounds."

Mrs. Dewsbury smiled. "Lady Dewsbury is liberal in all she does, Miss Arkell. I should not be surprised, were you to remain with her any considerable length of time, several years for instance, but she would double it."

But for the skeleton preying on Mildred Arkell's heart—the bitter agony that never left it by night or by day—she would have walked home, not knowing whether she trod on her head or her heels. The prospect of fifty pounds a-year to an inexperienced girl, who, perhaps, had never owned more than a few shillings at a time in her life, was enough to turn her head.

But it was not all to be quite plain sailing. Mildred had not disclosed the project to her aunt yet. Truth was, she shrunk from the task, foreseeing the opposition that would inevitably ensue. But it must no longer be delayed, for she was to depart for London that day week, and she went straight to Mrs. Arkell's. As she had expected, Mrs. Arkell met the news with extreme astonishment and anger.

"Do you know what you are doing, child! Don't talk to me about being a burden upon Peter! You——"

"Aunt, hear me!" she implored: and be it observed, that to Mrs. Arkell, Mildred put not forth one word of that convenient plea of "seeing the world," that she had filled Peter with. To Mrs. Arkell she urged another phase of the reasoning, and one, in truth, which had no slight weight with herself—Peter's interests. "I ought not to be a burden upon Peter, aunt, and I will not. You know how his heart is set upon going to the university; but he cannot get there if he does not save

for it ?   If I remain at home, the house must be
kept up the same as now; the housekeeping expenses must go on ; and it will take every shilling
of Peter's earnings to do all this.   Aunt, I could
not live upon him, for very shame.   While my
mother was here it was a different thing."

"But—to go to Peter's own affairs for a moment,"
cried Mrs. Arkell, irascibly—"what great difference will your going away make to his expenses ?
Twenty pounds a year at most.   Where's the use
of your putting a false colouring on things to me ?"

"I have not done so, aunt.   Peter and I have
talked these matters over since I resolved to go
out, and I believe he intends to let his house."

"To let his house !"

"It is large for him now; large and lonely.   He
means to let it, if he can, furnished ; just as it is."

"And take up his abode in the street ?"

"He will easily find apartments for himself,"
said Mildred, feeling for and excusing Mrs. Arkell's
unusual irritability.   "And, aunt, don't you see
what a great advantage this would be to him in his
plans ?   Saving a great part of what he earns, receiving money for his house besides, he will soon
get together enough to take him to college."

"I don't see anything, except that this notion of
going away, which you have taken up, is a very
wrong one.   It cannot be permitted, Mildred."

"Oh! aunt, don't say so," she entreated. " Peter must put by."

"Let him put by; it is what he ought to do. And you, Mildred, must come to us. Be a daughter to me and to your uncle in our old age. Since William left it, the house is not the same, and we are lonely. We once thought—you will not mind my saying it now—that you would indeed have been a daughter to us, and in that case William's home and yours would have been here. He should never have left us."

" Aunt——"

" Be still, and hear me, Mildred. I do not ask you this on the spur of the moment. because you are threatening to go out to service; and it is nothing less. Child! did you think we were going to neglect you? To leave you alone with Peter, uncared for? Your uncle and I had already planned to bring you home to us, but we were willing to let you stay a short while with Peter, so as not to take everybody from him just at once. Why, Mildred, are you aware that your *mother* knew you were to come to us?"

Mildred was not aware of it. She sat smoothing the black crape tucks of her dress with her fore-finger, making no reply. Her heart was full.

"A few days after I made that foolish mistake—but indeed the fault was William's, and so I have

always told him—I went and had it all out with
Mrs. Dan. I told her how bitterly disappointed I
and George both were ; but I said, in one sense it
need make no difference to us, for you should be
our daughter still, and come home to us as soon as
ever—I mean, when the time came that you would
no longer be wanted at home. And I can tell you,
Mildred, that your mother was gratified at the plan,
though you are not."

Mildred's eyes were swimming. She felt that if
she spoke, it would be to break into sobs.

"Your poor mother said it took a weight from
her mind. The house is Peter's, as you know, and
he can't dispose of it, but the furniture was hers,
left absolutely to her by your papa at his death.
She had been undecided whether she ought not to
leave the furniture to you, as Peter had the house ;
and yet she did not like to take it from him. This
plan of ours provided for you ; so her course was
clear, not to divide the furniture from the house.
As it turned out, she made no will, through delaying
it from time to time ; and in law, I suppose, the
furniture belongs as much to you as to Peter. You
must come home to us, Mildred."

"Oh, aunt, you and my uncle are both very
kind," she sobbed. "I should have liked much to
come here and contribute to your comforts : but,
indeed——"

"Indeed—what?" persisted Mrs. Arkell, pressing the point at which Mildred stopped.

"I cannot—I cannot come," she murmured, in her distress.

"But why?—what is your reason?"

"Aunt! aunt! do not ask me. Indeed I cannot stop in Westerbury."

They were interrupted by the entrance of William, and Mildred literally started from her seat, her poor heart beating wildly. She did not know of their return—had been in hopes, indeed, that she should have left the town before it; but, as she now learnt, they came home the previous night.

"I can make nothing of Mildred," cried Mrs. Arkell to her son; and in her anger and vexation, she gave him an outline of the case. "It is the most senseless scheme I ever heard of."

Mildred had touched the hand held out to her in greeting, and dried her tears as she best could, and altogether strove to be unconcerned and calm. *He* looked well—tall, noble, good, as usual, and very happy.

"See if you can do anything to shake her resolution, William. I have tried in vain."

Mrs. Arkell quitted the room abruptly, as she spoke. Mildred passed her handkerchief over her pale face, and rose from her seat.

Knowing what he did know, it was not a pleasant task for William Arkell. But for the extreme sensitiveness of his nature, he might have given some common-place refusal, and run away. As it was, he advanced to her with marked hesitation, and a flush of emotion rose to his face.

"Is there *anything* I can urge, Mildred, that will induce you to abandon this plan of yours, and remain in Westerbury?"

"Nothing," she replied.

"Why should you persist in leaving your native place?—why have you formed this strange dislike to remain in it?" he proceeded.

She would have answered him; she tried to answer him—any idle excuse that rose to her lips; but as he stood there, asking WHY she had taken a dislike to remain in the home of her childhood—he, the husband of another—the full sense of her bitter sorrow and desolation came rushing on, and overwhelmed her forced self-control. She hid her face in her hands, and sobbed in anguish.

William Arkell, almost as much agitated as herself, drew close to her. He took her hand—he bent down to her with a whisper of strange tenderness. "If *I* have had a share in causing you any grief, or—or—disappointment, let me implore your forgiveness, Mildred. It was not intentionally done. You cannot think so."

She motioned him away, her sobs seeming as if they would choke her.

"Mildred, I must speak; it has been in my heart to do it since—you know when," he whispered hoarsely, in his emotion, and he gathered both her hands in his, and kept them there. "I have begun to think lately, since my marriage, that it might have been well for both of us had we understood each other better. You talk of going into the world, a solitary wanderer; and my path, I fear, will not be one of roses, although it was of my own choosing. But what is done cannot be recalled."

"I must go home," she faintly interrupted; "you are trying me too greatly." But he went on as though he heard her not.

"Can we not both make the best of what is left to us? Stay in Westerbury, Mildred! Come home here to my father and mother; they are lonely now. Be to them a daughter, and to me as a dear sister."

"I shall never more have my home in Westerbury," she answered; "never more—never more. We can bid each other adieu now."

A moment's miserable pause. "Is there no appeal from this, Mildred?"

"None."

"Will you always remember, then, that you are very dear to me? Should you ever want a friend,

Mildred—ever want any assistance in any way—do not forget where I am to be found. I am a married man now, and yet I tell you openly that Westerbury will have lost one of its greatest charms for me, when you have left it."

"Let me go!" was all she murmured; "I cannot bear the pain."

He clasped her for a moment to his heart, and kissed her fervently. "Forgive me, Mildred—we are cousins still," he said, as he released her; "forgive me for all. May God bless and be with you, now and always!"

With her crape veil drawn before her face, with the cruel pain of desolation mocking at her heart, Mildred went forth; and in the court-yard she encountered Mrs. William Arkell, in a whole array of bridal feathers and furbelows, arriving to pay her first morning visit to her husband's former home. She held out her hand to Mildred, and threw back her white veil from her radiant face.

A confused greeting—she knew not of what—a murmured plea of being in haste—a light word of careless gossip, and Mildred passed on.

So there was to be no hindrance, and poor Mildred was to leave her home, and go forth to find one with strangers! But from that day she seemed to change—to grow cold and passionless;

and people reproached her for it, and wondered what had come to her.

How many of these isolated women do we meet in the world, to whom the same reproach seems due! *I* never see one of them but I mentally wonder whether her once warm, kindly feelings may not have been crushed; trampled on; just as was the case with those of Mildred Arkell.

CHAPTER XI.

MR. CARR'S OFFER.

RARE nuts for Westerbury to crack! So delightful a dish of gossip had not been served up to it since that affair of Robert Carr's. Miss Arkell was going out as lady's-maid!

Such was the report that spread, to the intense indignation of Mrs. Arkell. In vain that lady protested that her obstinate and reprehensibly-independent niece was going out as companion, not as lady's-maid; Westerbury nodded its head and knew better. It must be confessed that Mildred herself favoured the popular view: she was to be lady's-maid, she honestly said, as well as companion.

The news, indeed, caused real commotion in the town; and Mildred was remonstrated with from all quarters. What could she mean by leaving incapable Peter to himself?—and if people said true, Mr. and Mrs. Arkell would have been glad to adopt her. Mildred parried the comments, and shut herself up as far as she could.

But she could not shut herself up from all; she

12—2

had to take the annoyances as they came. A very especial one arrived for her only the morning previous to her departure. It was not intended as an annoyance, though, but as an honour.

There came to visit her Mr. John Carr, the son and heir of the squire. He came in state—a phæton and pair, and his groom beside him. John Carr was a little man, with mean-looking features and thin lips ; and there was the very slightest suspicion of a cross in his light eyes. Mildred was vexed at his visit : not because she was busy packing, but for a reason that she knew of. Some twelve months before, John Carr had privately made her an offer of his hand. She had refused it at once and positively, and she had never since liked to meet him. She could not escape now, for the servant said she was at home.

He had been shown upstairs to the drawing-room, an apartment they rarely used ; and he stood there in top-boots and a rose in his black frock coat. Mildred saw at once what was coming—a second offer. She refused him before he had well made it.

"But you must have me, Miss Arkell, you must," he reiterated. "You know how much I have wished for you; and—is it true that you think of going out to service in London ?"

"Quite true," said Mildred. "I am going as companion and maid to Lady Dewsbury."

"But surely that is not desirable. If there is no other resource left, you must come to me. I know you forbid me ever to renew the subject again ; but——"

"I beg your pardon, Mr. Carr. Your premises are wrong. I am not going out because I have no other resource. I have my home here, if I chose to stay in it. I have one pressed urgently upon me with my aunt and uncle. It is not that. I am going because I wish to go. I wish for a change. It is very kind of you to renew your offer to me ; but you must pardon my saying that I should have found it kinder had you abided by my previous answer."

" What is the reason you will not have me, Miss Arkell ? I know what it is, though : it is because I have had two wives already. But if I have, I made them both happy while they lived. They——"

" Oh, pray, Mr. Carr, don't talk so," she interrupted. " Pray take my answer, and let the subject be at an end."

But Mr. Carr was one who never liked any subject to be at an end, so long as he chose to pursue it ; and he was fond of diving into reasons for himself.

" I shall be Squire Carr after the old man's gone ; the owner of the property. I can make a settlement on you, Miss Arkell."

" I don't want it, thank you," she said in her

vexation. All Mildred's life, even when she was a little girl, she had particularly disliked Mr. John Carr.

"It's the children, I suppose," grumbled Mr. Carr. "But they need not annoy you. Valentine must stop at home; for it has not been the custom in our house to send the eldest son out. But Ben will go; I shall soon send him now. In fact, I did place him out; but he wouldn't stop, and came back again. Emma, I dare say, will be marrying; and then there's only the young children. You will be mistress of the house, and rule it as my late wife did. It is not an offer to be despised, Miss Arkell."

"I don't despise it," returned Mildred, wishing he would be said, and take himself away. "But I cannot accept it."

"Well, what is it, then? Do you intend never to marry?"

The question called up bitter remembrances, and a burning red suffused her cheeks.

"I shall never marry, Mr. Carr. At least, such is my belief now. Certainly I shall not marry until I have tried whether I cannot be happy in my life of dependence at Lady Dewsbury's."

Mr. John Carr's lucky star appeared not to be in the ascendant that day, and he went out considerably crest-fallen. Whipping his horses, he proceeded up the town to pay a visit to his uncle, Mr. Marmaduke Carr. None, save himself, knew how covetous were the eyes he cast to the good fortune his uncle had to bequeath to somebody; or that he would cast so long as the bequeathal remained in abeyance.

Lady Dewsbury lived in the heart of the fashionable part of London. Mildred went up alone. Mrs. Arkell had made a hundred words over it; but Mildred stood out for her independence : if she were not fit to take care of herself on a journey to London by day, she urged, how should she be fit to enter on the life she had carved out for herself? She found no trouble. Mr. Arkell had given instructions to the guard, and he called a coach for her at the journey's end. One of Mildred's great surprises on entering Lady Dewsbury's house was, to find that lady young. As the widow of the colonel's eldest brother—and the colonel himself was past middle age—Mildred had pictured in her mind a woman of at least fifty. Lady Dewsbury, however, did not look more than thirty, and Mildred was puzzled, for she knew there was a grown-up son, Sir Edward. Lady Dewsbury was a plain woman, with a sickly look, and teeth that projected very much ; but the expression of her face was homely and kindly, and Mildred liked her at the first glance. She was leaning back in an invalid chair; a peculiar sort of chair, the like of which Mildred had never seen, and a maid stood before her holding a cup of tea. Mildred found afterwards that Lady Dewsbury suffered from an internal complaint; nothing dangerous in itself, but tedious, and often painful. It caused her to live completely the life of an invalid; going out very little, and receiving few visitors. The medical men said if she could live over the next ten years or so, she might recover, and be afterwards a strong woman.

Nothing could be more kind and cordial than her reception of Mildred. She received her more as an equal than an attendant. It relieved Mildred excessively. Reared in her simple country home, a Lady Dewsbury, or Lady anybody else, was a formidable personage to Mildred; one of the high-born and unapproachable of the land. It must be confessed that Mildred was at first as timid as ever poor humble Betsey Travice could have been; and nearly broke down as she ventured on a word of hope that "My lady," "her ladyship," would find her equal to her duties.

"Stay, my dear," said Lady Dewsbury, detecting the embarrassment and smiling at it—"let us begin as we are to go on. I am neither my lady nor your ladyship to you, remember. When you have occasion to address me by name, I am Lady Dewsbury; but that need not be often. Mrs. Dewsbury said you were coming to be my maid, I think?"

" Yes," replied Mildred.

" I told her to say it, because I shall require many little services performed for me on my worst days that properly belong to a maid to perform; and I did not like to deceive you in any way. But can you understand me when I say that I do not wish you to do these things for me as a servant, but as a friend?"

" I shall be so happy to do them," murmured Mildred.

" I do not wish to keep two persons near me, a companion and a maid. I have tried it, and it does not answer. Until my sister married, she lived with me, my companion; and I had my maid. After my sister left, I engaged a lady to replace her, but she and the maid did not get on together; the one grew jealous of the other, and things became so unpleasant, that I gave both of them notice to leave. It then occurred to me that I might unite the two in one, if by good luck I could find a well-educated and yet domesticated lady, who would not be above waiting on an invalid. And I happened to mention this to Mrs. Dewsbury."

" I hope you will like me; I hope I shall suit," was Mildred's only answering comment.

" I like you already," returned Lady Dewsbury. " I am apt to take fancies to faces, and the contrary, and I have taken a fancy to yours. But

I will go on with my explanation. You will not be regarded in the light of a servant, or ever treated as one. You will generally sit with me, and take your meals with me when I am alone. If I have visitors, you will take them in the little sitting-room appropriated for yourself. The servants will wait upon you, and observe to you proper respect. I have not told them you are coming here as my maid, but as my friend and companion."

Mildred felt overpowered at the kindness.

"In reality you will, as I have said, in many respects be my maid; that is, you will have to do for me a maid's duties," proceeded Lady Dewsbury. "You will dress me and undress me. You will sleep in the next room to mine, with the door open between, so as to hear me when I call; for I am sorry to say, my sufferings occasionally require sudden attendance in the night. As my companion, you will read to me, write letters for me, go with me in the carriage when I travel, help me with my worsted work, of which I am very fond, do my personal errands for me out of doors, give orders to the servants when I am not well enough, keep the house-keeping accounts, and always be —patient, willing, and good-tempered."

Lady Dewsbury said the last words with a laugh.

Mildred gave one of her sweet smiles in answer.

"I really mean it though, Miss Arkell," continued Lady Dewsbury. "Patience is absolutely essential for one who has to be with a sufferer like myself; and I could not bear one about me for a day who showed unwillingness or ill-temper. The trouble that I am obliged to give, is sufficiently present always to my own mind; but I could not bear to have the expression of it thrown back to me. The last and worst thing I must now mention; and that is, the confinement. When I am pretty well, as I am now, it is not so much; but it sometimes happens that I am very ill for weeks together; never out of my room, scarcely out of my bed: and not once perhaps during all that time will you be able to go out of doors."

"I shall not mind it indeed, Lady Dewsbury," Mildred said, heartily. "I am used to confinement. I told Mrs. Dewsbury so. Oh, if I can but suit you, I shall not mind what I do. I think it seems a very, very nice place. I did not expect to meet with one half so good."

"How old do you think I am?" suddenly asked Lady Dewsbury. "Perhaps Mrs. Dewsbury mentioned it to you?"

"It is puzzling me," said Mildred, candidly, quite overlooking the last question. "I could not take you to be more than thirty; but I—I had fancied—I beg your pardon, Lady Dewsbury—that

you must be quite fifty. I thought Sir Edward
was some years past twenty."

"Sir Edward?—what has that to do with—oh, I
see! You are taking Sir Edward to be my son.
Why, he is nearly as old as I am, and I am thirty-
five. I was Sir John Dewsbury's second wife. I
never had any children. Sir Edward comes here
sometimes. We are very good friends."

Mildred's puzzle was explained, and Lady
Dewsbury sent her away, happy, to see her room.
It had been a gracious reception, a cordial welcome;
and it seemed to whisper an earnest of future
comfort, of length of service.

Lady Dewsbury was tolerably well at that period,
and Mildred found that she might take advantage
of it to pay an afternoon visit to Betsey Travice.
She sent word that she was coming, and Betsey
was in readiness to receive her; and Mrs. Dundyke,
a stout lady in faded black silk, had a sumptuous
meal ready: muffins, bread and butter, shrimps,
and water-cress.

The parlour, on a level with the kitchen, was
a very shabby one, and the bells of the house kept
clanging incessantly, and Mrs. Dundyke went in
and out to urge the servant to alacrity in answering
them, and two troublesome fractious children, of
eighteen months, and three years old, insisted on
monopolizing the cares of Betsey; and altogether

Mildred *wondered* that Betsey could or would stop there.

"But I like it," whispered Betsey, "I do indeed. Mrs. Dundyke is not handsome, but she's very kind-hearted, and the children are fond of me; and I feel at home here, and there's a great deal in that. And besides——"

"Besides—what?" asked Mildred, for the words had come to a sudden stand-still.

"There's David," came forth the faint and shame-faced answer.

"David?"

"Mrs. Dundyke's son. We are to be married sometime."

Mildred had the honour of an introduction to the gentleman before she left—for Mr. David came in—a young man above the middle height, somewhat free and confident in his address and manners. He was not bad-looking, and he was attired sufficiently well; for the house he was in, in Fenchurch-street, was one of the first houses of its class, and would not have tolerated shabbiness in any of its clerks. The shirt-sleeve episodes, the blacking-boot and carrying-up coal attire, so vivid in the remembrance of Charlotte Travice, were kept for home, for late at night and early morning. Of this, Mildred saw nothing, heard nothing.

"He has eighty pounds a year now," whispered

Betsey to Mildred; " his next rise will be a
hundred and fifty. And then, when it has got to
that——," the blush on the cheeks, the downcast
eyes, told the rest.

" 'Them there shrimps ain't bad ; take some more
of 'em."

Mildred positively started—not at the invitation
so abruptly given to her, but at the wording of it.
It was the first sentence she had heard him speak.
Had he framed it in joke ?

No ; it was his habitual manner of speaking.
She cast her compassionate eyes on Betsey Travice,
just as Charlotte would have cast her indignant
ones. But Betsey was used to him, and did not
feel the degradation.

" Now, mother, don't you worry your inside out
after that girl," he said, as Mrs. Dundyke, for the
fiftieth time, plunged into the kitchen, groaning
over the shortcomings of the servant. " You won't
live no longer for it. Betsey, just put them two
squalling chickens down, and pour me out a drop
more tea; make yourself useful if you can till
mother comes back. Won't you take no more,
Miss Arkell ?"

" Betsey," asked Mildred, in a low tone, as
they were alone for a few minutes when Mildred
was about to leave, " do you *like* Mr. David
Dundyke ?"

Betsey's face was sufficient answer.

" I think you ought not to be too precipitate to say you will do this or do the other. You are young, Mr. Dundyke is young, and—and—if you had had more experience in the world, you might not have engaged yourself to *him*."

" Thank you kindly ; that is just as Charlotte says. But we are not going to marry yet.",

" Betsey—you will excuse me for saying it : if I speak, it is for your own sake—do you consider Mr. Dundyke, with his—his apparently imperfect education, is suitable for you ?"

" Indeed," answered Betsey, " his education is better than it appears. He has fallen into this odd way of speaking from habit, from association with his mother. *She* speaks so, you must perceive. He rather prides himself upon keeping it up, upon not being what he calls fine. And he is so clever in his business ! "

Mildred could not at all understand that sort of " pride." Betsey Travice noticed the gravity of her eye.

"What education have *I* had, Miss Arkell? None. I learnt to read, and write, and spell, and I learnt nothing more. If I speak as a lady, it is because I was born to it, because papa and mamma and Charlotte so spoke, not from any advantages they gave me. I have been kept down all my life.

Charlotte was made a lady of, and I was made to work. When I was only six years old I had to wait on mamma and Charlotte. I am not complaining of this; I like work; but I mention it, to ask you in what way, remembering these things, I am better than David Dundyke?"

In truth, Mildred could not say.

"What am I now but a burden on his mother?" continued Betsey. "In one sense I repay my cost; for, if I were not here, she would have to take a servant for the two little children. I have no prospects at all; I have nobody in the world to help me; indeed, Miss Arkell, it is *generous* of David to ask me to be his wife."

"You might find a home with your sister, now she has one. You ought to have it with her."

Betsey shook her head. "You don't know Charlotte," was all she answered.

Mildred dropped the subject. She took a ring from her purse, an emerald set round with pearls, and put it into Betsey's hand.

"It was my mother's," she said, "and I brought it for you. She had two of these rings just alike; one of them had belonged to a sister of hers who died. I wear the other—see! My mother was very poor, Betsey, or she might have left something worth the acceptance of you, her god-daughter."

Betsey Travice burst into tears, partly at the kind words, partly at the munificence of the gift, for she had never possessed so much as a brass ring in all her life.

"It is too good for me," she said; "I ought not to take it from you. I would not, but for your having one like it. What have I done that you should all be so kind to me? But I will never part with the ring."

And, indeed, the contrast between the kindness to her of the Arkells generally and the unfeeling behaviour of her sister Charlotte, could but mark its indelible trace on even the humble mind of Betsey Travice.

"Has Charlotte come home?" she asked.

"Have you heard from her?" exclaimed Mildred in astonishment. "She came home before I left Westerbury."

Betsey shook her head. "We are not to keep up any correspondence; Charlotte said it would not do; that our paths in life lay apart; hers up in the world, mine down; and she did not care to own me for a sister. Of course I know I *am* inferior to Charlotte, and always have been; but still——"

Betsey broke down. The grieved heart was full.

CHAPTER XII.

MARRIAGES IN UNFASHIONABLE LIFE.

THE next twelvemonth brought little of event, if we except the birth of a boy to William Arkell and his wife.   In the month of March, nearly a year after their marriage, the child was born ; and its mother was so ill, so very near, as was believed, unto death, that Mrs. Arkell sent a despatch to bring down her sister, Betsey Travice.   Had Charlotte been able to have a voice in the affair, rely upon it Betsey had never come.

But Charlotte was not, and Betsey arrived ; the same meek Betsey as of yore.   William liked the young girl excessively, and welcomed her with a warm heart and open arms.   His wife was better then, could be spoken to, and did not feel in the least obliged to them for having summoned Betsey.

" I am glad to see you, Betsey," William whispered, " and so would Charlotte be, poor girl, if she were a little less ill.   You shall stand to the baby, Betsey; he is but a sickly little fellow, it seems, and they are talking of christening him at once. If it were a girl, we would name it after you; we'll call it—can't we call it Travice? That will be after you, all the same, and it's a very pretty name."

Betsey shook her head dubiously. She had an innate fondness for children, and she kissed the little red face nestled in her arms.

" Charlotte would not like *me* to stand to it," whispered.

" Not like it!" echoed William, who did not know his wife yet, and had no suspicion of the state of things. " Of course she would like it. Who has so great a right to stand to the child as you, her sister. Would you like it yourself?"

" Oh, very much ; I should think it was my own little boy all through life."

" Until you have little boys of your own," laughed William, and Betsey felt her face glow. " All right, his name shall be Travice."

And so it was ; the child was christened Travice George ; and Betsey had become his godmother before Charlotte knew the treason that was agate. She was bitterly unkind over it afterwards to Betsey, reproaching her with " thrusting herself forward unwarrantably."

A very, very short stay with them, only until

Charlotte was quite out of danger, and Betsey went back to London. "Do not, if you can help it, ever ask me down again, dear Mrs. Arkell," she said, with tears. "You must see how it is—how unwelcome I am; Charlotte, of course, is a lady, always was one, and I am but a poor working girl. It is natural she should wish us not to keep up too much intimacy."

"I call it very unnatural," indignantly remonstrated Mrs. Arkell.

Perhaps Betsey Travice yearned to this little baby all the more, from the fact that the youngest of the two children she had taken care of at Mrs. Dundyke's, had died a few months before. Fractious, sickly, troublesome as it had been, Betsey's fondness for it was great, and her sorrow heavy. There had been nobody to mourn it but herself; Mrs. Dundyke was too much absorbed in her household cares to spare time for grief, and everybody else, saving Betsey, thought the house was better without the crying baby than with it. These children were almost orphans; the mother, David's only sister, died when the last was born; the father, a merchant captain, given to spend his money instead of bringing it home, was always away at sea.

Death was to be more busy yet with the house of Mrs. Dundyke. A few months after Betsey's return from the short visit to Westerbury, when the hot weather set in for the summer, the other baby died. Close upon that, Mrs. Dundyke died—died in a fit.

The attack was so sudden, the shock so great, that for a short time those left—David and Betsey—were stunned. David had to go to Fenchurch-street all the same; and Betsey quietly took Mrs. Dundyke's place in the house, and saw that things went on right. Duty was ever first with Betsey Travice; what her hand found to do, that she did with all her might; and the whole care devolved on her now. A clergyman and his wife were occupying the drawing-rooms, and they took great interest in the poor girl, and were very kind to her; but they never supposed but that she was some near relative of the Dundykes. David, who did not want for plain sense —no, nor for self-respect either—saw, of course, that the present state of things could not continue.

" Look here, Betsey," he said to her, one evening that they sat together in silence; he busy with his account books, and Betsey absorbed in trying to make out and remember the various items charged in the last week's butcher's bill; " we must make a change, I suppose."

She looked up, marking the place she had come

to with her pencil. "What did you please to say, David?—make a change?"

"Well, yes, I suppose so, or we shall have the world about our ears. I mean to get rid of the house as soon as I can; either get somebody to come in and buy the good-will and the furniture; or else, if nobody wont do that, give up the house, and sell off the old things by auction, just keeping enough to furnish a room or two."

"It would be better to sell the good-will and the furniture, would it not?"

"Don't I say so? But I'm not sure of doing it, for houses is going down in Stamford-street: people that pay well for apartments, like to be fashionable, and get up to the new buildings westward. Any way, I'm afraid there wont be no more realized than will serve to pay what mother owed."

David stopped here and looked down on his accounts again. Betsey, who sat at the opposite side of the table, with the strong light of the summer evening lighting up its old red cloth, returned to hers. Before she had accomplished another item, David resumed—

"And all this will take time; three or four months, perhaps. And so, Betsey—if you don't mind being hurried into it—I think we had better be married."

"Be married!" echoed Betsey, dropping her book and her pencil. "Whatever do you mean?"

"I mean what I say," was David's sententious answer; "I don't mean nothing else. You and me must be married."

Betsey stared at him aghast. "Oh, David! how can you think of such a thing yet? It is not a month since your poor mother died."

"That's just it, her being dead," said David. "Don't you see, Betsey, neither you nor me can go out of the house until somebody takes to it, or till something's settled; and, in short, folks might get saying things."

Not for a full minute did she in the least comprehend his meaning. Then she burst into a passion of tears of anger; all her face aflame.

"Oh! David, how can you speak so? who would dare to be so cruel?"

"It's because I know the world better than you, and because I know how cruel it is, that I say it," added David. "Look here, Betsey, there's nobody left now to take care of you but me; and I *shall* take care of you, and I'm saying what's right. I shall buy a licence; it's a dreadful deal of money, when asking in church does as well, but that takes longer, and I'll spend the money cheerfully, for your sake. We'll go quietly to church next Sunday morning, and nobody need know, till it's all over, what we've been for. Unless you like to tell the servant, and the parson and his wife in the drawing-room. Perhaps you'd better."

" But, David——"

" Now, where's the good of contending?" he interrupted; "you don't want to give me up, do you?"

" You know I don't, David."

" Very well, then."

Betsey held out for some time longer, and it was only because she saw no other opening out of the dilemma—for, as David said, neither of them could leave the house if it was to go on—that she gave in at last. David at once entered upon sundry admonitions as to future economy, warning her that he intended they should live upon next to nothing for years and years to come. He did not intend to spend all his income, and be reduced to letting lodgings, or what not, when he should get old.

And a day or two after the marriage had really taken place, Betsey wrote a very deprecatory note to Charlotte, and another to Mrs. Arkell, with the news. But she did not give them an intimation of it beforehand. So that even had Charlotte wished to make any attempt to prevent it, she had not the opportunity. And from thenceforth she washed her hands of Betsey Dundyke, even more completely than she had done of Betsey Travice.

This first portion of my story is, I fear, rather inclined to be fragmentary, for I have to speak of the history of several; but it is necessary to do so, if you are to be quite at home with all our friends in it, as I always like you to be. The next thing we have to notice, was an astounding event in the life of Peter Arkell.

Peter Arkell was not a man of the world; he was a great deal too simple-minded to be anything of the sort. In worldly cunning, Peter was not a whit above Moses Primrose at the fair. Peter was getting on famously; he had let his house furnished, and the family who took it accommodated Peter with a room in it, and let him take his breakfast and dinner with them, for a very moderate sum. He worked at the bank, as usual, and he attended at Colonel Dewsbury's of an evening; that gentleman's eldest son had gone to college, but he had others coming on. Peter Arkell had also found time to write a small book, not *in* Greek, but touching Greek; it was excessively learned, and found so much favour with the classical world, that Peter Arkell grew to be stared at in his native city, as that very rare menagerie animal, a successful author; besides which, Peter's London publishers had positively transmitted him a sum of thirty pounds. I can tell you that the sum of thirty hundred does not appear so much to some people as that appeared to Peter. Had he gained thousands and thousands in his after life, they would have been to him as nothing, compared to the enraptured satisfaction brought to his heart by that early sum, the first fruits of his labours. Ask any author that ever put pen to paper, if the first guinea he ever earned was not more to him than all the golden profusion of the later harvest.

And so Peter, in his own estimation at any rate, was going on for a prosperous man. He put by all he could; and at the end of three years and a-half from Mildred's departure—for time is constantly on the wing, remember—Peter had saved a very nice sum, nearly enough to take him to Oxford, when he should find time to get there. For that, the getting there, was more of a stumbling block now than the means, since Peter did not yet see his way clear to resign his situation in the bank.

Meanwhile he waited, hoped, and worked. And during this season of patience, he had an honour conferred upon him by young Fauntleroy the lawyer: a gentleman considerably older than Peter, but called young Fauntleroy, in distinction to his father, old Fauntleroy the lawyer. Young Fauntleroy, who was as much given to spending as Peter was to saving, and had a hundred debts, unknown to the world, got simple Peter to be security for him in some dilemma. Peter hesitated at first. Four hundred pounds was a large sum, and would swamp him utterly should he ever be called upon to pay it; but upon young Fauntleroy's assuring him, on his honour, that the bank could not be more safe to pay its quarterly dividends than he was to provide for that obligation when the time came, Peter gave in. He signed his name, and from that hour thought no more of the matter. When a person promised Peter to do a thing he had the implicit faith of a child. And now comes the event that so astounded Westerbury.

You remember Lucy Cheveley, the young lady whose lovely face had so won on Mildred's admiration? How it came about no human being could ever tell, least of all themselves; but she and Peter Arkell fell in love with each other. It was not one of those ephemeral fancies that may be thrown off just as easily as they are assumed, but a passionate, powerful, lasting love, one that makes the bliss or the bane of a whole future existence. The chief of the blame was voted by the meddling town to Colonel and Mrs. Dewsbury. Why had they allowed Miss Cheveley to mix in familiar intercourse with the tutor? To tell the truth, Miss Cheveley had not been much better there than a governess. Her means were very small. She had only the pension of a deceased officer's daughter, and Mrs. Dewsbury, what with clothes and maintenance, was considerably out of pocket by her; therefore she repaid herself by making Miss Cheveley useful with the children. The governess was a daily one, and Lucy Cheveley helped the children at night to prepare their lessons for her. The study for both boys and girls was the same, and thus Lucy was in constant daily intercourse with Mr. Peter Arkell. Since the publication of Peter's learned book, and his consequent rise in public estimation, Colonel Dewsbury had once or twice invited him to dinner; and Miss Cheveley met him on an equality.

But the marvel was, how ever that lovely girl could have lost her heart to Peter Arkell—plain, shy, awkward Peter! But that such things have been known before, it might have been looked upon as an impossibility.

There was a fearful rumpus. The discovery came through Mrs. Dewsbury's bursting one night into the study in search of a book, when the children had left it, and she supposed it empty. Mr. Peter Arkell stood there with his arm round Lucy's waist, and both her hands gathered and held in his. For the first minute or so, Mrs. Dewsbury did not believe her own eyes. Lucy stood in painful distress, the damask colour glowing on her transparent cheek, and the explanation, as of right it would, fell to Peter.

These shy, timid, awkward-mannered men in every-day life, are sometimes the most collected in situations of actual embarrassment. It was so with Peter Arkell. In a calm, quiet way he turned to Mrs. Dewsbury, and told her the straightforward truth: that he and Miss Cheveley were attached to each other, and he had asked her to be his wife.

Mrs. Dewsbury was an excitable woman. She went back to the dining-room, shrieking like one in hysterics, and told the news. It aroused Colonel Dewsbury from his wine; and it was not a light thing in a general way that could do that, for the colonel was fond of it.

Then ensued the scene. Colonel and Mrs. Dewsbury heaped vituperation on the head of the tutor, asking what he could expect to come to for thus abusing confidence? Poor Peter, far more composed in that moment than he was in every-day matters, said honestly that he had not intended to abuse it; nothing would ever have been farther from his thoughts; but the mutual love had come to them both unawares, and been betrayed to each other without thought of the consequences.

All the abuse ever spoken would not avail to undo the past. Of course nothing was left now but to dismiss Mr. Peter Arkell summarily from his tutorship, and order Miss Cheveley never to hold intercourse by word or look with him again.

This might have mended matters in a degree had Miss Cheveley acquiesced, and carried the mandate out; but, encouraged no doubt secretly by Mr. Peter, she timidly declined to do so—said, in fact, she would not. Colonel and Mrs. Dewsbury were rampant as two chained lions, who long to get loose and tear somebody to pieces.

For Mr. Peter Arkell was not to be got at. The law did not sanction his imprisonment; and society would not countenance the colonel in beating or killing him. Neither could Mrs. Dewsbury lock up Miss Lucy Cheveley, as was the mode observed to refractory damsels in what is called the good old time.

The next scene in the play was their marriage. Lucy, finding that she could never hope to obtain the consent of her protectors to it, walked quietly to church from their house one fine morning, met Peter there, and was married without consent. Peter had made his arrangements for the event in a more sensible manner than one so incapable would have been supposed likely to do. The friends who had occupied his house vacated it previously to oblige him; he had it papered and painted, and put into thoroughly nice order, spending about a hundred pounds in new furniture, and took Lucy home to it. Never did a more charming wife enter on possession of a home; and

Westerbury, which of course made everybody's affairs its own, in the usual manner, was taken with a sudden fit of envy at the good fortune of Peter Arkell, when it had recovered its astonishment at Miss Cheveley's folly. One of her order marry poor Peter Arkell, the banker's clerk! The world must be coming to an end.

Colonel and Mrs. Dewsbury almost wished it *was* coming to an end, for the bride and bridegroom at any rate, in their furious anger. The colonel went to the bank, and coolly requested it to discharge Peter Arkell from its service. The bank politely declined, saying that Mr. Peter Arkell had done nothing to offend it, or of which it could take cognizance. Colonel Dewsbury threatened to withdraw his account, and carry it off forthwith to a sort of patent company bank, recently opened in the town. The bank listened with equanimity; it would be sorry of course, and hoped the colonel would think better of it; but, if he insisted, his balance (he never kept more than a couple of hundred pounds there) should then be handed to him. The colonel growled, and went out with a bang. He next wrote to Lady Dewsbury a peremptory letter, almost *requiring* her to discharge Miss Arkell from her service. Lady Dewsbury wrote word back that Mildred had become too valuable to her to be parted with;

and that if Peter Arkell was like his sister in goodness, Lucy Cheveley had not chosen amiss.

Lucy had been married about a fortnight, and was sitting one evening in all her fragile loveliness, the red light of the setting sun flickering through the elm trees on her damask cheeks, when a tall elegant woman entered. This was Mrs. St. John, whose family had been intimate with the Cheveleys. The St. Johns inhabited that old building in Westerbury called the Palmery, of which mention has been made, but they had been away from it for the past two years. Mrs. St. John had just returned to hear the scandal caused by the recent disobedient marriage.

Though all the world abandoned Lucy, Mrs. St. John would not. She had not so many years been a wife herself, having married the widower, Mr. St. John, who was more than double her age, and had a grown-up son. Lucy started up, with many blushes, at Mrs. St. John's entrance; and she told the story of herself and Peter very simply, when questioned.

"Well, Lucy, I wish you happy," Mrs. St. John said; "but it is not the marriage you should have made."

"Perhaps not. I suppose not. For Mr. Arkell's family is of course inferior to mine—"

"Inferior! Mr. Arkell's family!" interrupted

Mrs. St. John, all her aristocratic prejudices offended at the words. "What do you mean, Lucy? Mr. Arkell is of *no* family! They are tradespeople—manufacturers. We don't speak of that class as 'a family.' *You* are of our order; and I can tell you, the Cheveleys have had the best blood in their veins. It is a very sad descent for you; little less—my dear, I cannot help speaking —than degradation for life."

"If I had good family," spoke Lucy, "what else had I?"

"Beauty!" was Mrs. St. John's involuntary answer, as she gazed at the wondrously lustrous brown eyes, the bright exquisite features.

"*Beauty!*" echoed Lucy, in surprise. "Oh, Mrs. St. John! you forget."

"Forget what, Lucy."

"That I am deformed."

The word was spoken in a painful whisper, and the sensitive complexion grew carmine with the sense of shame. It is ever so. Where any defect of person exists, none can feel it as does its possessor; it is to the mind one ever-present agony of humiliation. Lucy Cheveley's spine was not straight; of fragile make and constitution, she had "grown aside," as the familiar saying runs; but at this early period of her life it was not so apparent to a beholder (unless the defect was known and searched for) as it afterwards became.

"You are not very much so, Lucy," was Mrs. St. John's answer. "And your face compensates for it."

Lucy shook her head. "You say so from kindness, I am sure. Do you know," she resumed, her voice again becoming almost inaudible, "I once heard Mrs. Dewsbury joking with Sir Edward about me. He was down for a week about a year ago, and she was telling him he ought to get married and settle down to a steady life. He answered that he could get nobody to have him, and Mrs. Dewsbury—of course you know it was only a jesting conversation on both sides—said, 'There's Lucy Cheveley, would she do for you?' '*She*,' he exclaimed; 'she's deformed!' Mrs. St. John, will you believe that for a long while after I felt sick at having to go out, or to cross a room?"

"Yes, I can believe it," said Mrs. St. John, sadly, for she was not unacquainted with this sensitive phase in human misfortune. "Well, Lucy, you cannot be convinced, I dare say, that your figure is *not* unsightly, so we will let that pass. But I do not understand yet, how you came to marry Peter Arkell."

Lucy laughed and blushed.

"Ah! I see; you loved him. And yet, few,

save you, would find Peter Arkell so lovable a man."

"If you only knew his worth, Mrs. St. John!"

"I dare say. But as a knight-errant he is not attractive. Of course, the chief consideration now, is—the thing being irrevocably done, and you here—what sort of a home will he be able to keep for you."

"I have no fear on that score; and I am one to be satisfied with so little. Colonel Dewsbury discharged him, but he soon found an evening engagement that is as good. He intends to go to Oxford when he can accomplish it, and afterwards take orders. When he is a clergyman, perhaps my friends, including you, Mrs. St. John, will admit that his wife can then claim to be in the position of a gentlewoman."

"But, meanwhile you must live."

Lucy smiled. "If you knew how entirely I trust and may trust to Peter, you would have no fear. We shall spend but little; we have begun on the most economical plan, and shall continue it. We keep but one servant——"

"But one servant!" echoed Mrs. St. John. "For *you!*"

"I did not bring Peter a shilling. I brought him but myself and the few poor clothes I possess, for my bit of a pension ceased at my marriage.

14—2

You cannot think that I would run him into any expense not absolutely necessary. We have no need of more than one servant, for we shall certainly be free from visitors."

" How do you know that ?"

" Peter has lived too retired a life to entertain any. "And there's no fear that my friends will visit me. I have put myself beyond their pale."

" I cannot say that you have not. But how you will feel this, Lucy !"

"I shall not feel it. Mrs. St. John, when I chose my position in life as Peter Arkell's wife, I chose it for all time," she emphatically added. "Neither now, nor at any future period, shall I regret it. Believe me, I shall be far happier here, in retirement with him, although I have the consciousness of knowing that the world calls me an idiot, than I could have been had I married in what you may call my own sphere. For me there are not two Peter Arkells in the world."

And Mrs. St. John rose, and took her leave; deeply impressed with the fact, that though there might not be two Peter Arkells in the world, there was a great deal of infatuation. She could not understand how it was possible for one, born as Lucy Cheveley had been, to make such a marriage, and to live under it without repentance.

CHAPTER XIII.

GOING ON FOR LORD MAYOR.

THE years rolled on, bringing their changes. Indeed, the first portions of this history are more like a panorama, where you see a scene here, and then go on to another scene there; for we cannot afford to relate these earlier events consecutively.

That good and respected man, Mr. George Arkell, had passed away with the course of time to the place which is waiting to receive us all. His wife followed him within the year. A handsome fortune, independently of the flourishing business at the manufactory, was left to our old friend William; and there was a small legacy to Mildred of a hundred pounds.

William Arkell had taken possession of all: of his father's place, his father's position, and his father's house. No son ever walked more entirely in his father's steps than did he. He was honoured throughout Westerbury, just as Mr. Arkell had been. His benevolence, his probity, his high character, were universally known and appreciated. And Mrs. William Arkell, now of course, Mrs. Arkell, was a very fine lady, but liked on the whole.

They had three children, Travice, Charlotte, and Sophia Mary. Travice bore a remarkable resemblance to his father, both in looks and disposition; the two girls were more like their mother. They were young yet; but no expense, even now, was spared upon them. Indeed, expense, had Mrs. Arkell had her way, would not have been spared in anything. Show and cost were not to William's taste; they were to hers: but he restrained it with a firm hand where it was absolutely essential.

Peter had not got to college yet, and Peter had not on the whole prospered. The great blow to him was the having to pay the four hundred pounds for which he had become security for Mr. Fauntleroy the younger. Mr. Fauntleroy the younger's affairs had come to a crisis; he went away for a time from Westerbury, and Peter was called upon to pay. There's no doubt that it was the one great blight upon Peter Arkell's life. He never recovered it. It is true that the money was afterwards refunded to him by degrees; but it seemed to do him no good; the blight had fallen.

He became ill. Whether it was the blow of this, that suddenly shattered his health, or whether illness was inherent in his constitution, Westerbury never fully decided; certain it was, that Peter Arkell became a confirmed invalid, and had to resign his appointment at the bank. But he had excellent teaching, and was paid well; and he brought out a learned book now and then, so that he earned a good living. He had two children, Lucy, and a boy some years younger.

Never since she quitted the place some ten or twelve years before, had Mildred Arkell paid a visit to Westerbury. She was going to do so now. Lady Dewsbury, whose health was better than usual, had gone to stay with her married sister, and Mildred thought she would take the opportunity of going to see her brother Peter, and to make acquaintance with his wife. It is probable that, without that tie, she would never have re-entered her native place. The pain of going now would be great; the pain of meeting William Arkell and his wife little less than it was when she first left it. But she made her mind up, and wrote to Peter to say she was coming.

It was on a windy day that Mildred Arkell—had anybody known her—might have been seen picking her way through the mud of the streets of London. She went to a private house in the neighbourhood of Hatton Garden, rang one of its bells, and walked upstairs without waiting for it to be answered. Before she reached the third floor, a young woman, with a coarse apron on, and a quantity of soft flaxen hair twisted round her head, which looked like a lady's head in spite of the accompaniment of the apron, came running down it.

"Oh, Miss Arkell! if you had but sent me word you were coming!"

The tone was a joyous one, mixed somewhat with vexation; and Mildred smiled.

"Why should I send you word, Betsey? If you are busy, you need not mind me."

On the third floor of this house, in two rooms, Mr. and Mrs. David Dundyke had lived ever since their marriage. David himself had chosen it from the one motive that regulated most actions of his life — economy. The two lower floors of the house were occupied by the offices of a solicitor; the underground kitchen and attic by a woman who kept the house clean; and David had taken these two rooms, and got them very cheap, on condition that he should always sleep at home as a protection to the house. Not having any inducement to sleep out, David acceded readily; and here they had been for several years. It was, in one sense, a convenient arrangement for Betsey, for they kept no servant, and the woman occasionally did cleaning and other rough work for her, receiving a small payment weekly.

Will you believe me when I say that David Dundyke was ambitious? Never a more firmly ambitious man lived than he. There have been men with higher aims in life, but not with more pushing, persevering purpose. He wanted to become a rich man; he wanted to become one of importance in this great commercial city; but the highest ambition of all, the one that filled his thoughts, sleeping and waking, was a higher ambition still—and I hope you will hold your breath with proper deference while you read it—he aspired to become, in time, the LORD MAYOR!

He was going on for it. He truly and honestly believed that he was going on for it; slowly, it is true, but not less sure. Rome, as we all know was not built in a day; and even such men as the Duke of Wellington must have had a beginning— a first start in life.

Whatever David Dundyke's short-comings might be, in—if you will excuse the word—gentility, he made up for it by a talent for business. Few men have possessed a better one; and his value in the Fenchurch-street tea-house, was fully known and appreciated. This wholesale establishment, which had tea for its basis, was of undoubted respectability. It took a high standing amidst its fellows, and was second in its large dealings to none. It was not one of your advertising, poetry-puffing, here-to-day and gone-to-morrow houses, but a genuine, sound firm, having real dealings with Chaney, as the respected white-haired head of the house was in the habit of designating the Celestial Empire. Mr. Dundyke sometimes presumed to correct the " Chaney," and hint to his indulgent master and head, that that pronunciation was a little antediluvian, and that nobody now called it anything but " Chinar."

David Dundyke had gone into this house an errand boy; he had risen to be a junior clerk. He was now not a junior one, but took rank with the first. Steady, taciturn, persevering, and industrious to an extent not often seen, thoroughly trustworthy, and in business dealings of strict honour, perhaps David Dundyke was one who could not fail to prosper, wherever he might have been placed. These qualities, combined with rare business foresight, had brought him into notice, and thence into favour. The faintest possible hint had been dropped to him by the white-haired old man, that perseverance, such as his, had been known to meet its reward in an association with the firm; a share in the business. Whether he meant anything, or whether it was but a casual remark, spoken without intention, David did not know; but he saw from thenceforth that one great ambition, of his, coming nearer and nearer. From that moment it was sure; it fevered his veins, and coloured his dreams; the massive gold chain of the Lord Mayor was ever dancing before his eyes and his brain; to be called "my lord" by the multitude, and to sit in that arm-chair, dispensing justice in the Mansion House, seemed to him a very heaven upon earth. Every movement of his mind had reference to it; every nerve was strained on the hope for it! For that he saved; for that he pinched; for that he turned sixpences into shillings, and shillings into pounds: for he knew that to be elected a Lord Mayor he must first of all be a rich man, and attain to the honour through minor gradations of wealth. He was judged to be a hard griping man by the few acquaintances he possessed, possessing neither sympathy for friends, nor pity for enemies; but he was not hard or griping at heart; it was all done to further this dream of ambition. For money in the abstract he really did not very much care; but as a stepping-stone to civic importance, it was of incalculable value.

He had four hundred pounds a year now, and they lived upon fifty. Betsey, the most generous heart in the world, saw but with his eyes, and was as saving and careful as might be, because it pleased him. Many and many a time he had taken home a red herring and made his dinner of it, giving his wife the head and the tail to pick for hers. Not less meek than of yore was Mrs. Dundyke, and felt duly thankful for the head and the tail.

Mrs. Dundyke had been at some household work when Mildred entered, but she soon put it aside and sat down with Mildred in the sitting-room, a cheerful apartment with a large window. Betsey was considerably over thirty years of age now, but she looked nearly as young as ever, as she sat bending her face a little down over her sewing while she talked, the stitching of a wristband; for she was one who thought it a sin to lose time. Mildred told her the news she had come to tell— that she was going on the morrow to Westerbury.

"Going to Westerbury!" echoed Mrs. Dundyke in great surprise; for it had seemed to her that Miss Arkell never meant to go to her native place again.

Mildred explained. She had a holiday for the first time since going to Lady Dewsbury's, and should use it to see her brother and his wife. " I came to tell you, Betsey," she added, " thinking you might have some message you would like me to carry to your sister."

A faint change, like a shadow, passed over Betsey Dundyke's face. "She would not thank you for it, Miss Arkell. But you may give my best love to her. She never came to see me, you know, when they were in London."

"When were they in London?" asked Mildred, quickly.

"Last year. Did you not know of it? Perhaps not, for you were in Paris with Lady Dewsbury at the time, and the reminiscence to me is not so pleasing as to make me mention it gratuitously. She came up with Mr. Arkell and their boy; they were in London about a week: he had business, I believe. The first thing *he* did was to come and see us, and he brought Travice; and he said he hoped I and my husband would make it convenient to be with them a good deal while they were in town, and would dine with them often at their hotel. Well, David, as you know, has no time to spare in the day, for business is first and foremost with him, but I went the next day to see Charlotte. She was very cool, and she let me unmistakably know in so many words that she could not make an associate of Mr. Dundyke. It was not nice of her, Miss Arkell."

"No, it was not. Did you see much of her?"

"I only saw her that once. William Arkell was terribly vexed, I could see that; and as if to atone for her behaviour, he came here often and brought Travice. Indeed, Travice spent nearly the whole of the time with us, and David would have

let me keep him after they went home, but I knew
it was of no use to ask Charlotte. He is the nicest
boy! I—I know it is wrong to break the tenth
commandment," she said, looking up and laughing
through her tears, " but I envy Charlotte that boy."

It was an indirect allusion to the one great
disappointment of Betsey Dundyke's life: she had
no children. She was getting over the grief
tolerably now; we get reconciled to the worst
evil in time ; but in the first years of her marriage
she had felt it keenly. It may be questioned if Mr.
Dundyke did. Children must have brought expense with them, so he philosophically pitted the
gain against the loss.

" Why should Mrs. Arkell dislike to be on
sisterly terms with you ?" asked Mildred. " I have
never been able to understand it."

" Charlotte has two faults—pride and selfishness,"
was Mrs. Dundyke's answer : " though I cannot
bear to speak against her, and never do to David.
When she first married, she feared, I believe, that
I might become a burden upon her ; and she did
not like that I should be in the position I was at
Mrs. Dundyke's ; she thought it reflected in a degree
upon her position as a lady. *Now* she shuns us,
because she thinks we are altogether beneath her.
Were we living in style, well established and all
that, she would be glad to come to us ; but we are

in these two quiet rooms, living humbly, and Charlotte would cut off her legs before she'd come near us. Don't think me unkind, Miss Arkell; it is Charlotte who has forced this feeling upon me. I worshipped her in the old days, but I cannot be blind to her faults now."

David Dundyke came in. He shook hands cordially with Mildred, whom he was always glad to see. He had begun to dress like a city magnate now: in glossy clothes, and a white neckcloth; and a fine gold cable chain crossed on his waistcoat, in place of the modest silver one he used to wear. He had become more personable as he gained years, was growing portly, and altogether was a fine, gentlemanly-looking man. But his mode of speech! *That* had very little changed from the earlier style: perhaps David Dundyke was one who did not care to change it; or had no ear to catch the accents of others. If he had but never opened his mouth!

"I'm a little late, Betsey. Shouldn't ha' been, though, if I'd known who was here. Get us some tea, girl; and here's something to eat with it."

He pulled a paper parcel of shrimps out of his pocket as he spoke: a delicacy he was fond of. Some of them fell on the carpet in the process, and Betsey stooped to pick them up. David did not trouble himself to help her. He sat down and talked to Mildred.

"The last time you were here, I remember, something kept me out: extra work at the office, I think that was. I have been round now to Leifchild's. He is my stock-broker."

Mildred laughed. She supposed he was saying it for jest. But the keen look came over Mr. Dundyke's face that was usual to it when he spoke of money.

"Leifchild is a steady-going man; he's no fool, he isn't. There's not a steadier nor a keener on the stock exchange. I've knowed him since he was that high, for we was boys together; and, like me, he began from nothing. There was one thing kept him down—want of capital; if he had had that, he'd ha' been a rich man now, for many good things fell in his way, and he had to let 'em slip by him. I turned the risk over in my mind, Miss Arkell; for, and against; and I came to the conclusion to put a thousand pound in his hands, on condition——"

"A thousand pounds," involuntarily interrupted Mildred. "Had you so much—to spare?"

"Yes, I had that," said David Dundyke, with a little cough that seemed to say he might have found more, if he had cared to do so. "On condition that I went shares in whatsoever profit my thousand pound should be the means of realizing," he resumed where he had broken off. "And my thousand pound has not done badly yet."

Mildred could not help noting the significant satisfaction of the tone. "I should have fancied you too cautious to risk your money in speculating, Mr. Dundyke."

"And you fancied right. 'Tain't speculating: leastways not now. There might be some risk at first, but I knew Leifchild. In three months after that there thousand pound was in his hand, he had made two of it for me, and I took the one back from him, leaving him the other to go on with again. *That* hasn't done badly neither, Miss Arkell; it's paying itself over and over again. And I'm safe; for if he lost it all, I'm only where I was afore I began, and my first risked thousand is safe."

"And if failure should come, is there no risk to you?"

"Not a penny risk. Trust me for that. But failure won't come. My head's a pretty long one for seeing my way clear, and Leifchild lays every thing before me afore he ventures. It's better, this is, than your five per cent. investments."

"I think it must be," assented Mildred. "I wish I could employ a trifle in the same manner."

She spoke without any ulterior motive, but David Dundyke took the words literally. He had no objection to do a good turn where it involved no outlay to himself, and he really liked Mildred. He drew his chair an inch nearer, and talked to her long and earnestly.

"Let's say it's a hundred pound," he said. "Risk it. And when Leifchild has doubled that for you, take the first hundred back. If you lose the rest, it won't hurt; and if it multiplies its ones into tens, you'll be so much the better off."

It cannot be denied that Mildred was struck with the proposition. "But does Mr. Leifchild do all this for nothing?" she asked.

"In course he don't. Leifchild ain't a fool. He gets his percentage—and a good fat percentage too. The thing can afford it. Do as you like, you know, Miss Arkell; but if you take my advice, you mayn't find cause to be sorry for it in the end."

"Thank you," said Mildred, "I will think of it."

"Give Aunt Betsey's dear love to Travice," whispered Mrs. Dundyke, when Mildred was leaving, "and my best and truest regards to Mr. Arkell. And oh, Miss Mildred, if you could prevail upon them to let Travice come back with you to visit me, I should not know how to be happy enough! I have always so loved children; and David would like it, too."

"Is there any chance, think you?" returned Mildred.

"No, no, there is none; his mother would be indignant at the presumption of the request," concluded Betsey in her bitter conviction.

And she was not mistaken.

CHAPTER XIV.

OLD YEARS BACK AGAIN.

MILDRED'S heart ached with the changes; Peter was growing into a middle-aged man, his hair beginning to silver, his tall back bowed with care.

They were gathered in the old familiar sitting-room the night of her arrival at Westerbury. Peter and Mildred sat at the table, Mrs. Peter Arkell lay on her sofa; the children remained orderly on the hearth rug. Lucy was getting a great girl now; little Harry—a most lovely child, his face the counterpart of his mother's—was but three years old.

Never but once in her life had Mildred seen the exquisite face of Miss Lucy Cheveley; it had never left her memory. The same, same face was before her now, looking upwards from the sofa, not a whit altered—not a shade less beautiful. But Mildred had now become aware of a fact which she had not known previously—Peter had kept it from her in his letters—that the defect in Mrs. Peter Arkell's back had become more formidable, giving her pain nearly always. They had had a hard, reclining sofa made, a little raised at the one end; and here she had to lie a great deal, some days only getting up from it to meals.

"I am half afraid to encounter your wife," Mildred had said, as she walked home with Peter from the station—for there was a railway from London now, and the old coaching days had vanished for ever. "She is one of the Dewsbury family —of Mrs. Dewsbury's, at any rate—and I am but a dependent in it."

"Oh, Mildred! you little know my dear wife; but she is one in a thousand. She is very poorly this evening, and is so vexed at it; she says you will not think she welcomes you as she ought."

"What is it that is really the matter with her? Is it the spine? You did not tell me all this in your letters."

"It is the spine. She was never strong, you may be aware; and I believe there occurred some slight injury to it when the boy was born. The doctors think she will get stronger again; but I don't know."

"Is she in pain? Does she walk out?"

"She is not in pain when she lies, but it comes on if she exerts herself. Sometimes she walks out, but not often. She is so patient—so anxious to make the best of things; lying there, as she is often obliged to do, for hours, and going without any little thing she may want, because she will not disturb the servant from her work to get it. I don't think anyone was ever blessed with so patient and sweet a temper."

And when Mildred entered and saw the bright expectancy of the well-remembered face, the eager hands held out to welcome her, she knew that they were true sisters from that hour. The invalid drew down her face to her own flushed one.

"I am so grieved," she whispered, the tears rising in her earnest eyes; "this is one of my worst days, and I am unable to rise to welcome you."

"Do not think of it," answered Mildred; "I am glad to be here to wait upon you. I am used to nursing; I think it is my *specialité*," she added, with one of her old sunny smiles. "I will try and nurse you into health before I go back again."

"You shall make the tea, and do all those things, now you are here, Mildred," interposed Peter. "I am as awkward as an owl when I have to attempt anything, and Lucy lies and laughs at me."

"Which is to be my room?" asked Mildred. "I will go and take my things off, and come down to hear all the news of the old place."

"The blue room," said Mrs. Peter. "You will find little Lucy——"

"Your own old room, Mildred," interposed Peter. "Lucy, my dear, when Mildred left home the room was not blue, but a sort of dirty yellow."

Mildred went and came down again, bringing the children with her, little orderly things; steady Lucy quite like a mother to her baby brother. Mildred made acquaintance with them, and she and Peter gossiped away to their hearts' content; the one telling the news of the "old place," and its changes, the other listening.

"We think Lucy so much like you," Peter observed in the course of the evening, alluding to his little daughter.

"Like me!" repeated Mildred.

"It strikes us all. William never sees her but he thinks of you. He says we ought to have named her 'Mildred.'"

"*His* daughters are not named Mildred, either of them," she answered, hastily—an old sore sensation, that she had been striving so long to bury, becoming very rife within her.

"His wife chose their names—not he. She has a will of her own, and likes to exercise it."

"How do you get on with William's wife?"

"Not very well. She and Lucy did not take to each other at first, and I suppose never will. She is quite a fine lady now; and, indeed, always was, to my thinking; and William's wealth enables them to live in a style very different from what we can do. So Mrs. Arkell looks down upon us. We are invited to a grand, formal dinner there once a year, and that is about all our intercourse."

"A grand, formal dinner!" echoed Mildred. "For you!"

Peter nodded. "She makes it so on purpose, no doubt; a hint that we are not to be every-day visitors. She invites little Lucy there sometimes to play with Charlotte and Sophy; but I am sure the two girls despise the child just as their mother despises us."

"And does William despise you?" inquired Mildred, a touch of resentment in her usually gentle tone.

"How can you ask it, Mildred?" returned Peter, warmly. "I thought you knew William Arkell better than that. He grows so like his father— good, kindly, honourable. There's not a man in all Westerbury liked and respected as he is. He comes in sometimes in an evening; glad, I fancy, of a little peace and quietness. Between ourselves, Mildred, I fancy that in marrying Charlotte Travice, William found he had caught a Tartar."

"And so they are grand!" observed Mildred,

waking out of a fit of musing, and perhaps hardly conscious of what she said.

"Terribly grand. *She* is. They keep their close carriage now. It strikes me—I may be wrong—but it strikes me that he lives up to every farthing of his income."

"My Uncle George did not."

"No, indeed! Or there'd not have been the fortune that there was to leave to William."

"But, Peter, I gather a good deal now and then from the local papers of the distress that exists in Westerbury, of the depressed state that the trade is falling into ; more depressed even than it was when I left, and that need not be. Does not this state of things affect William Arkell?"

"It must affect him ; though not, I conclude, to any great extent. You see, Mildred, he has what so many of the other manufacturers want—plenty of money, independent of his business. William has not to force his goods into the market at unfavourable moments ; be his stock ever so large, he can hold it until the demand quickens. It is the being obliged to send their goods into the market at low prices, that swamps the others."

"Will the prosperity of the town ever come back to it, think you?"

"Never. And I am not sure that the worst has come yet."

Mildred sighed. She called Lucy to her and held her before her, pushing the hair from her brow as she looked attentively into her face. It was not a beautiful or a handsome face; but it was fair and gentle, the features pale, the eyes dark brown, with a sweet, sad, earnest expression : just such a face as Mildred's.

"Do you like your cousins, Charlotte and Sophia, Lucy?" asked Mildred.

"I like Travice best," was the little lady's unblushing answer. "Charlotte and Sophy tease me; they are not kind ; but Travice wont let them tease me when he is there. He is a big boy, but he plays with *me ;* and he says he loves me better than he does them."

"I really believe he does," said Peter, amused at the answer. "Travice is just like his father, as this child is like you—the same open, generous, noble boy that William himself was. When I see Travice playing with Lucy, I could fancy it was you and William over again—as I used to see you play in the old days."

"Heaven grant that the ending of it may not be as mine was !" was the inward prayer that went up from Mildred's heart.

"Travice is in the college school, I suppose, Peter?"

"Oh, yes. With a private evening tutor at home.

The girls have a resident governess. William spares no money on their education."

"Would it not be a nice thing for Lucy if she could go daily and share their lessons?"

"Hush, Mildred! Treason!" exclaimed Peter, while Mrs. Peter Arkell burst into a laugh, her husband's manner was so quaint. "I have reason to know that William was hardy enough to say something of the same sort to his wife, *and he got his answer.* I and my wife, between us, teach Lucy. It is better so; for the child could not be spared from her mother. You don't know the use she is of, already."

"I am of use to mamma too, I am!" broke in a bold baby voice at Mildred's side.

She caught the little fellow on her knee: he thought no doubt he had been too long neglected. Mildred began stroking the auburn curls from his face, as she had stroked Lucy's.

"And I am like mamma," added the young gentleman. "Everybody says so. Mamma says so."

Indeed "everybody" might well say it. As the mother's was, so was the child's, the loveliest possible type of face. The same, the exquisite features, the refined, delicate look, the lustrous brown eyes and hair, the rose-flush on the cheeks. "No, I never did see two faces so much alike, allowing for the difference in age," cried Mildred, looking from the mother on the sofa to the child on her knee. "Tell me again what your name is."

"It's Harry Cheveley Arkell."

"Do you know," exclaimed Mildred, looking up at Mrs. Peter, "it strikes me this child speaks remarkably plain for his age."

"He does," was the answer. "Lucy did not speak so well when she was double his age. He is unusually forward and sensible in all respects. I fear it sometimes," she added in a lower tone.

"By why do you fear it?" quickly asked Mildred.

"Oh—you know the old saying, or superstition," concluded Mrs. Arkell, unable further to allude to it, for the boy's earnest eyes were bent upon her with profound interest.

"Those whom the gods love, die young," muttered Peter. "But the saying is all nonsense, Mildred."

Peter had been getting his books, and was preparing to become lost in their pages, fragrant as ever to him. Mildred happened to look to him and scarcely saved herself from a scream. He had put on a pair of spectacles.

"Peter! surely you have not taken to spectacles!"

"Yes, I have."

"But why?"

Peter stared at her. "Why does anybody take to them, Mildred? From failing sight."

"Oh, dear!" sighed Mildred. "We seem to have

gone away altogether from youth—to be gliding into old age without any interregnum."

"But we are not middle-aged yet, Mildred," said Mrs. Peter.

A sudden opening of the door—a well-known form, tall, upright, noble, but from which a portion of the youthful elasticity was gone—and Mildred found herself face to face with her cousin William. How loved still, the wild beating of her heart told her! His simply friendly greeting, warm though it was, recalled her to her senses.

"What a stranger you have been to us, Mildred!" he exclaimed. "Never to come near Westerbury all these years! When my father was dying, he wished so much to see you."

"I would have come then had I been able, but Lady Dewsbury was very ill, and I could not leave her. Indeed, I wish I could have seen both my aunt and uncle once more."

"They felt it, I can tell you, Mildred."

"Not more than I did; not indeed so much. They could not: they had others with them nearer than I."

"Perhaps none dearer," he quietly answered. "My father's death was almost sudden at the last. The shock to me was great: I did not think to lose him so early."

"A little sooner or a little later!" murmured

Mildred. "What does it matter, provided the departure be a hopeful one. As his must have been."

"As his *was*," said William. "Mildred, you are not greatly changed."

"Not changed!"

"I said, not greatly changed. It is still the same face."

"Ah, you will see it by daylight. My hair is turning grey."

"Mildred, which day will you spend with us?" he asked, when leaving. "To-morrow?"

Mildred evaded a direct reply. Even yet, though years had passed, she was scarcely equal to seeing the old home and its installed mistress; certainly not without great emotion. But she knew it must be overcome, and when Mr. Arkell pressed the question, she named, not the morrow, but the day following.

William Arkell went home, and had the nearest approach to a battle with his wife that he ever had had. Mrs. Arkell was alone in their handsome drawing-room; she did not keep it laid up in lavender, as the old people had done. She was as pretty as ever; and of genial manners, when not put out. But unfortunately she got put out at trifles, and the unpleasantness engendered by it was frequent.

"Charlotte, I have seen Mildred," he began as he entered. "She will spend the day with us on

Friday, but I suppose you will call upon her to morrow."

"No, I shan't," returned Mrs. Arkell. "She's nothing but a lady's-maid."

William answered sharply. Something to the effect that Mildred was a lady born and bred, a lady formerly, a lady still, and that he respected her beyond anyone on earth : in his passion, he hardly knew what he said. Mrs. Arkell was even with him.

"I know," she said—"I know you would have been silly enough to make her your wife, but for your better stars interposing and sending me to frustrate it. I don't suppose she has overcome the disappointment yet. Now, William, that's the truth, and you need not look as if you were going to beat me for saying it. And you need not think that I shall pay court to her, for I shall not. Whether as Mildred Arkell, your disappointed cousin, or as Mildred Arkell, Lady Dewsbury's maid, I am not called upon to do it."

William Arkell felt that he really could beat her. He did not answer temperately.

Mrs. Arkell could be aggravating when she chose; ay, and obstinate. She would not call on Mildred the following day, but three separate times did her handsome close carriage parade before the modest house of Mr. Peter Arkell, and never once, of all the three times, did she condescend to turn her eyes towards it, as she sat inside. Late that evening there arrived a formal note requesting the pleasure of Mr. and Mrs. Peter Arkell's accompanying Miss Arkell to dinner on the following day.

"She's going to do it grand, Peter," said Lucy to her husband with a laugh, in the privacy of their chamber at night. "She's killing two birds with one stone, impressing Mildred with her pomp, and showing her at the same time that she must not expect to be admitted to unceremonious intimacy."

Only Mildred went. Lucy said she was not well enough, and Peter had lessons to give. The former unpretentious and, for Mr. Arkell, convenient dinner hour of one o'clock had been long changed for a late one. Mildred, fully determined *not* to make a ceremony of the visit, went in about four o'clock, and found nobody to receive her. Mrs. Arkell was in her room, the maid said. She had seen Miss Arkell's approach, and hastened away to dress, not having expected her so early. Would Miss Arkell like to go to a dressing room and take her bonnet off? Miss Arkell replied that she would take it off there, and she handed it to the maid with her shawl.

The drawing-room had been newly furnished since old Mrs. Arkell's time, as Mildred saw at a glance. She was touching abstractedly some of its elegant trifles, musing on the changes that years

bring, when the door flew open, and a tall, pre-
possessing, handsome boy entered, whistling a song
at the top of his voice, and trailing a fishing line
behind him. There was no need to ask who he
was; the likeness was too great to the beloved face
of her girlhood: it was the same manner, the same
whistle; all as it used to be.

"You are Travice," she said, holding out her
hand; "I should have known you anywhere."

"And you must be Mildred," returned the boy,
impetuously taking the hand between both of his,
and letting his cherished fishing line drop anywhere.
"May I call you Aunt Mildred, as Lucy does?"

"Call me anything,' was Mildred's answer. "I
am so glad to see you at last. And to see you
what you are! How like you are to your father!"

"All the world says that," said the boy with a
laugh. "But how is it that nobody's with you?
Where are they all? Where's mamma?"

Springing to the door he called out in the hall
that there was nobody with Miss Arkell, that she
was waiting in the drawing-room alone. His voice
echoed to the very depths of the house, and two
slender, pretty girls came running downstairs in
answer to its sound. There was a slight look of
William in both of them, but the resemblance to
their mother was great, and Mildred's heart did not
go out yearning to them as it had to Travice. She

kissed them, and found them pleasant, lady-like
girls; but with a dash of coquetry in their manner
already.

"I hope I see you well, Miss Arkell."

Mildred was bending over the girls, and started
at the well-remembered tones, so superlatively
polite, but freezing and heartless. Charlotte was
radiant in beauty and a blue silk dinner-dress, with
flowing blue ribbons in her bright hair. Mildred
felt plain beside her. Her rich black silk was
made high, and its collar and cuffs were muslin,
worked with black. Nothing else, save a gold
chain; the pretty chain of her girlhood that
William had given her; nothing in her hair. She
was in mourning for a relative of Lady Dewsbury.

"You have made acquaintance with the children, I see, Miss Arkell."

"Yes; I am so glad to do it. Peter has sometimes mentioned them in his letters; and I have
heard much of Travice from Betsey—Mrs. Dundyke. Your sister charged me to give you her best
love, Mrs. Arkell. I saw her on Friday."

"She's very kind," coldly returned Mrs. Arkell;
"but I don't quite understand how you can have
heard much of my son from her; that is, how she
can have had much to say. Mrs. Dundyke had
not seen him since he was an infant, until we were
in town last year."

" I think Travice has been in the habit of writing to her."

" In the habit of writing to Aunt Betsey,—of course I have been!" interposed Travice. " And she writes to me, too. I like Aunt Betsey. And I can tell you what, mamma, for all you go on against him so, I like Mr. Dundyke."

" Your likings are of very little consequence at present, Travice," was the languidly indifferent answer of his mother. " You will learn better as you grow older. My sister forfeited all claim on me when she married so low a man as Mr. Dundyke," continued Mrs. Arkell to Mildred ; " and she knows that such is my opinion. I shall never change it. She married him deliberately, with her eyes open to the consequences, and of course she must take them. I said and did what I could to warn her, but she would not listen. And now look at the way in which they are obliged to live !"

" Mr. Dundyke earns an excellent income ; in fact, I believe he is making money fast," observed Mildred. " Their living in the humble way they do is from choice, I think, not from necessity."

Mrs. Arkell shrugged her pretty shoulders with contempt.

" We will pass to another topic, Miss Arkell, that one does not interest me. What are the new fashions for the season ? You must get them at

16—2

first hand, from your capacity in Lady Dewsbury's household."

Mildred would not resent the hint.

"Indeed, Mrs. Arkell, if you only knew how little the fashions interest either Lady Dewsbury or me, you would perhaps laugh at us both," she answered. "Lady Dewsbury lives too much out of the world to need its fashions. She is a great invalid."

Peter's wife was right in her conjecture, for Mrs. Arkell had hastily summoned a dinner party. Mr. Arkell took his revenge, and faced his wife in a morning coat. Ten inclusive; and the governess and Travice were desired to sit down in the place of Mr. and Mrs. Peter. It may be concluded that Mildred was of the least consequence present, in social position; nevertheless, Mr. Arkell took her in to dinner, and placed her at his right hand. All were strangers to her, excepting old Marmaduke Carr. Squire Carr was dead, and his son John was the squire now.

It was not the quiet evening Mildred had thought to spend with them. She slipped from the drawing-room at ten, Mrs. Peter's health being the excuse for leaving early. Mr. Arkell had his hat on at the hall door waiting for her, just as it used to be in the days gone by.

"But, William, I do not wish to take you out," she remonstrated. "You have your guests."

"'They are not my guests to-night," was his quiet answer, as he gave his arm to Mildred.

Travice came running out. "Oh, papa, let me go with you!"

"Get your trencher, then."

He stuck the college cap on his head and went leaping on, through the gates and up the street, just in the manner that college boys like to leap. Mr. Arkell and Mildred followed more soberly, speaking of indifferent things. Mildred began talking of Mr. Carr.

"How well he wears!" she said. "Peter tells me he has retired from business."

"These three or four years past. He did wisely. Those who keep on manufacturing, only do it at a loss."

"You keep it on, William."

"I know. But serious thoughts occur to me now and then of the wisdom of retiring. There are reasons against it, though. Were I to give up business, we should have to live in a very different style from what we do now; for my income would be but a small one, and that would not suit Mrs. Arkell. Besides, I really could not bear to turn my workmen adrift. There are too many unemployed already in the town; and I am always hoping, against my conviction, that times will mend."

"But if you only make to lose, how would the retiring from business lessen your income?"

William laughed. "Well, Mildred, of course I do get something still by my business; but in speaking of the bad times, we are all apt to make the worst of it. I dare say I make about half what we spend; but that you know, compared to the profits of old days, is as nothing."

"If you do make that, William, why think at all of giving up?"

"Because the doubt is upon me whether worse times may not come, and bring ruin with them to all who have kept on manufacturing. Were I as Marmaduke Carr is, a lonely man, I should give up to-morrow; but I have my wife and children to provide for, and I really do not know what to do for the best."

"What has become of Robert Carr? Has he ever been home?"

"Never. He is in Holland still for all I know. I have not heard his name mentioned for years in the town. Old Marmaduke never speaks of him; and others, I suppose, have forgotten him. You know that the old squire's dead?"

"Yes; and that John has succeeded him. Did John's daughter—Emma, I mean—ever marry?"

"She married very well indeed; a Mr. Lewis. Valentine, the son and heir, is at home with his

father ; steady, selfish, mean as his father was before him ; but I fancy John Carr has trouble with
the second, Ben."

"Ben promised to be a spendthrift, I remember,"
remarked Mildred. "What is Travice gazing at."

Travice had come to a stand-still, and was standing with his face turned upwards. Mr. Arkell
laughed.

"Do you remember my propensity for star-
gazing, Mildred ? Travice has inherited it. But
with him it is more developed than it was with me.
I should not be surprised at his turning out an
astronomer one of these days."

Did she remember it ! Poor Mildred fell into a
reverie that lasted until William said good night
to her at her brother's door.

She was not sorry when her visit to Westerbury
came to an end. The town seemed to look cold
upon her. Of those she had left in it, some had
died, some had married, some had quitted the place
for ever. The old had vanished, the middle-aged
were growing old, the children had become men
and women. It did not seem the same native place
to Mildred : it never would seem so again. Some of
the inhabitants of her own standing had dwindled
down to obscurity ; others who had *not* been of her
standing, had gone up and become very grand
indeed. These turned up their noses at Mildred,

just as did Mrs. William Arkell; and thought it
excessive presumption in a lady's maid to come
amongst them as an equal. She had persisted in
going out to service in defiance of all her friends,
and the least she could do was to keep her distance
from them.

Mildred did not hear these gracious comments,
and would not have cared very much if she had
heard them. She returned to her post at Lady
Dewsbury's, and a few more years passed on.

CHAPTER XV.

THE DEAN'S DAUGHTER.

THE tender green of early spring was on the new leaves of the cathedral elm trees. Not sufficient to afford a shade yet; but giving promise of its fulness ere the sultry days of summer should come.

The deanery of Westerbury was a queer old building to look at, especially in front. It had no lower windows. There were odd-looking patches in the wall where the windows ought to have been, and three or four doors. These doors had their separate uses. One of them was the private entrance of the dean and his family; one was used by the servants; one was allotted to official or state occasions, at the great audit time, for instance, when the dean and chapter held their succession of dinners for ever so many days running; and one (a little one in a corner) was popularly supposed to be a sham. But the windows above were unusually large, and so they compensated in some degree for the lack of them below.

Standing at the smallest of the windows on this spring day, was a young lady of some ten or twelve years old. She had a charming countenance, rather saucy, and great blue eyes as large as saucers. She wore a pretty grey silk frock, trimmed with black velvet—perhaps, as slight mourning—and her light brown hair fell on her neck in curls, that were apt to get untidy and entangled. It was Georgina Beauclerc, the only child of the Dean of Westerbury.

The window commanded a good view of the grounds, as the space here at the back of the cathedral was called—a large space; the green, inclosed promenade, shaded by the elm-trees, in the middle; well-kept walks outside; and beyond, all around, the prebendal and other houses. Opposite to the deanery, on the other side the walks, the elm-trees, and the grassy promenade, was the house of the Rev. Mr. Wilberforce, minor canon and sacrist of the cathedral, rector of St. James the Less, and head-master of the college school. Side by side with it was the quaint and small house once inhabited by the former rector of St. James the Less, an old clergyman, subject to gout, now dead and gone. The Rev. Wheeler Prattleton lived in the house now : he was also a minor canon, and chanter to the cathedral—that is, he held the office of what was called the chanter, which gave

him the right to fix upon the services for the choir
when the dean did not, but he only took his turn
for chanting in rotation with the rest of the minor
canons. On the other side the head-master's house
was a handsome, good-sized dwelling, tenanted by
a gentleman of the name of Lewis, who held a good
and official position in connexion with the bishop,
and had married the daughter of old Squire Carr,
the sister to the present squire, and niece to
Marmaduke. Beyond this, in a corner, was the
quaintest house in the grounds, all covered with
ivy, and seeming to have nothing belonging to it
but a door ; but the fact was, although the door
was here, the house itself was built out behind,
and could not be seen—its windows facing, some
the river, some the open country, and catching a
view of St. James the Less in the distance. Mr.
Aultane, Westerbury's greatest lawyer, so far as
practice went, though not perhaps in honour, lived
here ; and he held up his head and thought himself
above the minor canons. In this one nook of the
grounds a few private individuals congregated—it
is not necessary to mention them all ; but the rest
of the houses were mostly occupied by the prebendaries and minor canons. In some lived the
widows and families of prebendaries deceased.

Looking to the left, as Georgina Beauclerc stood
at the deanery window, just beyond the gate that

inclosed the grounds on that side, might be seen
the tall red chimneys of the Palmery. It was,
perhaps, inside, the worst of all the larger houses;
but the St. John's came to it often because they
owned it. They (the St. John's) were the best
family in Westerbury, and held sway as such. Mr.
St. John had died some years ago, leaving one son,
about thirty years of age, greatly afflicted; and a
young little son, by his second wife. But that
young son was growing up now : time flies.

Georgina Beauclerc's great blue eyes, so clear
and round, were fixed on one particular spot, and
that appeared to be one rather difficult to see.
She had her face and nose pressed against the
glass, looking toward the college school-room, a
huge building on the right of the deanery, just
beyond the cloisters.

"They are late again!" she exclaimed, in a
soliloquy of resentment. "I wish that horrid old
Wilberforce was burnt!"

"Georgina!"

The tone of the reproof, more fractious than surprised, came from a recess in the large room, and
Georgina turned hastily.

"Why, when did you come in, mamma? I
thought you were safe in your bed room."

Mrs. Beauclerc came forward, a thin woman with
a somewhat discontented look on her face, and a

little nose, red at the tip. She had long given up all real rule of Georgina, but she had not given up attempting it. And Georgina, a wild, spoilt child, was in the habit of saying and doing very much what she liked. She made great friends of the college school-boys, and had picked up many of their sayings; and this was particularly objectionable to the reserved Mrs. Beauclerc.

"What did you say about Mr. Wilberforce?"

"I *said* I wished he was burnt."

"Oh, Georgina!"

"I *do* wish he was scorched. It has struck one o'clock and the boys are not out! What business has he to keep them in? He did it once before."

"May I ask what business it is of yours, Georgina? But it has not struck one."

"I'm sure it has," returned Georgina.

"It has *not*, I tell you. How dare you contradict me? And allow me to ask why Miss Jackson quitted you so early to-day?"

"Because I dismissed her," returned the young lady, with equanimity. "I had the headache, mamma; and I can't be expected to attend to my studies when I have *that*."

"You have it pretty often," grumbled Mrs. Beauclerc; and indeed upon this plea, or upon some other, Georgina was perpetually contriving, when not watched, to get rid of her daily governess. "My opinion is, you never had the headache in your life."

"Thank you, mamma. That is just what Miss Jackson herself said yesterday afternoon. I paid her out for it. I sent her away with Baby Ferraday's kite fastened to her shawl behind."

"What ?" exclaimed Mrs. Beauclerc.

"The kite was small, not bigger than my hand, but the tail was fine," continued the imperturbable Georgina. "You cannot imagine how grand the effect was as she walked along the grounds, and the wind took the tail and fluttered it. The college boys happened to come out of school at the moment; and they followed her, shouting out 'kites for sale; tails to sell.' Miss Jackson couldn't think what was the matter, and kept turning round. She'd have had it on till now, I hope, only Fred. St. John went and tore it off."

Mrs. Beauclerc had listened in speechless amazement. When Georgina talked on in this rapid way, telling of her exploits—and to do the young lady justice, she never sought to hide them—Mrs. Beauclerc felt powerless for correction.

"What is to become of you?" groaned Mrs. Beauclerc.

"I'm sure I don't know, mamma; something good, I hope," returned the saucy girl. "Little Ferraday —I had called him up here to give him some cakes—

could not think where his kite had vanished, and
began to roar; so I found him sixpence and sent
him into the town to buy another. I don't know
whether he got lost or run over. The nurse seemed
to think it would be one of the two, for she went
into a fit when she found he had gone off alone."

"Georgina, I tell you these things cannot be
permitted to continue. You are no longer a child."

The colloquy was interrupted by the entrance of
the dean : a genial-looking man, with silver buckles
in his shoes, and a face very much like Georgina's
own. He had apparently just come in, for he had
his shovel hat in his hand. The girl loved her
father above everything on earth; to *his* slightest
word she rendered implicit homage ; though she
waged hot war with all others in authority over her,
commencing with Mrs. Beauclerc. She flew to the
dean with a beaming face, and he clasped his arms
round her with a gesture of the fondest affection.
Mrs. Beauclerc left the room. She never cared to
enter into a contest with her daughter before the
dean.

"My Georgina!" came forth the loving whisper.

"Papa, *is* it one o'clock ?"

"Not yet, my dear."

"I'm sure I heard the college clock strike."

"You thought you did, perhaps. It must have
been the quarters."

"Oh, dear! I have been calling Mr. Wilberforce hard names for nothing."

"What has Mr. Wilberforce done to you, my Georgie?"

"I thought he was keeping the school in; and I want to speak to Frederick St. John."

They were interrupted. One of the servants appeared, and said a gentleman was asking permission to see the dean. The dean took the credential card handed to him: "Mr. Peter Arkell."

"Show Mr. Arkell up," said the dean. "Georgina, my dear, you can go to your mamma."

"I'd rather stay here, papa," she said, boldly.

One word of explanation as to this visit of Peter Arkell's. It had of course been his intention to get his son Henry entered at the college school, and to this end had the boy been instructed. Of rare capacity, of superior intellect, of sense and feeling beyond his years, it had been a pleasure to his teachers to bring him on: and they consisted of his father and mother. From the one he learnt the classics and figures; from the other music and English generally. Henry Arkell was apt at all things: but if he had genius for one thing more than another, it was certainly music. The sole luxury Mrs. Peter Arkell had retained about her, was her piano; and Henry was an apt pupil. Few boys are gifted with so rare a voice for singing, as was he ; and his mother had cultivated it well : it was intended that he should enter the cathedral choir, as well as the school.

By the royal charter of the school, its number was confined to forty boys, king's scholars ; of these, ten were chosen to be choristers : but the head master had the privilege of taking private pupils, who paid him handsomely. The dean had the right of placing in ten of these king's scholars, but he rarely exercised it ; leaving it in the hands of the head master. Mr. Peter Arkell had applied several times lately to Mr. Wilberforce ; and had received only vague answers from that gentleman—" when there was a vacancy to spare, he would think of his son"—but Peter Arkell grew tired. Henry was of an age to be in the school now, and he resolved to speak to the dean.

He came in, leading Henry by the hand. Georgina fell a little back, struck—awed—by the boy's wondrous beauty. The dean, one of the most affable men that ever exercised sway over Westerbury cathedral, shook hands with Peter Arkell, whom he knew slightly.

" I don't know that there's a vacancy," said the dean, when Mr. Arkell told his tale. " Your son shall have it, and welcome, if there is. I have left these things to Mr. Wilberforce."

At this juncture Miss Beauclerc threw the window up, and beckoned to some one outside. Had her mother been present she would have administered a reprimand, but the dean was absorbed with the visitors, and he was less particular than his wife. Georgina was but a child, he reasoned ; she might be too careless in her manners now, but it would all come right with years. Better, far better see her genuine and truthful, if a little brusque, than false, mincing, affected, as young ladies were growing to be. And the dean checked her not.

"I know Mr. Wilberforce well, sir, and he has said he will do what he can," said Peter Arkell, in reply to the dean. "But I fear that I may have to wait an indefinite period. There are others in the town of far greater account than I, who are anxious to get their sons into the school ; and who have, no doubt, the ear of Mr. Wilberforce. A word from you, Mr. Dean, would effect all, I am sure : if you would only kindly speak it in my behalf."

Dr. Beauclerc turned his head to see who was entering the room, for the door had opened. It was a handsome stripling, growing rapidly into manhood—Frederick, heir of the St. John's. He was already keeping his terms at Oxford ; Mrs. St. John had sent him there too early ; and in the intervals, when they were sojourning at Westerbury, he was placed in the college; not as an ordinary scholar; the private pupil, and the chief one too, of Mr. Wilberforce.

The dean gave him a nod, and took the hand of the eager, exquisite face turned to him. Like his daughter, he was a great admirer of beauty in the human face: it would often give him a thrill of intense pleasure.

"What is your name, my boy?"

"Henry Cheveley Arkell, sir."

The dean glanced at Peter Arkell with a half smile. He remembered yet the commotion caused in Westerbury when Miss Cheveley married the tutor, and the name brought it before him.

"How old are you?"

"Nearly ten, sir."

"If I could paint faces, I'd paint his," cried Georgina to young St. John, in a half whisper. "Why don't *you* do it?"

"I suppose you mean his portrait?"

"You know I do. But, Fred, is he not beautiful?"

"You may get sent away if you talk," was the gentleman's answer.

"Has he been brought on well in his Latin? Is he fit to enter as a king's scholar?" inquired the dean of Peter Arkell.

"He has been brought on well in all necessary

17—2

studies, Mr. Dean; I may say it emphatically, *well*. I was in the college school myself, and know what is required. But learning has made strides of late, sir; boys are brought on more rapidly; and I can assure you that many a lad has quitted the college school in my days, his education finished, not as good a scholar as my son is now. I have taken pains with him."

"And we know what that implies from you, Mr. Arkell," said the dean, with a kindly smile. "You would like to be a king's scholar, my brave boy?"

"Oh yes, sir," said Henry, his transparent cheek flushing with hope.

"Then you shall be one. I will give you the first vacancy under myself."

They retired with many thanks; Frederick St. John giving Henry's bright waving hair a pull, as he passed him, by way of parting salutation.

"Papa! if you don't put that child into the college school, I will," began Georgina; her tone one of impassioned earnestness. "I will; though I have to beg it of old Wilberforce. I never saw such a face. I have fallen in love with it."

"I am going to put him in, Georgie. I like his face myself. But he can't go in until there's a vacancy. I must ask Mr. Wilberforce."

"There are two vacancies now, Dr. Beauclerc,"

spoke up Frederick St. John. "One of them is under you, I know."

"Indeed!"

"That is, there will be to-morrow. Those two West Indian boys, the Stantons, are sent for home suddenly: their mother's dying, or something of that. The master had the news this morning, and the school is in a commotion over it. If you do wish to fill the vacancy, sir, you should speak to Mr. Wilberforce at once, or he may stand it out that he has promised it," concluded Frederick St. John, with that freedom of speech he was fond of using, even to the dean.

"Stanton?" repeated the dean. "But were they not private pupils of the master's?"

"Oh dear no, sir, they are on the foundation. You might have seen them any Sunday in their surplices in college. They board at the master's house; that's all."

"Two dark boys, papa, the ugliest in the school," struck in Georgina, who knew a great deal more about the school than the dean did.

When Mr. Peter Arkell and Henry quitted the deanery, the former turned to the cloisters; for he had an errand to do in the town, and to go through the cloisters was the shortest way. He encoun-tered some of the college boys in the cloisters, whooping, hallooing, shouting; their feet and their tongues a babel of confusion. Mr. Arkell looked back at them with strange interest. It did not seem so very long since he and his cousin William had been college boys themselves, and had shouted and leaped as merrily as these. Two or three of them touched their trenchers to Mr. Arkell: they were evening pupils of his.

Henry had turned the other way, towards his home. At the gate, when he reached it, the boundary of the cathedral grounds on that side, he found a meek donkey drawn up, the drawer of a sort of truck, holding a water barrel. A woman was in the habit of bringing this water every day from a famous spring outside the town, to supply some of the houses in the grounds. The water was drawn out by means of a contrivance called a spigot and faucet, and she was stooping over this, filling a can. Henry, boy like, halted to watch the process, for the water rushed out full force.

Putting in the spigot when the can was full, she was proceeding to carry it up the old stairs belonging to the gateway, above which lived one of the minor canons, when the first shout of the college boys broke upon her ear.

" Oh, mercy !" she screamed out, as if in abject fear ; and Henry Arkell, who was then continuing his way, halted again and stared at her.

"Young gentleman," she said in a voice of appeal, "would you do me a charity?"

"What is it?" he asked. He was tall and manly for his years.

"If you would but stand by the barrel and guard it! The day afore yesterday, while my donkey and barrel was a stopped in this very spot, and I was a going up these here stairs with this very can, them wild young college gents came trooping by, and they pulled out the spigot and set the water a running. There warn't a drop left in the barrel when I got down. It was a loss to me I haven't over got."

"Go along," said Henry, "I'll guard it for you."

Unconscious boast! The boys came on in a roar of triumph, for they had caught sight of the water barrel. A young gentleman of the name of Lewis, a little older than Henry, was the first to get to the barrel, and lay his hand on the spigot.

"Oh, if you please, you are not to touch it," said Henry; "I am taking care of it."

"Halloa! what youngster are you? The donkey's brother?"

"Oh, don't take it out—don't!" pleaded Henry. "I promised the woman I'd guard it for her."

At this moment the woman's head was protruded through one of the small, deep, square loopholes

of the ancient staircase; and she apostrophized the
crew in no measured terms, and rather contradic-
tory. They were a set of dyed villains, of young
limbs, of daring pigs; and they were dear, good,
young gentlemen, that she prayed for every night;
and that she'd be proud to give a drink of the
beautiful spring water to any thirsty day.

You know school-boys; and may, therefore,
guess the result of this. The derisive shouts increased; the woman was ironically cheered; and
Henry Arkell had a struggle with Master Lewis for
possession of the spigot, which ended in the former's
ignominious discomfiture. He lay on the ground,
the water pouring out upon him, when a tall form
and authoritative voice dashed into the throng, and
laid summary hands on Lewis.

"Now then, Mr. St. John! Please to let me
alone, sir. It's no affair of yours."

"I choose to make it my affair, young Lewis.
You help that boy up that you have thrown
down."

Lewis rebelled. The rest of the boys had drawn
back beyond reach of the splashing water. St.
John stooped for the spigot, and put it in; and
then treated Lewis to a slight shaking.

"You be quiet, Mr. St. John. If you cock it
over us boys in school, it's no reason why you
should, out."

Another instalment of the shaking.

"Help him up, I tell you, Lewis."

Perhaps as the best way of getting out of it, Lewis jerked himself forward, and did help him up. Henry had been unable to rise of himself, and for a few moments he could not stand: his knee was hurt. It was a curious coincidence that the first fall, when he was entering the school, and the last fall——But it may be as well not to anticipate.

"Now, mind you, Mr. Lewis: if you attempt a cowardly attack on this boy again—you are bigger and stronger than he is—I'll thrash you kindly."

Lewis walked away, leaving a mental word behind him—not spoken, he would not have dared that—for Frederick St. John. The woman came down wailing and lamenting at the loss of the water, and the boys scuttered off in a body. St. John threw the woman half-a-crown, and helped Henry home.

The dean held to his privilege for once, and gave Mr. Wilberforce notice that he had filled up the vacancy by bestowing it on the son of Mr. Peter Arkell. Mr. Wilberforce, privately believing that the world was about to be turned upside-down, could only bow and acquiesce. He did it with a good grace, and sent a courteous message for

Henry to be there on the following Monday, at early school.

Accordingly, at seven o'clock, Henry was there. He did not like to troop in with the college boys, but waited until the head master had come, and entered then. Mr. Wilberforce called him up, inscribed his name on the school-roll, put a few questions to him as to the state of his studies, and then assigned him his place.

The boy was walking to it with that self-consciousness of something like a thousand eyes being on him—so terrible to the mind of a sensitive nature, and his was eminently one—when the head-master's voice was heard.

" Arkell, junior."

Never supposing " Arkell, junior," could be meant for him, he went timidly on ; but the voice rose higher.

" Arkell, junior."

It was so peremptory that Henry turned, and found it *was* meant for him. The sensitive crimson dyed his face deeper and deeper as he retraced his steps to the head-master's desk.

" Are you lame, Arkell, junior ?"

" Oh, it's nothing, sir. It's nearly well."

" What's the matter, then ?"

" I fell down last week, sir, and hurt my knee a little."

"Oh. Go to your desk."

"What a girl's face!" cried one, as Henry recommenced his promenade, for the indicated place was far down in the school.

"I'm blest if I don't believe it is the knight of the water-barrel!" exclaimed a big boy at the first desk. "Wont Lewis take it out of him! I hope he may get off with whole bones; but I'd not bet upon it."

"Lewis had better not try it on, or you either, Forbes," quietly struck in the second senior of the school, who was writing within hearing.

"Why, do you know him, Mr. Arkell?"

"Never you mind. I intend to take care of him."

The boys were trooping through the cloisters when school was over, and met the dean. Georgina was with him. She caught sight of Henry's face, and in her impulsive fashion dashed through the throng of boys to his side.

"Papa, he's here! Papa! he *is* here."

The dean, in his kindly manner, shook Henry by the hand. "Be a good boy, mind," he said. "Remember, you are under me."

"I'll try, sir," replied Henry. .

"Do. I shall not lose sight of you." And, with a general nod to the rest, he departed, taking his daughter's hand.

For a full minute there was a dead silence. It was so entirely unusual a thing for the dean to shake hands familiarly with a college boy, that those gentry did not at first decide how to take it. Then one of them, more impudent than the rest, bowed his body down before the new junior with mock gravity.

"If you please, sir, wouldn't you be pleased to make yourself cock of the school after this, and cut out St. John?"

"Take care of your tongue, Marshall," admonished St. John, who made one of the throng.

"I *am* blowed, though!" returned Marshall. "*Did* anybody ever see such a go as this?"

"What's the row?" demanded Hennet, a fine youth, one of Mr. Wilberforce's private pupils, and who only now came up.

"Oh, my! you should have been here, Hennet," responded Marshall. "We have got a lord, or something else, among us. The Dean of Westerbury has been bowing down to worship him."

Hennet, not understanding, looked at St. John.

"No. Trash!" explained St. John. "Marshall is putting his tongue and his foot into it to-day. I'm off to breakfast."

The word excited anticipations of the meal, and all the rest were off to breakfast too—making the grounds echo with their shouts as they ran.

CHAPTER XVI.

A CITY'S DESOLATION.

HENRY ARKELL had been in the college school rather more than a year, and also in the choir—for he entered the two almost simultaneously, his fine voice obtaining him the place before any other candidate—when the rank and fashion of Westerbury found itself in a state of internal, pleasurable commotion, touching an amateur concert about to be given for the benefit of the distressed Poles.

Mrs. Lewis, the daughter of the late Squire Carr, Mrs. Aultane, and a few more of the lesser satellites residing near the cathedral clergy, suddenly found themselves, from some cause never clearly explained to Westerbury, aroused into a state of sympathy and compassion for that ill-starred country, Poland, and its ill-used inhabitants. Casting about in their minds what they could do to help those *misérables* —the French word slipped out at my pen's end— they alighted on the idea of an amateur morning concert, and forthwith set about organizing one.

Painting in glowing colours the sufferings and hardships of this distant people, they contrived to gain the ear of the good-natured dean, and of Mrs. St. John of the Palmery, and the rest was easy. Canons and minor canons followed suit; all the gentry of the place took the concert under their especial patronage ; and everybody with the slightest pretension to musical skill, intimated that they were ready to assist in the performances, if called upon. In fact, the miniature scheme grew into a gigantic undertaking ; and no expense, trouble, or time was spared in the getting up of this amateur concert. Ladies of local rank and fashion were to sing at it ; the mayor accorded the use of the guildhall ; and Westerbury had not been in so delightful a state of excited anticipation for years and years.

But it is impossible to please everybody—as I dare say you have found out for yourselves at odd moments, in going through life. So it proved with this concert ; and though it was productive of so much satisfaction to some, it gave great dissatisfaction to others. This arose from a cause which has been a bone of contention even down to our own days : the overlooking near distress, to assist that very far off. There are ill-conditioned spirits amidst us who protest that the dear little interesting black Ashantees should not be presented with nice fine warm stockings, while our own common-place young Arabs have to go without shoes. While the destitution in Westerbury was palpably great, crying aloud to Heaven in its extent and helplessness, it seemed to some inhabitants of the city— influential ones, too—that the movement for the relief of the far-off Poles was strangely out of place; that the amateur concert, if got up at all, ought to have been held for the relief of the countrymen at home. This opinion gained ground, even amidst the supporters of the concert. The dean himself was heard to say, that had he given the matter proper consideration, he should have advised postponement of this concert for the foreigners to a less inopportune moment.

You, my readers, may know nothing of the results following the opening of the British ports for the introduction of French goods, as they fell on certain local places. When the bill was brought into the House of Commons by Mr. Huskisson, these results—ruin and irrecoverable distress—were foreseen by some of the members, and urged as an argument against its passing. Its defenders did not deny the probable fact; but said that in all great political changes the FEW must be content to suffer for the good of the MANY. An unanswerable argument; all the more plain that those who had to discuss it were not of the few. That the few did suffer, and

suffered to an extremity, none will believe who did
not witness it, is a matter of appalling history.
Ask Coventry what that bill did for it.   Ask
Worcester.   Ask Yeovil.   Ask other places that
might be named.   These towns lived by their staple
trade; their respective manufactures; and when a
cheaper, perhaps better article was introduced from
France, so as to supersede, or nearly so, their own,
there was nothing to stand between themselves and
ruin.

Ah! my aged friends! if you were living in those
days, you may have taken part in the congratulations
that attended the opening of the British ports to
French goods.   The popular belief was, that the
passing of the measure was as a boon falling upon
England; but you had been awed into silence had
you witnessed, but for a single day, the misery and
confusion it entailed on these local isolated places.
Take Westerbury: half the manufacturers went to
total ruin, their downfall commencing with that
year, and going on with the following years, until
it was completed.   It was but a question of the extent of private means.   Those who had none to fly
to, sunk at once in a species of general wreck; their
stock of goods was sold for what it would fetch;
their manufactories and homes were given up;
their furniture was seized; and with beggary staring
them in the face, they went adrift upon the cold

world. Some essayed other means of making their
living; essayed it as they best could without money
and without hope, and struggled on from year to
year, getting only the bread that nourished them.
Others, more entirely overwhelmed with the blow,
made a few poor efforts to recover themselves, in
vain, in vain : and their ending was the workhouse.
Honourable citizens once, good men, as respectable
and respected as you are, who had been reared and
lived in comfort, bringing up their families as well-
to-do manufacturers ought ; these were reduced to
utter destitution. Some drifted away, seeking only
a spot where they might die, out of sight of men ;
others found an asylum in their old age in the
paupers' workhouse ! You do not believe me ?
you do not think it could have been quite so bad as
this ? As surely as that this hand is penning the
words, I tell you but the truth.' For no fault of
theirs did they sink to ruin ; by no prudence could
they have averted it.

The manufacturers who had private property—
that is, property and money apart from the capital
employed in their business—were in a different
position, and could either retire from business, and
make the best of what they had left, or keep on
manufacturing in the hope that they should retrieve
their losses, and that times would mend. For a
very, very long time—for years and years—a great

many cherished the delusive hope that the ports would be reclosed, and English goods again fill the markets. They kept on manufacturing; content, perforce, with the small profit they made, and drawing upon their private funds for what more they required for their yearly expenditure. How they could have gone on for so many years, hoping in this manner, is a marvel to them now. But the fact was so. There were but very few who did this, or who, indeed, had money to do it; but amidst them must be numbered Mr. Arkell.

But, if the masters suffered, what can you expect was the fate of the workmen? Hundreds upon hundreds were thrown out of employment, and those who were still retained in the few manufactories kept open, earned barely sufficient to support existence; for the wages were, of necessity, sadly reduced, and they were placed on short work besides. What was to become of this large body of men? What did become of them? God only knew. Some died of misery, of prolonged starvation, of broken hearts. *Their* end was pretty accurately ascertained; but those who left their native town to be wanderers on the face of the land, seeking for employment to which they were unaccustomed, and perhaps finding none—who can tell what was their fate? The poor rates increased alarmingly, little able as were the impoverished population to bear an increase; the workhouses were filled, and lamentations were heard in the streets. Poor men! They only asked for work, work; and of work there was none. Small bodies of famished wretches, deputations from the main body, perambulated the town daily, calling in timidly at the manufactories still open, and praying for a little work. How useless! when those manufactories had been obliged to turn off many of their own hands.

It will not be wondered at, then, if, in the midst of this bitter distress, the grand scheme for the relief of the Poles, which was turning the town mad with excitement, did not find universal favour. The workmen, in particular, persisted in cherishing all sorts of obstinate notions about it. Why should them there foreign Poles be thought of and relieved, while *they* were starving? Would the Polish clergy and the grand folks, over there, think of *them*, the Westerbury workmen, and get up a concert for 'em, and send 'em the proceeds? There was certainly rough reason in this. The discontent began to be spoken aloud, and altogether the city was in a state of semi-rebellion.

Some of the men were gathered one evening at a public-house they used; their grievances, as a matter of course, the theme of discussion. So many years had elapsed since the blow had first fallen on the city by the passing of the bill, almost

18—2

a generation as it seemed, that the worn-out theme
of closing the ports was used threadbare ; and the
men chiefly confined themselves to the hardships
of the present time. Bad as the trade was at
Westerbury, it was expected to be worse yet, for
the more wealthy of the manufacturers were beginning to say they should be forced at last to close
their works. The men lighted their pipes, and
called for pints or half pints of ale. Those who
were utterly penniless, and could, in addition, neither
beg nor borrow money for this luxury, sat gloomily
by, their brows lowering over their gaunt and
famished cheeks.

"James Jones," said the landlord, a surly sort of
man, speaking in reply to a demand for a half pint
of ale, "I can't serve you. You owe five and
fourpence already."

What Mr. James Jones might have retorted in
his disappointment, was stopped by the entrance
of several men who came in together. It was the
"deputation ;" the men chosen to go round the
city that day and ask for work or alms. The interest aroused by their appearance overpowered petty
warfare.

"Well, and how have ye sped ?" was the eager
general question, as the men found seats.

"We went round, thirteen of us, upon empty
stomachs, and we left them at home empty too,"

replied a tidy-looking man with a stoop in his shoulders; "but we've done next to no good. Thorp, he has gone home; we gave him the money out of what we've collected for a loaf o' bread, for his wife and children's bad a-bed, and nigh clammed besides. The tale goes, too, that things are getting worse."

"They can't get worse, Read."

"Yes, they can; there was a meeting to-day of the masters. Did you hear of it?"

Of course the men had heard of it. Little took place in the town, touching on their interests, that they did not hear of.

"Then perhaps you've heard the measure that was proposed at it—to reduce the wages again. It was carried, too. George Arkell & Son's was the only firm that held out against it."

"Nobody has held out for us all along like Mr. Arkell," observed one who had not yet spoken. "He was a young man when these troubles first fell on the city, and he's middle-aged now, but never once throughout all the years has his voice been raised against us."

"True," said Read; "and when he speaks to us it is kindly and sympathizingly, like the gentleman he is, and as if *we* were fellow human beings, which they don't all do. Some of the masters don't care whether we starve or live; they

are as selfish as they are high. Mr. Arkell has
large means and an open hand ; it's said he has
the interests of us operatives at heart as much as
he has his own; for my part, I believe it. His
contribution to-day was a sovereign—more than
twice as much as anybody else gave us."

"And why not!" broke in Mr. James Jones
"If Arkells have got plenty—and it's well known
they have—it's only right they should help us."

"As to their having such plenty, I can't say
about that," dissented Markham—a superior man,
and the manager of a large firm. "They have
kept on making largely, and they must lose at
times. It stands to reason, as things have been.
Of course they had plenty of money to fall back
upon. Everybody knows that; and Mr. Arkell
has preferred to sacrifice some of that money—all
honour to him—rather than turn off to destitution
the men who have grown old in his service, and
in his father's before him."

"It's true, it's true," murmured the men.
"God bless Mr. William Arkell!"

"It's said that young Mr. Travice is to be
brought up to the business, so things can't be
very bad with them."

"Yah! bad with 'em!" roared a broad-shouldered
old man. "It riles me to sit here and hear you
men talk such foolery. Haven't he got his close

carriage and his horses? and haven't he got his fine house and his servants? Things bad with the Arkells!"

"You should not cast blame to the masters," continued Markham. "How many of them are there who still keep on making, but whose resources are nearly exhausted!"

"No, no, 'taint right," murmured some of the more just-thinking of the men. "The masters' troubles must be ten-fold greater than ours."

"I should be glad to hear how you make that out?" grumbled a malcontent. "I have got seven mouths to feed at home, and how am I to feed 'em, not earning a penny? We was but six, but our Betsey, as was in service as nuss-girl at Mrs. Omer's, came home to-day. I won't deny that Mrs. Omer have been kind to her, keeping her on after they failed, and that; but she up and told her yesterday that she couldn't afford it any longer. I remember, brethren, when Mr. and Mrs. Omer held up their heads, and paid their way as respectable as the first manufacturer in Westerbury. Good people they was."

"Mr. Omer came to our place to-day," interrupted Markham, "to pray the governor to give him a little work at his own home, as a journeyman. But we had none to give, without robbing them that want it worse than he. I think I never saw our governor so cut up as he was, after being obliged to refuse him."

"Ay," returned the former speaker ; " and our Betsey declares that her missis cried to her this morning, and said she didn't know but what they should come to the parish. Betsey, poor girl," he continued, "can't bear to be a burden upon us ; but there ain't no help for it. There be no places to be had ; what with so many of the girls being throwed out of employment, and the famerlies as formerly kept two or three servants keeping but one, and them as kept one keeping none. There's nothing that she can do, brethren, for herself or for us."

"The Lord keep her from evil courses!" uttered a deep, earnest voice.

"If I thought as her, or any of my children, was capable of taking to *them*," thundered the man, his breast heaving as he raised his sinewy, lean arm in a threatening attitude, "I'd strike her flat into the earth afore me !"

"Things as bad with the masters as they be with us ! " derisively resumed the broad-shouldered old man. "Yah! Some on you would hold a candle to the devil himself, though he appeared among ye horned and tailed ! Why, I mind the time—I'm older nor some o' you be—when there warn't folks wanting to defend Huskisson ! And

I mind," he added, dropping his voice, " the judgment that come upon him for what he done."

" It's of no good opening up that again," cried
Thomas Markham. " What Huskisson did, he
did for his country's good, and he never thought it
would bring the ill upon us that it did bring. I
have told you over and over again of an interview
our head governor—who has now been dead these
ten years, as you know—had with Huskisson in
London. It was on a Sunday evening in summer ;
and when the governor went in, Huskisson was
seated at his library table, with one of the petitions
sent up from Westerbury to the House of Commons, spread out before him. It was the one sent
up in the May of that year, praying that the ports
might be closed again—some of you are old enough
to recollect it, my friends—the one in which our sufferings and wrongs were represented in truer and
more painful colours than they were, perhaps, in any
other of the memorials that went up. It was reported, I remember, that Mr. William Arkell had the
chief hand in drawing out that petition : but I don't
know how that might have been. Any way, it told
on Mr. Huskisson ; and the governor said afterwards, that if ever he saw remorse and care seated
on a brow, it was on his."

" As it had cause to be !" was echoed from all
parts of the room.

"Mr. Huskisson began speaking at once about the petition," continued the manager. "He asked if the sufferings described in it were not exaggerated; but the governor assured him upon his word of honour, as a resident in Westerbury and an eye-witness, that they were underdrawn rather than the contrary; for that no pen, no description, could adequately describe the misery and distress which had been rife in Westerbury ever since the bill had passed. And he used to say that, live as long as he would, he should never forget the look of perplexity and care that overshadowed Mr. Huskisson's face as he listened to him."

"It was repentance pressing sore upon him," growled a deep bass voice. "It's to be hoped our famished and homeless children haunted his dreams."

"The next September he met with the accident that killed him," continued Thomas Markham; "and though I know some of us poor sufferers were free in saying it was a judgment upon him, I've always held to my opinion that if he had foreseen the misery the bill wrought, he would never have brought it forward in the House of Commons."

"Here's Shepherd a coming in! I wonder how his child is? Last night he thought it was dying. Shepherd, how's the child?"

A care-worn, pale man made his way amid the throng. He answered quietly that the child was well.

"Well ! why, you said last night that it was as bad as it could be, Shepherd ! You was going off for the doctor then. Did he come to it?"

"One doctor came, from up there," answered Shepherd, pointing to the sky. "He came, and He took the child."

The words could not be misunderstood, and the room hushed itself in sympathy. "When did the boy die, Shepherd?"

"To-day, at one; and it's a mercy. Death in childhood is better than starvation in manhood."

"Could Dr. Barnes do nothing for him?" inquired a compassionate voice.

"He didn't try; he opened his winder to look out at me—he was undressing to go to bed—and asked whether I had got the money to pay him if he came."

"Hiss—iss—ss !" echoed from the room.

"I answered that I had not; but I would pay him with the very first money that I could scrape together; and I said he might take my word for it, for that had never been broken yet."

"And he would not come?"

"No. He said he knew better than to trust to promises. And when I told him that the boy was dying, and very precious to me, the rest being girls, he said it was not my word he doubted but my ability, for he didn't believe that any of us men would ever be in work again. So he shut down his winder and douted his candle, and I went home to my boy, powerless to help him, and I watched him die."

"Drink a glass of ale, Shepherd," said Markham, getting a glass from the landlord, and filling it from his own jug.

"Thank ye kindly, but I shall drink nothing tonight," replied Shepherd, motioning back the glass. "There's a sore feeling in my breast, comrades," he continued, sighing heavily; "it has been there a long while past, but it's sorer far to-day. I don't so much blame the surgeon, for there has been a deal of sickness among us, and the doctors have been unable to get their pay. Hundreds of us are nigh akin to starvation; there's scarcely a crust between us and death; we desire only to work honestly, and we can't get work to do. As I sat to-day, looking at my dead boy, I asked what we had done to have this fate thrust upon us?"

"What have we done? That's it!—what have we done?"

"But I did not come here to-night to grumble," resumed Shepherd, "I came for a specific purpose, though perhaps I mayn't succeed in it. I went down to Jasper, the carpenter, to-day, to ask him to come and take the measure for the little coffin. Well, he's like all the rest, he won't trust me; at last he said, if anybody would go bail he should be paid later, he'd make it; and I have come down to ye, friends, to ask who'll stand by me in this?"

A score of voices answered, each that he would— eager, sympathizing voices—but Shepherd shook his head. There was not one among them whose word the carpenter would take, for they were all out of work. In the silence that ensued, Shepherd rose to leave.

"Many thanks for the good-will, neighbours," he said. "And I don't grumble at my unsuccess, for I know how powerless many of ye are to aid me. But it's a bitter trial. I would rather my boy had never been born than that he should come to be buried by the parish. God knows we have heavy burdens to bear."

"Shepherd!" cried the clear voice of Thomas Markham, "I will stand by you in this. Tell Jasper I pass my word to see him paid."

Shepherd turned back and grasped the hand of Thomas Markham.

"I can't thank you as I ought, sir," he said; "but you have took a load from my heart. Though you were never repaid here, you would be hereafter; for I have come to feel a certainty that if our good deeds are not brought home to us in this world, they are only kept to speak for us in the next."

"I say, stop a minute, Shepherd," called out James Jones, as the man was again making his way to the door. "What made you go to Jasper? He's always cross-grained after his money, he is. Why didn't you go to White?

"I did go to White first," answered Shepherd, turning to speak; "but White couldn't take it. He has got the job for all the new wooden chairs that are wanted for this concert at the town-hall, and hadn't time for coffins."

The mention was the signal for an outburst. It came from all parts of the room, one noise drowning another. Why couldn't a concert be got up for them? Weren't they as good as the Poles? Hadn't they bodies and souls to be saved as well as the Poles? Wasn't there a whole town of 'em starving under the very noses of them as had got up the concert? They could tell the company that French revolutions had growed out of less causes.

"And I'll tell ye what," roared out the old man with the broad shoulders, bringing his fist down on the table with such force that the clatter amidst the cups and glasses caused a sudden silence. "Every gentleman that puts his foot inside that there concert room, is no true man, and I'd tell him so to his face, if 'twas the Lord Lieutenant. What do our people want a fattening up of them there Poles, while we be starving ?   I wish the Poles was——"

"Hold your tongue, Lloyd," interposed Markham. "It's not the fault of the Poles, any more than it's ours ; so where's the use of abusing them ?"

"Yah !" responded Mr. Lloyd.

CHAPTER XVII.

A DIFFICULTY ABOUT TICKETS.

AMIDST those who held a strong opinion on the subject of the concert—and it did not in any great degree differ from the men's—was Mr. Arkell. Mrs. Arkell knew of this, but never supposed it would extend to the length of keeping her away from it: or perhaps she wilfully shut her eyes to any suspicion of the sort.

On the morning preceding the concert, she was seated making up some pink bows, intended to adorn the white spotted muslin robes of her daughters, when the explanation came. She said something about the concert—really inadvertently—and Mr. Arkell took it up.

"You are surely not thinking of going to the concert?" he exclaimed.

"Indeed I am. I shall go and take Lottie and Sophy."

"Then, Charlotte, I desire that you will put away all thoughts of it," he said. " I could not allow my wife and daughters to appear at it."

"Why not? why not?" she asked in irritation.

"There is not the least necessity for my going over the reasons ; you have heard me say already what I think of this concert. It is a gratuitous insult on our poor starving people, and neither I nor mine shall take part in it."

"All the influential people in the town are supporting it, and will be there."

"Not so universally as you may imagine. But at any rate what other people do is no rule for me. I should consider it little less than a sin to purchase tickets, and I will not do it, or allow it to be done."

Mrs. Arkell gave a flirt at the ribbon in her hand, and sent it flying over the table.

"What will Charlotte and Sophy say? Pleasant news this will be for them! These bows were for their white dresses. I might have spared myself the time and trouble of making them up. Travice goes to it," she added, resentfully.

"But Travice goes as senior of the college school. It has pleased Mr. Wilberforce to ask that the four senior boys shall be admitted ; it has been accorded, and they have nothing to do but make use of the permission in obedience to his wishes. That is a different thing. If I had to buy a ticket for Travice, I assure you, Charlotte, the concert would wait long enough before it saw him there."

" Our tickets would cost only fifteen shillings," she retorted.

" I can't afford fifteen shillings," said Mr. Arkell, getting vexed. " Charlotte, hear me, once for all; if the tickets cost but one shilling each, I would not have you purchase them. Not a coin of mine, small or large, shall go to swell the funds of the concert. If you and the girls feel disappointed, I am sorry," he continued, in a kind tone. " It is not often that I run counter to your wishes; but in this one instance—and I must beg you distinctly to understand me—I cannot allow my decision to be disputed."

To say that Mrs. Arkell was annoyed, would be a very inadequate word to express what she felt. She had been fond of gaiety all her life; was fond of it still; she was excessively fond of dress; any project offering the one or the other was eagerly embraced by Mrs. Arkell. Though of gentle birth herself—if that was of any service to her—as the wife of William Arkell, the manufacturer, she did not take her standing in what was called the society of Westerbury—and you do not need, I presume, to be reminded what " society " in a cathedral town is : or are ignorant of its pretentious exclusiveness. There was not a more

respected man in the whole city than Mr. Arkell;
the dean himself was not more highly considered;
but he was a manufacturer, the son of a manufacturer, and therefore beyond the pale of the visiting
society. It never occurred to him to wish to enter
it; but it did to his wife. To have that barrier
removed, she would have sacrificed much; and
now and again her reason would break out in
private complaint against it. She could not see
the justice of it. It is true her husband was a
manufacturer; but he had been reared a gentleman; he was a brilliant scholar, one of the most
accomplished men of his day. His means were
ample, and their style of living was good. Mrs.
Arkell glanced to some of the people revelling in
the *entrée* of that society, with their poor pitiful
income of a hundred pounds, or two, a year; their
pinching and screwing; their paltry expedients to
make both ends meet. Why should they be
admitted and she excluded, was the question she
often asked herself. But Mrs. Arkell knew perfectly well, in the midst of her grumbling, that one
might as well try to alter the famed laws of the
Medes and Persians, as the laws that govern
society in a cathedral town: or indeed in
any town. This concert she had looked forward to with more interest than usual, because
it would afford her the opportunity of hearing

19—2

some of the great ones of the county play and
sing.

But she did not now see how to get to it; and
her disappointment was bitter. It had fallen upon
her as a blow. Mrs. Arkell had her faults, but
she was a good wife on the whole; not one to run
into direct disobedience. She generally enjoyed
her own way; her husband rarely interfered to
counteract it; certainly he had never denied her
anything so positively as this. She sat, the image
of discontent, listlessly tossing the pink bows
about with her fingers, when her eldest daughter, a
tall, elegant girl, came in.

"Oh, mamma! how lovely they are! won't they
look well on the white dresses!"

"Well!" grunted Mrs. Arkell, "I might have
spared myself the trouble of making them. We
are not to go to the concert now."

"Not to go to the concert!" echoed Charlotte,
opening her eyes in utter astonishment. "Does
papa say so?"

"Yes; he will not allow tickets to be purchased.
He does not approve of the concert. And he says,
if the tickets cost but a shilling each, he should
think it a sin to give it."

Charlotte sat down, the picture of dismay.

"Where will be the use of our new dresses
now!" she exclaimed.

" Where will be the use of anything," retorted Mrs. Arkell. " Don't whirl your chain round like that, Charlotte, giving me the fidgets !"

Charlotte dropped her chain. A bright idea had occurred to her.

" If papa's objection lies in the purchase of tickets, let us ask Henry Arkell for his, mamma. Mrs. Peter is sure to be too ill to go."

One minute's pause of thought, and Mrs. Arkell caught at the suggestion, as a famished outcast catches at the bread offered to him. If a doubt obtruded itself, that their appearing at the concert at all would be almost as unpalatable to her husband as their spending money upon its tickets, she conveniently put it out of sight.

The gentlemen forming the choir of the cathedral, both lay-clerks and choristers, had been solicited to give their services to the concert ; as an acknowledgment two tickets were presented to each of them, in common with the amateur performers. Henry Arkell had, of course, two with the rest, and these were the tickets thought of by Charlotte.

Not a moment lost Mrs. Arkell. Away went she to pay a visit to Mrs. Peter—a most unusual condescension ; and it impressed Mrs. Peter accordingly, who was lying on her sofa that day, very poorly indeed. Mrs. Arkell at once proclaimed

the motive of her visit; she did not beat
about the bush, or go to work with crafty diplo-
macy, but she plunged into it with open frank-
ness, telling of their terrible disappointment,
through Mr. Arkell's objecting, on principle, to
buy tickets.

"If you do not particularly wish to go yourself,
Mrs. Peter—I know how unequal you are to exer-
tion—and would give Henry's tickets to myself
and Charlotte, I should feel more obliged than I
can express."

There was one minute's hesitation on Mrs. Peter
Arkell's part. She had really wished to go to this
concert; she was nursing herself up to be able to
go ; and she knew how greatly Lucy, who had but
few chances of any sort of pleasure, was looking
forward to it. But the hesitation lasted the minute
only ; the next, the coveted tickets, with their
pretty little red seal in the corner, were in the
hand of Mrs. Arkell.

She went home as elated as though she had
taken an enemy's ship at sea, and were sailing into
port with it.

"Sophy must make up her mind to stay at home,"
she soliloquized. "It is her papa's fault, and I
shall tell her so, if she's rebellious over it, as she
is sure to be. This gives one advantage, however:
there will be more room in the carriage for me and

Charlotte. I wondered how we should all three cram in, with new white dresses on."

About the time that she was hugging this idea complacently to herself, the college clock struck one; and the college boys came pelting, pell-mell, down the steps of the school-room, their usual mode of egress. Travice Arkell, the senior boy of the school now—and the senior of that school possessed great power, and ruled his followers with an iron hand, more or less so according to his nature—waited, as he was obliged, to the last; he locked the door, and went flying across the grounds to leave the keys at the head master's. Travice Arkell was almost a man now, and would quit the school very shortly.

Bounding along as fast as he could go when he had left the keys—taking no notice of a knot of juniors who were quarrelling over marbles—Travice made a detour as he turned out of the grounds, and entered the house of Mrs. Peter Arkell. He was rather addicted to making this detour, but he burst in now at an inopportune moment. Lucy was in tears, and Mrs. Arkell was remonstrating against them in a reasoning, not to say a reproving tone. Henry, who had got in previously, was nursing his leg, a very blank look upon his face.

"What's the matter?" asked Travice, as Lucy made her escape.

"I thought Lucy had more sense," was the vexed rejoinder made by Mrs. Peter. "Don't ask, Travice. It is nothing."

"What is it, Harry, boy?" cried Travice, with scant attention to the "don't ask." "She can't be crying for nothing."

"It's about the concert," returned Henry, ruefully, his disappointment being at least equal to Lucy's. "Mamma has given away the tickets, and Lucy can't go."

"Whatever's that for?" asked Travice, who was as much at home at Mrs. Peter's as he was at his own house. "Who has got the tickets?"

"Mrs. Arkell."

"Mrs. Arkell!" shouted Travice, staring at the boy as if he questioned the truth of the words. "Do you mean my mother? What on earth does she want with your tickets?"

As he put the question he turned to Mrs. Peter, lying there with the sensitive crimson on her cheeks. She had certainly not intended to betray this to Travice: it had come out in the suddenness of the moment, and she strove to make the best of it now.

"I am glad it has happened so, Travice. I feel so weak to-day that I was beginning to think it would be imprudent, if not impossible, for me to venture to go to-morrow. To say the least, I am better away. As to Lucy, she is very foolish to cry over so trifling a disappointment. She'll forget it directly."

"But what does my mother want with your tickets?" reiterated Travice, unable to understand that point in the matter. "Why can't she buy tickets for herself?"

"Mr. Arkell has scruples, I believe. But, Travice, I am happy to——"

"Well, I shall just tell my mother what I think of this!" was the indignant interruption.

"Don't, Travice," said Mrs. Arkell. "If you only knew how *glad* I am to have the opportunity of rendering any little service to your home!" she whispered, drawing him to her with her gentle hand; "if you knew but half the kindness my husband and I receive from your father! I am only sorry I did not think to offer the tickets at first; I ought to have done so. It is all right; let us say no more about it."

Travice bent his lips to the flushed cheek: he loved her quite as much as he did his own mother.

"Take care, or you will get feverish; and that would never do, you know."

"My dear boy, I am feverish already; I have been a little so all day; and I am sure there could be no concert for me to-morrow, had I a roomful of tickets. It has all happened for the best, I say.

I should only have been at the trouble of finding somebody to take Lucy."

As he was leaving the room he came upon Lucy in the passage, who was returning to it—the tears dried, or partially so; and if the long dark eyelashes glistened yet, there was a happy smile upon the sweet red lips. Few could school themselves as did that thoughtful girl of fifteen, Lucy Arkell.

Travice stopped her as he closed the door.

"You'll trust me, will you not, Lucy?"

"For what?" she asked.

"To put this to rights. It——"

"Oh pray, pray don't!" she cried, fearing she hardly knew what. "Surely you are not thinking of asking for the tickets back again! I would not use them for the world. And they would be of no use to us now, for mamma says she shall not be well enough to go, and I don't think she will. I shall not mind staying at home."

Travice placed his two hands on her shoulders, and looked into her face with his sweet smile and his speaking eyes; she coloured strangely beneath the gaze.

"I'll tell you what it is, Lucy: you are just one of those to get put upon through life and never stand up for yourself. It's a good thing you have me at your side."

"You can't be at my side all through life," said Lucy, laughing.

"Don't make too sure of that, Mademoiselle." And the colour in her face deepened to a glowing crimson, and her heart beat wildly, as the significance of the tone made itself heard, in conjunction with his retreating footsteps.

He dashed home, spending about two minutes in the process, and dashed into the room where his mother was, her bonnet on yet, talking to Charlotte, and impressing upon her the fact that their going to the concert must be kept an entire secret from all, until the moment of starting arrived, but especially from papa and Sophy. Charlotte, in a glow of delight, acquiesced in everything.

"I say, mamma, what's this about your taking Mrs. Peter's tickets?"

He threw his trencher on the table, as he burst in upon them with the question, and his usually refined face was in a very unrefined glow of heat. The interruption was most unwelcome. Mrs. Arkell would have put him down at once, but that she knew, from past experience, Travice had an inconvenient knack of not allowing himself to be put down. So she made a merit ·of necessity, and told how Mr. Arkell had interdicted their buying tickets.

"Well, of all the cool things ever done, that was about the coolest—for you to go and get those tickets from Mrs. Peter!" he said, when he had heard her to an end. "They don't have so many opportunities of going out, that you should deprive them of this one. I'd have stopped away from concerts for ever before I had done it."

"You be quiet, Travice," struck in Charlotte; "it is no business of yours."

"You be quiet," retorted Travice. "And it is my business, because I choose to make it mine. Mother, just one question: Will you let Lucy go with you to the concert? Mrs. Peter fears she shall be too ill to go. I'm sure I don't wonder if she is," he continued, with a spice of impertinence; "I should be, if I had had such a shabby trick played upon me."

"It is like your impudence to ask it, Travice. When do I take out Lucy Arkell? She is not going to the concert."

"She is going to the concert," returned Travice, that decision in his tone, that incipient rebellion, that his mother so much disliked. "You have deprived them of their tickets, and I shall, therefore, buy them two in place of them. And when my father asks me why I spent money on the concert against his wish, I shall just lay the whole case before him, and he will see that there was no help for it. I shall go and tell him now, before I——"

"You will do no such thing, Travice," interrupted Mrs. Arkell, her face in a flame. "I forbid you to carry the tale to your father. Do you hear me? *I forbid you;*—and I am your mother. How dare you talk of spending your money on this concert? Buy two tickets, indeed!"

The first was a mandate that Travice would not break; the latter he conveniently ignored. Flinging his trencher on his head, he went straight off to buy the tickets, and carried them to Mrs. Peter Arkell's. There was not much questioning as to how he obtained them, for Mrs. St. John was sitting there. That they were fresh tickets might be seen by the numbers.

"My dear Travice," cried Mrs. Peter, "it is kind of you to bring these tickets; but we cannot use them. I shall be unable to go; and there is no one to take Lucy."

"Nonsense, there are plenty to take her," returned Travice. "Mrs. Prattleton would be delighted to take her; and I dare say," he added, in his rather free manner, as he threw his beaming glance into the visitor's face, "that Mrs. St. John would not mind taking charge of her."

"I *will* take charge of her," said Mrs. St. John —and the tone of the voice showed how genuinely ready was the acquiescence—"that is, if I go myself. But Frederick is ill to-day, and I am not sure that I can leave him to-morrow. But Lucy shall go with some of us. My niece, Anne, will be here, I expect, to-night. She is coming to pay a long visit."

"What is the matter with Frederick?" asked Travice, quickly.

"It appears like incipient fever. I suppose he has caught a violent cold."

"I'll go and see him," said Travice, catching up his trencher, and vaulting off before anyone could stop him.

Mrs. St. John rose, saying something final about the taking Lucy, and the arrangements for the morrow. She was the only one of the acquaintances of Miss Lucy Cheveley who had not abandoned Mrs. Peter Arkell. It is true the St. Johns were not very often at the Palmery, but when they were there, Mrs. St. John never failed to be found once a week sitting with the wife of the poor tutor, so neglected by the world.

And, after all, when the morrow came, Mrs. Peter Arkell *was* too ill to go. So she folded the spare ticket in paper, and sent it with her love, to Miss Sophia Arkell.

CHAPTER XVIII.

THE CONCERT.

NEVER did there rise a brighter morning than the one on which the amateur concert was to take place. And Westerbury was in a ferment of excitement ; carriages were rolling about, bringing the county people into the town ; and fine dresses, every colour of the rainbow, crowded the streets.

Three parts of the audience walked to the concert, nothing loth, gentle and simple, to exhibit their attire in the blazing sunlight. It was certainly suspiciously bright that morning, had people been at leisure to notice it.

The Guildhall was filled to overflowing, when three ladies came in, struggling for a place. One was a middle-aged lady, quiet looking, and rather dowdy ; the other was an elegant girl of seventeen, with clear brown eyes and a pointed chin : the third was Lucy Arkell.

There was not a seat to be found. The elder lady looked annoyed ; but there was nothing for it but to stand with the mass. And they were standing when they caught—at least Lucy did— the roving eye of Travice Arkell.

Now, it happened that the four senior pupils of the college school—not the private pupils of Mr. Wilberforce, but the king's scholars—were being made of much account at this concert; and, by accident, or design, a side sofa, near to the orchestra—one of the best places—was assigned to them. Travice Arkell suddenly darted from his seat on it, and began to elbow his way down the room, for every avenue was choked. He reached Lucy at last.

"How late you are, Lucy! But I can get you a seat—a capital one, too. Will you allow me to pilot you to a sofa?" he courteously added to bad the two ladies with her.

The elder lady turned at the address, and saw a tall, slender young man, with a pale, refined face. The college cap under his arm betrayed that he belonged to the collegiate school; otherwise, she had thought him too old for a king's scholar.

"You are very kind. In a few moments. But we ought to wait until this song that they are beginning is over."

It was not a song, but a duet—and a duet that had given no end of trouble to the executive management—for none of the ladies had been found suitable to undertake the first part in it. It required a remarkably clear, high, bell-like voice, to do it justice; and the cathedral organist, privately wishing the concert far enough—for he had never been so much pestered in all his life as since he undertook the arrangements — proposed Henry Arkell. And Mrs. Lewis, who took the second part, was fain to accept him : albeit, the boy was no favourite of hers.

"How singularly beautiful!" murmured the elder lady to Travice Arkell, as the clear voice burst forth.

"Yes, he has an excellent voice. The worst of him is, he is timid. He will out-grow that."

"I did not allude to the voice; I spoke of the boy himself. I never saw a more beautiful face. Who is he?"

Travice smiled. "It is Henry Arkell, Lucy's brother, and my cousin."

"Ah! I knew his mother once. Mrs. St. John was telling me her history last night. Anne, my dear, you have heard me speak of Lucy Cheveley: that is her son, and it is the same face. Then you," she continued, "must be Mr. Travice Arkell? Hush!"

For the duet was in full force just then, and Mrs. Lewis's rich contralto voice was telling well.

"Who is she?" asked Travice of Lucy in a whisper.

"Mrs. James. She's the governess," came the answer.

When the duet was over, Travice Arkell held out his arm to Mrs. James. "If you will do me the honour of taking it, the getting through the crowd may be easier for you," he said. But Mrs. James drew back, as she thanked him, and motioned him towards the younger lady with her. So Travice took the younger lady; not being quite certain, but suspecting who she was; and Mrs. James and Lucy followed as they best could.

And his reward was a whole host of daggers darted at him—if looks can dart them. The two ladies were complete strangers to the aristocracy of the grounds; and seeing Peter Arkell's daughter in their wake, the supposition that they belonged in some way to that renowned tutor, but obscure man, was not unnatural. Mrs. Lewis, who had come down to her sofa then, and Mrs. Aultane, who sat with her, were especially indignant. How dared that class of people thrust themselves at the top of the room amidst them?

"Travice," said Mrs. Arkell, bending forward from one of the cross benches, and pulling his sleeve as he passed on, "you are making yourself too absurd!"

" Am I ! I am very sorry."

But he did not look sorry ; on the contrary, he looked highly amused : and he bent his head now and again to say a word of encouragement to the fair girl on his arm, touching the difficulties of their progress. On, he bore, to the sofa he had quitted, and ordered the three seniors he had left on it to move off. In school or out, they did not disobey him ; and they moved off accordingly. He seated the two ladies and Lucy on it, and stood near the arm himself; never once more sitting down throughout the concert. But he stayed with them the whole of the time, talking as occasion offered.

But, oh ! that false morning brightness ! Before the concert was over, the rain was coming down with fury, pelting, as the college boys chose to phrase it, cats and dogs. Very few had given orders for their carriages to be there ; and they could only wait in hopes they would come, or send messengers after them. What, perhaps, rendered it more inconvenient was, that the concert was over a full half-hour earlier than had been expected.

The impatient company began to congregate in the lower hall ; its folding doors of egress and its large windows looking to the street. Some one had been considerate enough to have a fire lighted at the upper end ; and most inviting it was, now the day had turned to damp. The head master, who had despatched one of the boys to order his close carriage to be brought immediately, gave the fire a vigorous poke, and turned round to look about him. He was a little man, with silver-rimmed spectacles.

Two causes were exciting some commotion in the minds of the lesser satellites of the grounds. The one was the presuming behaviour of those people with Lucy Arkell, and the unjustifiable folly of Travice; the other was the remarkable absence of the Dean of Westerbury and his family from the concert. It, the absence, was put down to the dean's having at the last moment refused to patronize it, in consequence of its growing unpopularity; and Mrs. St. John's absence was attributed to the same cause. People knew later that the dean and Mrs. Beauclerc had remained at home in consequence of the death of a relative; but that is of no consequence to us.

"The dean is given to veering round," remarked Mrs. Aultane in an under tone to the head master. "Those good-natured men generally are."

The master cleared his throat, as a substitute for a reply. It was not his place to speak against the dean. And, indeed, he had no cause. He walked to the window nearest him, and looked out at the carriages and flies as they came tardily up.

Travice Arkell seemed determined to offend. He

was securing chairs for those ladies now near the fire ; and Mrs. Lewis put her glass to her eye, and surveyed them from head to foot. Her wild brother, Benjamin Carr, could not have done it more insolently.

"Who is that lady, Arkell ?" demanded the master, of Travice, when he got the opportunity.

"It is a Mrs. James, sir."

"Oh. A friend of yours ?"

"No, sir. I never saw her until to-day."

Mrs. Aultane bent her head. "Mrs. James ? Who *is* Mrs. James ? And the other one, too ? I should be glad to know, Mr. Travice Arkell."

"I can't tell you much about them, Mrs. Aultane," returned Travice, suppressing the laugh of mischief in his eye. "I saw them for the first time in the concert-room."

"They came with your relative, Peter Arkell's daughter."

"Exactly so. That is, she came with them."

"Some people from the country, I suppose," concluded Mrs. Aultane, with as much hauteur as she thought it safe to put into her tone. "It is easy to be seen they have no style about them."

Travice laughed and went across the room. He was speaking to the ladies in question, when a gentleman of three or four-and-twenty came up and tapped him on the back.

"Won't you speak to me? It *is* Travice Arkell, I see, though he has shot up into a man."

One moment's indecision, and Travice took the hand in his. "Anderson! Can it be?"

"It can, and is. *Captain* Anderson, if you please, sir, now."

"No!"

"It's true. I have been lucky, and have got my company early."

"But what brings you here? I did not know you were in Westerbury."

"I arrived only this morning. Hearing of your concert when I got here, I thought I'd look in; but it was half over then, and I barely got inside the room. You don't mean to say that you are in the school still?"

Travice laughed, and held out the betraying cap. "It is a shame. I am too big for it. I have only a month or two longer to stay."

"But you must have been in beyond your time."

"I know I have."

"And who is senior?"

"Need you ask, looking at my size. This is Lucy; have you forgotten her?"

Captain Anderson turned. He had been educated in the college school, a private pupil of the head master's. Travice Arkell was only a junior in it when Anderson left; but Anderson had been intimate at the houses of both the Arkells.

"Miss Lucy sprung up to this! You were the prettiest little child when I left. And your sisters, Travice? I should like to see them."

Lucy laughed and blushed. Captain Anderson began talking to Mrs. James, and to the young lady who sat between her and Lucy.

"I can't stop," he presently said. "I see the master there. And that—yes, that must be Mr. and Mrs. Prattleton. There! the master is scanning me through his spectacles, wondering whether it's me or somebody else. I'll come back to you, Arkell."

He went forward, and was beset at once. People were beginning to recognise him. Anderson, the private pupil, had been popular in the grounds. Mrs. Aultane on one side, Mrs. Lewis on the other, took forcible possession of him, ere he had been a minute with the head master and his wife. It was hard to believe that the former somewhat sickly, fair-haired private pupil, who had been coddled by Mrs. Wilberforce with bark and flannel and beaten-up eggs, could be this fine soldierly man.

"Those ladies don't belong to you, do they?" cried Mrs. Aultane, beginning to fear she had made some mistake in her treatment of the ladies in question, if they did belong to Anderson.

" Ladies ! what ladies ?"

" Those to whom Travice Arkell is talking. He has been with them all day."

" They don't belong to me. What of them ?"

" Nothing. Only these inferior people, strangers, have no right to push themselves amidst us, taking up the best places. We are obliged to draw a line, you know, in this manufacturing town ; and none but strangers, ignorant of our distinctions, would dare to break it."

Captain Anderson laughed ; he could not quite understand. " I don't think they are inferior," he said, indicating the two ladies. " Anything but that, although they may belong to manufacturers, and not be in your set. The younger one is charming ; so is Lucy Arkell."

Mrs. Aultane vouchsafed no reply. It was rank heresy. The college boys were making a noise and commotion at the other end of the hall, and the master called out sharply—

" Arkell, keep those boys in order."

Travice sauntered towards them, gave his commands for silence, and returned to the place from whence he came. Henry Arkell came into the hall from the upper room, and there was a lull in the proceedings. The carriages came up but slowly.

" Don't you think we might walk home, Mrs. James ?" inquired the younger lady. " I do not

care to stay here longer to be stared at. I never
saw people stare so in my life."

She said it with reason. Many were staring, and
not in a lady-like manner, but with assuming
manner and eye-glass to eye.

"They look just as though they thought we had
no right to be here, Mrs. James."

"Possibly, my dear. It may be the Westerbury
custom to stare at strangers. But I cannot allow
you to walk home; you have thin shoes on. Mrs.
St. John is certain to send your carriage, or hers."

"You did well, Harry," cried Travice Arkell,
laying his hand on the young boy's shoulders.
"Many a fair dame would give her price for your
voice."

"And for something else belonging to you,"
added Mrs. James, taking the boy's hand and
holding him before her as she gazed. "It is the
very face; the very same face that your mother's
was at your age."

"Did you know mamma then? Then, you
must be a friend of hers," was Henry Arkell's eager
answer.

"No, I never was her friend—in that sense. I
was a governess in a branch of the Cheveley family,
and Miss Lucy Cheveley and her father the colonel
used to visit there. She had a charming voice, too:
just as you have. Ah, dear me! speaking to you

and your sister here, her children, it serves to remind me how time has flown."

"I am reminded of that, when I look at Captain Anderson here," said Travice Arkell, with a laugh. "Only the other day he was a schoolboy."

"If you want to be reminded of that, you need only look at yourself," retorted Anderson. "You have shot up into a maypole."

"Will you see me to the carriage, Travice, if you are not too much engaged?" cried out a voice which Travice knew well.

It was his mother's. She had seen the approach of her carriage from the windows of the upper hall, and was going down to it. Travice turned in obedience to the summons; and Captain Anderson sprang forward to renew his former friendship.

"You might set down Lucy on your way," said Travice, as they were stepping in. "I don't know how she'll get home through this pouring rain."

"And how would our dresses get on?" returned Mrs. Arkell, in hot displeasure. "Lucy, it seems, could contrive to get to the concert, and she must contrive to get from it. You can come in, Travice; you take up no room."

"Thank you, I'd not run the chance of damaging your dresses for all the money they cost."

As he returned to the hall, the boys, gathered

round the door, were making a great noise, and Mr.
Wilberforce spoke in displeasure.

"*Can't* you keep those boys in order, Mr.
Arkell?"

Travice dealt out a very significant nod, one
bespeaking punishment for the morrow, and the
boys subsided into silence.

"Please, sir, your carriage is coming up the
street," said Cockburn, junior, a little fellow of
ten, to the head master, rather gratified possibly to
be enabled to say it. "Somebody else's is coming
too."

The windows became alive with heads. But
the "somebody else's" proved to be of no interest,
for it did not belong to any of the concert goers,
and it went on past the Guildhall. Of course all
the attention was then concentrated on the master's.
It was a sober, old fashioned, rather shabby brown
chariot; and it came up the street at a sober pace.
The master, full of congratulation that the imprisonment was over, looked at it complacently.
What then was his surprise to see another carriage
dash before it, just as it was about to draw up, and
usurp the place it had been confidingly driving to.
A dashing vision of grandeur; an elegant yellow
equipage bright as gold; its hammer-cloth gold
also; its servants displaying breeches of gold
plush, with powdered hair and gold-headed canes.

"Why, whose is it?" exclaimed the discomfited master, almost forgetting in his surprise the eclipse his own chariot had received.

"Whose can it be?" repeated the gazers in puzzled wonder. The livery was that of the St. John family; the colour was theirs; and, now that they looked closely, the arms were the St. Johns'. But the St. Johns' panels did not display a coronet! And there was not a single head throughout the hall, but turned itself in curiosity to await the announcement of the servant. He came in with his powder and his cane, and the college boys made way for him.

"The Lady Anne St. John's carriage."

She, Lady Anne, the fair girl of seventeen, looked at Travice Arkell, appearing to expect his arm as a matter of course. Travice gave it. Mrs. James tucked Lucy's arm within her own, in an old-fashioned manner, and followed them out.

They stepped into the carriage. Lady Anne waiting in her stately courtesy for Lucy to take the precedence; she followed; Mrs. James went last. And Travice Arkell lifted his trencher as they drove away.

The head master, smoothing his ruffled plumes, came out next, and Travice returned to the hall. Mrs. Aultane, feeling fit to faint, pounced upon him.

"Did *you* know that it was Lady Anne St. John?"

"Not at first," he answered, suppressing his laughter as he best could, for the whole thing had been a rich joke to him. "I guessed it: because I heard Mrs. St. John tell Mrs. Peter Arkell yesterday that Lady Anne was coming."

"And you couldn't open your mouth to say it! You could let us treat her as if—as if—she were a nobody!" gasped Mrs. Aultane. "If you were not so big, Travice Arkell, I could box your ears."

The next to come down from the upper hall was a group, of whom the most notable was Marmaduke Carr. A hale, upright man still, with a healthy red upon his cheeks: a few more years, and he would count fourscore. With him, linked arm in arm, was a mean little chap, looking really nearly as old as Marmaduke: it was Squire Carr. His eldest son, Valentine, was near him, a mean-looking man also, but well-dressed, with a red rose in his button-hole. Mrs. Lewis, the squire's daughter, came forward and joined them, putting her arm within her husband's, a big man with a very ugly face; and the squire's younger children, the second family, women grown now, followed. Old Marmaduke Carr—he was always open-handed —had treated every one of these younger children, six of them, and all girls, to the concert, for he knew the squire's meanness; and he was taking the whole party home to a sumptuous dinner. All the family were there except one, Benjamin, the second son. The Reverend Mr. Prattleton and his wife were of the group; the two families were on intimate terms; and if you choose to listen to what they are saying, you may hear a word about Benjamin.

The rain was coming down fiercely as ever, so there was nothing for it but to wait until some of the flies came back again. Mr. Prattleton, the squire, and Marmaduke Carr sought the embrasure of a window, where they could talk at will, and watch the approach of any vehicle that could be seized upon. Squire Carr was a widower still; he had never married a third wife. It may be, that the persistent rejection of Mildred Arkell in the days long gone by, had put him out of conceit of asking anybody else. Certain it was, he had not done it.

"And where is he now?" asked Mr. Prattleton of the squire, pursuing a conversation which had reference to Benjamin.

"Coming home," growled the squire; "so he writes us word. I thought how long this American fever would last."

"I never clearly understood what it was he went to do there," observed the clergyman.

"Nor I," said Squire Carr, drawing down the thin lips of his discontented mouth. "All I know is, it has cost me two hundred pounds, for he took a heap of things out there on speculation, which I have since paid for. He wrote word home that the things were a dead loss; that he sold them to a rogue who never paid him for them. That's six months ago."

"Then how has he lived since?" asked Mr. Prattleton.

"Heaven knows. I don't."

"Perhaps he has lived as he lived at Homberg, John," put in old Marmaduke, who had a trick of saying home truths to the squire, by no means palatable. "You know how he lived *there,* for two seasons."

"I don't know what he's doing, and I don't care," repeated the squire to Mr. Prattleton, completely ignoring Marmaduke's interruption. "I have tried to throw him off, but he wont be thrown off. He is coming home now, in the hope that I will put him into a farm; I know he is, though he has not said so. Pity but the ship would go cruizing round the world and never come back again."

"You did put him into a farm once."

"I put him into one twice, and had to take them on my own hands again, to save the land from being ruined," returned Squire Carr, wrathfully. " He——"

" But you know, John, Ben always said that the fault was partly yours," again put in old Marmaduke; " you would not allow proper money to be spent upon the land."

" It's not true. Ben said it, you say ?—tush ! it's not much that Ben sticks at. When he ought to have been over the farm in the early morning, he was in bed, tired out with his doings of the night. He was never home before daylight; gambling, drinking; evil knows what his nights would be spent in. The fact is, Ben Carr was born with an antipathy to work, and so long as he can beg or borrow a living without it, he wont do any."

" It is a pity but he had been put to some regular profession," said the minor canon.

"I put him to fifty things, and he came back from all," said the squire, tartly.

"He was never put regularly to anything, John," dissented Marmaduke. "You sent him to one thing—' Go and try whether you like it, Ben,' said you; Ben tried it for a week or two, and came back and said he didn't like it. Then you put him to another—' Try that, Ben,' said you; and Ben came back as before. The fact is, he ought to have been fixed at some one thing off hand, and

my brother, the old squire, used to say it; not
have had the choice of leaving it given him over
and over again. 'You keep to that, Mr. Ben, or
you starve,' would have been my dealings with
him."

John Carr cast his thoughts back, and there was
a sneer upon his thin lips; old Marmaduke had
not dealt so successfully with his own son that he
need boast. But John did not say it; for many
years the name of Robert Carr had dropped out of
their intercourse. Had he been dead—and, indeed, for all they heard of Robert, he might be
dead—his name could not have been more completely sunk in silence. Marmaduke Carr never
spoke of him, and the squire did not choose to
speak: he had his reasons.

"It was the premium you stuck at, John. We
can't put young men out without one, when they
get to the age Ben was. *There* was another
folly!—keeping the boy at home till he was twenty
years of age, doing nothing except just idling about
the land. But it's your affair, not mine; and Ben
has certainly gone on a wrong tack this many a
year now. I should have discarded him long ago,
had he been my son."

"I should have felt tempted to do the same,"
observed the clergyman. "Benjamin has entailed
so much trouble on you."

"And he'll entail more yet," was the consolatory prediction of old Marmaduke.

The squire made no reply. He had his arm on the window-frame supporting his chin, and looking dreamily out. His thoughts were with Benjamin. Why had he not yet discarded this scapegrace son— he, the hard man? Simply because there was a remote corner in his heart where Benjamin was cherished—cherished beyond all his other children. Petty, mean, hard as John Carr was, he had passionately loved his first wife; and Benjamin, in features, was her very image. His eldest son, Valentine, resembled him, the squire; Mrs. Lewis was like nobody but herself; his other children were by a different mother. He only cared for Benjamin. He did not care for Valentine, he did not care for the daughters, but he loved Benjamin; and the result was, that though Ben Carr brought home grief continually, and had done things for which Valentine, had *he* done them, would never have been pardoned, the squire, after a little holding out, was certain to take him into favour again, and give him another chance.

"When does George go out?" asked the squire of Mr. Prattleton, alluding to that gentleman's half-brother, who was nearly twenty years younger than himself.

"Immediately. And very fortunate we have

been in getting him so good a thing. I hope the
climate will agree with him."

"Grandpapa," said young Lewis, running up to
the squire, "here are two flies coming down the
street now. Shall I rush out and secure them
first?"

"Ask Mr. Carr, my boy. He may like to stay
longer, and give a chance to the rain to abate."

Mr. Carr, old Marmaduke, laughed. He knew
John Carr of old, and his stingy nature. He would
not order the flies to be retained lest the payment
of them should fall to him.

"Go and secure them both, boy," said old
Marmaduke; "and there's a shilling for your own
trouble."

Young Lewis galloped out, spinning the shilling
in his hand. "Don't I hope old Marmaduke will
leave all his money to me!" quoth he, mentally.
To say the truth, the whole family of the Carrs
indulged golden dreams of this money more frequently than they need have done—apart from the
squire, who was the most sanguine dreamer of all.

They were going out, to stow themselves in the
two flies as they best could, when Marmaduke's
eye fell on Travice Arkell. The old man caught
his hand.

"Will you come home and dine with us, Travice?
Five o'clock, sharp!"

" Thank you, sir—I shall be very glad," replied Travice, who liked good dinners as well as most schoolboys, and Mr. Carr's style of dinner, when he did entertain, was renowned.

" If you don't want these flies to be taken by somebody else, you had better come!" cried out young Lewis, putting his wet head in at the entrance door. " Mamma, I am stopping another for you."

Travice Arkell for once imitated the junior college boys, and splashed recklessly through the puddles of the streets, as fast as his legs would carry him, on his way to the Palmery, for he wanted to see Frederick St. John : he had just time. His nearest road led him past Peter Arkell's, and he spared a minute to look in.

" So you have got home safely, Lucy ?"

" As if I could get home anything but safely, coming as I did !" returned Lucy, in merriment. " Such a commotion it caused when the carriage dashed up ! The elm-trees became alive with rooks'- heads, not to speak of the windows. You should have seen the footman and his cane marshalling me to the door ! But oh, Travice ! when I got inside, the gilt was taken off the gingerbread !"

" How so ?"

" You know how badly papa sees now without his spectacles. He did not happen to have them on, and he took it to be the old beadle of St. James the Less, with his laced hat and staff. He said he could not think what he wanted."

Travice laughed, laughed merrily, with Lucy. He stayed a minute, and then splashed on to the Palmery.

Frederick St. John was sitting up, but he had been really ill in the morning. Mrs. James and Lady Anne were giving him and Mrs. St. John the details of the concert. It was not surprising that no one had known Lady Anne. She had paid a long visit to Westerbury several years before, when she was a little girl; but growing girls alter, and her face was not recognised again. She had come for a long visit now, bringing, as before, her carriage and three or four servants—for she was an orphan, and had her own establishment.

"I say, Arkell, I'm glad you are come. Anne is trying to enlighten us about the grand doings this morning, and she can't do it at all. She protests that Mr. Wilberforce sang the comic song."

Lady Anne eagerly turned to Travice. "That little gentleman in silver spectacles, who was looking so impatiently for his carriage—who told you once or twice to pay attention to the college boys—was it not Mr. Wilberforce?"

"Undoubtedly."

LONDON :
SAVILL AND EDWARDS, PRINTERS, CHANDOS STREET,
COVENT GARDEN.

MESSRS. TINSLEY BROTHERS'
NEW WORKS,
Obtainable at all the Libraries.

NEW NOVEL BY THE AUTHOR OF "DENIS DONNE."

THEO LEIGH: A NOVEL. By ANNIE THOMAS, Author of "Denis Donne." In 3 vols. *[Now ready.*

BITTER SWEETS: A LOVE STORY. By JOSEPH HATTON. In 3 vols. *[Now ready.*

SHOOTING AND FISHING IN THE RIVERS, PRAIRIES, AND BACKWOODS OF NORTH AMERICA. By B. H. REVOIL. In 2 vols. *[Now ready.*

MR. SALA'S

MY DIARY IN AMERICA IN THE MIDST OF WAR. By GEORGE AUGUSTUS SALA. In 2 vols. 8vo.

"In two large volumes Mr. Sala reproduces a portion of the correspondence from America which he lately published in a London daily paper. He has added, however, a good deal which did not appear in the columns of that journal. Mr. Sala's is decidedly a clever, amusing, and often brilliant book."—*Morning Star.*

THE THIRD EDITION OF

"GEORGE GEITH OF FEN COURT," THE NOVEL. By G. F. TRAFFORD, author of "City and Suburb," "Too Much Alone," &c. In 3 vols. *[Now ready.*

"Rarely have we seen an abler work than this, or one which more vigorously interests us in the principal characters of its most fascinating story."—*Times.*

MASANIELLO OF NAPLES. By Mrs. HORACE ST. JOHN. In 1 vol.

This day is published, in 1 vol.

WIT AND WISDOM FROM WEST AFRICA; OR, A BOOK OF PROVERBIAL PHILOSOPHY, IDIOMS, ENIGMAS, AND LACONISMS. Compiled by RICHARD F. BURTON, late H. M.'s Consul for the Bight of Biafra and Fernando Po, author of "A Pilgrimage to El Medinah and Meccah," "A Mission to Dahomey," &c.

NEW STORY OF LANCASHIRE LIFE, BY BENJAMIN BRIERLY.
This day is published, in 2 vols.

IRKDALE: A LANCASHIRE STORY. By BENJAMIN BRIERLY.

NEW NOVEL BY THE AUTHOR OF "THE FIELD OF LIFE."

Shortly will be published, in 3 vols.

A WOMAN'S WAY. By the Author of "The Field of Life."

NEW EDITION OF "DENIS DONNE."

Shortly will be published, in 1 vol., price 6s.

DENIS DONNE: A NOVEL. By ANNIE THOMAS, author of "Theo Leigh."

FACES FOR FORTUNES. By AUGUSTUS MAYHEW, author of "How to Marry, and Whom to Marry," "The Greatest Plague in Life," &c.

A MISSION TO DAHOMEY, BEING A THREE MONTHS' RESIDENCE AT THE COURT OF DAHOMEY, IN WHICH ARE DESCRIBED THE MANNERS AND CUSTOMS OF THE COUNTRY, INCLUDING THE HUMAN SACRIFICE, &c. By Capt. R. F. BURTON, late H. M. Commissioner to Dahomey, and the Author of "A Pilgrimage to El Medinah and Meccah." In 2 vols., with Illustrations. Second Edition, revised.

THE MARRIED LIFE OF ANNE OF AUSTRIA, QUEEN OF FRANCE, MOTHER OF LOUIS XVI.; AND THE HISTORY OF DON SEBASTIAN, KING OF PORTUGAL. Historical Studies; from numerous Unpublished Sources. By MARTHA WALKER FREER. In 2 vols. 8vo., with Portrait. Second Edition.

TODLEBEN'S DEFENCE OF SEBASTOPOL: BEING A REVIEW OF GENERAL TODLEBEN'S NARRATIVE, 1854-5. By WILLIAM HOWARD RUSSELL, LL.D., Special Correspondent of the *Times* during the Crimean War. 10s. 6d.

*** A portion of this Work appeared in the *Times;* it has since been greatly enlarged, and may be said to be an abridgment of General Todleben's great work.

NEW EDITION OF "THE WORLD IN THE CHURCH."

This day is published, in 1 vol., 6s.,

THE WORLD IN THE CHURCH. By the Author of "George Geith of Fen Court," "Too Much Alone," &c.

Also, uniform with the above, New Editions of—

CITY AND SUBURB. 6s.	BARREN HONOUR. 6s.
JOHN MARCHMONT'S LEGACY. 6s.	BORDER AND BASTILE. 6s.
SEVEN SONS OF MAMMON. 6s.	SWORD AND GOWN. 4s. 6d.
RECOMMENDED TO MERCY. 6s.	TOO MUCH ALONE. 6s.
ELEANOR'S VICTORY. 6s.	ARNOLD'S LIFE OF MACAULAY.
BUCKLAND'S FISH HATCHING. 5s.	7s. 6d.
MAURICE DERING. 6s.	DUTCH PICTURES. By Sala. 5s.
TREVLYN HOLD. 6s.	TWO PRIMA DONNAS. 5s.
GUY LIVINGSTONE. 5s.	BUNDLE OF BALLADS. 6s.

www.ingramcontent.com/pod-product-compliance
Lightning Source LLC
Chambersburg PA
CBHW020945030726
47496CB00005B/1366